D1207434

7-17

TO THE VICTOR

A NOVEL OF LOUISIANA POLITICS

BY JOHN WYETH SCOTT

Baton Rouge

CLAITOR'S PUBLISHING DIVISION

Copyright, 1986
by
John Wyeth Scott

ISBN Number 0-87511-771-6

Published and for sale by:
CLAITOR'S PUBLISHING DIVISION
3165 S. Acadian
P.O. Box 3333
Baton Rouge, Louisiana 70821
Phone 1-800-535-8141 (in Louisiana 1-504-344-0476)

With love, to Dee Dee, Popsy and Cyndy;
    With appreciation, to the people of Alexandria, Louisiana.

Acknowledgments

I owe thanks to many people who provided various forms of assistance to this project, especially Theresa DeSelle for her tireless work on the word processor; Julie Irwin for her suggestions and proofreading; Leigh Harris for her valuable research.

I offer special thanks to my good friend Ken Juneau of Ken Juneau and Associates Public Relations Firm for his advice and his creative skills in designing the cover of this book. I am indebted to and appreciate the confidence of Bob Claitor in investing the efforts and talents of Claitor's Publishing Company in publishing *To The Victor*.

This is a novel. The characters, the families and the events are imaginary. However, the plight of Louisiana is real. Her future is clouded by many of the problems and political realities addressed in this book.

Table of Contents

CHAPTER ONE
Victor Berger
"The herd instinct..."   p.   1

CHAPTER TWO
Rubaiyat of Omarkhayam
"The Moving Finger writes..."   p.   7

CHAPTER THREE
Hans Zinsser
*"It seems that somewhere in the
legendary past of louse history..."*   p.   13

CHAPTER FOUR
Samuel Butler
"Self-preservation is..."   p.   18

CHAPTER FIVE
John Peter Altgeld
*"All great reforms, great movements,
come from..."*   p.   22

CHAPTER SIX
Woodrow Wilson
*"Sometimes people call me
an idealist..."*   p.   26

CHAPTER SEVEN
Theodore Roosevelt
"Power undirected..."   p.   32

CHAPTER EIGHT
American Political Formula
"Poor man's candidate and ..."   p.   39

CHAPTER NINE
Thomas Jefferson
"I hold a little rebellion..."   p.   45

CHAPTER TEN
Albert Einstein
*"The ideals which have lighted
my way..."*   p.   49

CHAPTER ELEVEN
Marcus Tullius Cicero
"When you have no basis..."   p. 52

CHAPTER TWELVE
Leonid Andreyev
*"I want to do away with everything
behind man..."*   p. 56

CHAPTER THIRTEEN
Robert Frost
"At bottom the world isn't a joke..."   p. 64

CHAPTER FOURTEEN
Thomas Alva Edison
"Genius is one percent inspiration..."   p. 69

CHAPTER FIFTEEN
Louis D. Brandeis
"Crime is contagious..."   p. 72

CHAPTER SIXTEEN
Frank Lloyd Wright
*"If capitalism is fair then
unionism..."*   p. 81

CHAPTER SEVENTEEN
Mark Twain
"Get your facts first,..."   p. 93

CHAPTER EIGHTEEN
Michel de Montaigne
"On the loftiest throne..."   p. 98

CHAPTER NINETEEN
Abraham Lincoln
"Let us have faith that Right..."   p. 103

CHAPTER TWENTY
Harry S. Truman
"I never did give anybody hell..."   p. 107

CHAPTER TWENTY-ONE
H. C. Meneken
*"The men the American people
admire..."*   p. 112

CHAPTER TWENTY-TWO
Harry S. Truman
"Last night the moon, the stars..."   p. 117

CHAPTER TWENTY-THREE
Walt Whitman
"A great city is..."   p. 124

CHAPTER TWENTY-FOUR
Robert Burns
"God knows, I'm not the thing I
should be..."   p. 131

CHAPTER TWENTY-FIVE
Alan Barth
"Character assassination is at
once easier..."   p. 141

CHAPTER TWENTY-SIX
George Bernard Shaw
"Lack of money is..."   p. 144

CHAPTER TWENTY-SEVEN
Anouih
"You're in the ocean..."   p. 148

CHAPTER TWENTY-EIGHT
F. Scott Fitzgerald
"The victor belongs..."   p. 153

CHAPTER TWENTY-NINE
Edmund Burke
"Facts are to the mind..."   p. 159

CHAPTER THIRTY
Edward Law
"The greater the truth..."   p. 169

CHAPTER THIRTY-ONE
Seven Wise Men, Delphi
"Know thyself..."   p. 175

CHAPTER THIRTY-TWO
Abraham Lincoln
"I desire to so conduct the affairs
of this Administration..."   p. 179

EPILOGUE
  Virgil
    "Sing Goddess..." p. 184

GLOSSARY OF TERMS p. 189

TO KEEP SILENT WHEN WE SHOULD PROTEST,
MAKES COWARDS OF MEN

Abraham Lincoln

TO THE VICTOR

ONE

"The herd instinct makes the average man afraid to stand alone; he is always afraid to stand alone for an idea, no matter how good, simply as a matter of prejudice. Our herd, like every other herd, when stampeded is liable to trample under its' feet anybody who does not run with it."

Victor Berger
Socialist leader
(1860-1929)

"Senator Flint, you are recognized for the floor to present your amendment," said the presiding officer of the Louisiana State Senate.

Louisiana State Senator Darin Flint's tall, lanky frame unfolded itself from behind his senate desk and walked to the microphone at the front of the chamber. The very thin, wiry limbs of his body contrasted with the large head, the large nose and ears. His head was capped by black hair swept straight back from his forehead. There was not a grey hair in his scalp. Despite his large, disproportional features, the face was dominated by thoughtful, penetrating grey eyes and a straight, gentle mouth. Only the deep lines reaching from the corners of his eyes and mouth revealed the fact that Darin Flint was approaching sixty years of age.

"Mr. President, members of the Senate, this is my last amendment," Flint began in a strong clear voice. A smattering of sarcastic applause rose from the ranks of senators.

Flint had worn out his welcome at the microphone hours ago as he had proposed reduction after reduction to the state budget (the appropriations bill). Flint's many amendments were aimed at balancing the budget, which was over $150 million in deficit. Every one of his amendments had failed and his efforts were now clearly a lost cause. But Flint would not stop. He wanted to force the Senate to debate and vote on every dollar of his $200 million of

1

proposed reductions. Senate President Sonny Stokes had been openly hostile as he presided over proceedings. Flint had attacked many spending proposals of Governor René Reynolds, thereby incurring the wrath of the Senate leadership. Most other senators were avoiding him like a pariah.

But it was old hat for Flint. He had been at it for twenty-seven years. This was an annual ritual for him. For years he had made efforts to cut wasteful spending from the budget a special project with a handful of other independent legislators.

Virtually all of the Senate members had items in the budget that were politically important to have funded. If a senator offended the governor or the Senate leadership by voting with Flint to reduce spending, then perhaps the governor's influence would not protect that senator if Flint's next amendment hit the spending item dear to that senator's heart. Offending the governor might bring retribution in a variety of forms.

Flint grimly looked upon his impatient, aggravated, and, in a few instances, even angry audience. His amendment was minor, but typical of the long list of cost cutting measures he had been presenting during the debate.

Flint spoke in his resonant, patient voice. "I'd like you to approve this amendment because it will save Louisiana over $10 million per year in our medicine prescription reimbursement program for the poor. Under that program, pharmacists are paid a service charge or fee for every prescription that is filled; this fee is in addition to reimbursement or payment to the pharmacist for the drug or medication. This disbursement fee is paid again each time a recipient fills or refills a prescription."

Flint paused and cleared his throat for a moment to allow his words to be absorbed.

"We've had numerous instances when excessive prescriptions or refills occur, thereby increasing the cost of the program to the state. There are also instances when the reimbursement paid to the pharmacist for the cost of the medicine is much greater than the actual competitive cost of the medicine. This is not the pharmacist's fault but, nevertheless, it is unfair to the taxpayer. Our system is too expensive because reimbursement to the pharmacist is not based on the actual cost paid by the pharmacist for the drug."

Flint again paused to let his words sink in.

"This amendment would do two things. First, a recipient would be allowed to fill or refill prescriptions free of charge six times per month. After six prescriptions, the recipient would shoulder part of the cost by paying the disbursing fee to the pharmacist for these additional prescriptions. The state would continue to pay the cost of the medicine in the additional prescriptions.

"Secondly, this amendment would establish a restricted generic drug formulary to better assure that the price the state pays to pharmacists for drugs accurately reflects the competitive cost of the drug. The formulary has been approved by the L.S.U. Medical Center, the Medical Care Advisory Committee and the Louisiana Medical Association."

Then Flint closed his remarks.

"This budget bill is deep in the red and over $150 million out of balance. My amendment will reduce that deficit by over $10 million. Isn't that our responsibility .... to adopt amendments to get our spending in line with revenues? This amendment is only one example of the many ways we can save money and balance this budget. I request your approval."

There were no questions and Flint returned to his desk. State Senator Colbert Freeman, chief floor leader for Governor René Reynolds, was recognized for the floor. Freeman's squat, heavyset appearance, his loud, nasal voice and his wide fleshy face contrasted dramatically with the lanky image of Flint he replaced at the rostrum.

"Mr. President and members of the Senate. Flint has finally brought some good news to this chamber. He says this is finally his last amendment, thank Heavens."

Flint smiled along with his colleagues at Freeman's attempt at humor. As he spoke, Freeman's expression changed repeatedly from a broad, toothy smile that reminded Flint of a cheshire cat to deep scowls accentuated by his graveled voice reaching for higher decibel levels. His manner of speech dripped with distain for both Flint, who he viewed as a tiresome nemesis, and Flint's amendment.

"So let's kill this amendment, then approve the budget bill so we can adjourn for supper. This amendment is an insult to both your pharmacists and to the sick, poor people who need this program. I'm not sure if Flint is calling the pharmacists of Louisiana a bunch of crooks or if he believes poor people are trafficking drugs. Either way, it's a bad amendment.

"Election day is coming up October 22nd. Maybe you don't have any poor people who need their medicine in your district. But I'm not going to tell someone in need that 'No, you can't refill that prescription because you've already had it refilled too many times this month.' This is a bad amendment. Let's defeat it. I move the previous question on the entire subject matter."

Several of Flint's colleagues rose to their feet to object. The previous question would end debate on both the amendment and the bill. Flint's small band of fiscal conservatives had planned hard-hitting speeches against this unbalanced budget. But the electronic voting board suddenly illuminated to reveal the lopsided vote. The previous question was ordered.

Under the Senate rules, Flint returned to the podium and gave the closing argument on his amendment. It would also be his last chance to speak against the $6 billion budget. The frustration and compressed anger of having over $200 million of his proposed reduction amendments defeated over the past five days burned in his chest. He wanted to shout his closing remarks to castigate the pathetic performance of the Senate. But anger, he knew, would do no good.

He controlled and suppressed himself.

His speech was again deliberate, patient. He again explained the amendment; that no needy recipient would be deprived of medicine; that many other states put far more severe limitations on the number of prescriptions allowable for a recipient; that Louisiana's drug reimbursement program costs more per recipient than virtually any state in America; that the restricted generic drug formulary would reduce costs while assuring a fair price is paid for appropriate medication.

Because debate on both the amendment and the bill had been shut off by the vote for the previous question, Flint also used this last opportunity to remind the Senate that this deeply in deficit budget violated the Legislature's constitutional obligation to the people of Louisiana to balance the budget. He wanted his amendment to cut spending to pass; he wanted the oversized budget bill defeated.

4

"I urge you to approve my amendment because it will save $10 million. But even with my amendment, the budget remains deep in the red. So, more important than my amendment, I urge you to find within your consciences the strength and conviction your constituents deserve from their senator to vote against this wasteful budget bill," he said. "Don't allow the further abuse of the public's tax dollars. We must stop spending money we don't have. Whatever you do on the amendment, I urge you to protest this budget and vote against its approval."

His closing speech concluded, Flint returned to his desk on the Senate floor.

The voting machine opened and the Senate voted first on Flint's amendment then on the overall budget bill. Flint's amendment was crushed. The budget, bloated with excessive spending and over $150 million in deficit, was overwhelmingly approved. Flint lost both votes by lopsided margins.

The Senate President then announced the Senate was adjourning for the day. Flint began putting his files away.

From over the railing that divided the restricted floor of the Senate from the public seating for visitors, lobbyists or other non-members, Flint heard a voice say, "Damn good try, Darin." He looked up into the handsome, brown face of Terrell Franks, a black man who had made his reputation as an investigative reporter for the Baton Rouge Morning Advocate and as a spokesman for civil rights causes. Franks had left the Morning Advocate to join the public relations consulting firm of Jon Douglas and Associates.

Flint picked up his briefcase and stepped past the railing to join Franks.

"What brings you to the Senate, Terrell?"

"Curiosity and force of habit, I guess. I miss covering you guys for the Advocate."

"Well, I'm still taking my medicine from Stokes and Reynolds on a regular basis," Flint joked.

Franks laughed. "Don't get discouraged Darin. You're the best man in this place and they know it. We need you fighting in here."

Flint looked at Terrell Franks' youthful, intelligent face. Franks was in his mid-thirties, slim with a neatly trimmed beard covering the angular features of his firm jaw and chin. He was tall, though not as tall as Flint, with a muscular, athletic frame. Franks had excelled in football during his college days fifteen years earlier and still appeared fit and trim. Flint was reminded of his lost youth and his frustrated hopes for Louisiana, hopes which seemed more bogged down in the quagmire of petty, selfish politics than ever before. He had been here for twenty-seven years and it was time for new blood, Flint thought to himself. But it was encouraging that a black man like Franks, an avowed liberal, was supportive of his efforts to cut waste.

"Thanks for the compliment, Terrell. What we really need is a bunch of young fighters like you in here instead of tired, old men like me."

Flint and Franks talked for awhile longer before they went their separate ways. Flint took the senate elevator downstairs to his office to telephone his wife Susan at home in New Orleans. It was 8:00 p.m. He told her he would be home by 10 p.m. and that he would stop for a sandwich along the way. Flint hung up the phone, leaned back in his chair, stretching his arms wide with his eyes closed allowing his mind to relax, to wander.

TWO

The Moving Finger writes; and, having writ
Moves on: nor all your Piety and Wit
Shall lure it back to cancel half a line,
Nor all your Tears wash out a Word of it.

RUBAIYAT
OF OMARKHAYAM
The Astronomer-Poet of Persia
Twelfth Century, A.D.

Darin Flint had arrived twenty-seven years ago in Baton Rouge as a thirty year old freshman state senator on a crusade to lift the quality of government and politics. In many ways, it seemed things were now worse than when he had arrived.

Flint never planned to spend his career in the Legislature. He had hoped to someday run for governor. But he himself had made that dream virtually impossible. He had alienated too many groups over the years.

The political groups that make or break a politician were not great fans of Darin Flint. They included the sheriffs; the teachers' unions; the political hierarchy of parish and city governments who were generally uncomfortable with a maverick like Flint. He had also managed to offend the welfare bureaucracy; the organized business leadership and the organized labor leadership. He had even managed to annoy people who often were his allies, such as fundamentalist church leaders when he opposed scientific creationism being taught in public schools. Many other groups had periodically found themselves at odds with Flint. For instance, his last budget amendment that evening had offended the Pharmacist Association members.

Flint unconsciously smiled as he recalled some of those confrontations such as his advocacy of placing all sheriff's offices, except for top assistants, under civil service job protection. That reform would have all but ended political patronage among sheriff's employees.

The teacher unions had opposed almost every new innovation

and education reform proposed over his twenty-seven years in Baton Rouge .... the competency testing of teachers before granting a teacher's certificate; a generous salary schedule for teachers based in part on satisfactory teaching performance in the classroom; a testing program as a major factor in determining whether the child should be placed in a summer remedial program or promoted to the next grade level. The teacher unions had even opposed an intense evaluation system aimed at identifying weaknesses, disadvantages or shortcomings that may exist in individual schools so that corrections could be implemented. They opposed all forms of merit pay.

Flint had advocated virtually every education reform. It did not matter that time had proven many such votes to be good ones. Flint's sin was that he had disagreed with union leadership at the time of the vote.

Flint further damaged himself politically with his proposal to establish an employment training and job referral program for welfare recipients. The bill required able bodied welfare recipients to accept satisfactory job training or an available job. Flint's purpose was to help people who were jobless and stuck on welfare by giving them a job skill and finding them a job. It would also relieve the crowded welfare roles, thereby saving money by helping the dependent become self-reliant. Welfare advocates had berated him before House and Senate committees as cruel, callous and devious.

After three years of legislative battles and many compromising alterations, Flint's bill had been approved as the work incentive program (WIN program). That had been ten years ago. The moderate success of the program had not dimmed the memories of the harsh legislative battles with the influential welfare establishment.

Flint realized he was also viewed with skepticism by both organized labor and the business lobby. In Louisiana, the rivalry of business and labor was the most fundamental battle occuring in politics. Inevitably, politicians had to choose sides. The issues were so emotional, compromises by either side so unlikely, and the votes so controversial that deviations from the hard line were not tolerated by either side.

But Flint was an enigma. He voted with business on numerous controversial issues, such as unemployment insurance and Right to Work while supporting labor on such major issues as collective bargaining and prevailing wage legislation. His votes on worker's compensation issues were split. Flint resented the discord between business and labor; the fact that the Legislature found itself stuck in the middle on these bitter confrontations year after year; that the emotional attitudes of both groups always made logical, fair conclusions to such issues virtually impossible.

Flint's ambition of serving in higher office had reluctantly faded as the years passed. Aside from the politics of his legislative record, Flint knew only too well the expense of a statewide campaign. To mount a serious bid for governor, a minimum of $5 million dollars had been necessary for major candidates in the past four elections. Flint had no hope of raising such sums of money. He was not a wealthy man. He had built his grocery store business in New Orleans from scratch over the past thirty-five years. He and Susan were in a comfortable financial position but not wealthy. Yet, perhaps unrealistically, Flint clung to the hope that he could somehow ignite a political uprising, a revolt of the Louisiana people to turn the state's political world upside down, to cleanse the system of those who use public office to enrich themselves and those who sustain such politicians.

Flint had vocally made his viewpoint clear. If a person's goal was to make money and wealth, then that person should be in private business where such goals were appropriate. Not in government, where self interest meant conflict of interest. Time had forced Darin Flint to face the stark realities of politics, the "real world" as his more sceptical colleagues referred to it. Tempered by years of dealing with this real world, Flint clung to his ideals. But his dream of real change, of his revolution, seemed far, far away.

Flint deeply disapproved of Governor René Reynolds, whose term in office had been characterized by sophisticated power politics, and extravagant spending practices. Favoritism and influence peddling thrived in his administration. René Reynolds would not, or could not, say "no" to his financial and political friends.

Flint believed Reynolds had perhaps been too inexperienced at thirty-five years of age when he became governor. His rise in politics had been meteoric. Blessed with youth, good looks and a wealthy family, Reynolds had easily won a spot on the Public Service Commission at the precocious age of thirty-two. He had proven to be an exceptional candidate, with a knack for hilarious one liners and crowd pleasing jokes. He had been politically pragmatic as a member of the Commission. Two years later, he had won the runoff for the vacant governorship with a strong, media oriented image campaign, strong black and quiet labor support.

The image Reynolds projected was of youth, humor, vitality, progressiveness and family. Reynolds was now only thirty-nine years old and running for his second term as governor. An easy re-election would provide an opportunity to enter the national political arena as a dynamic new force from the South.

Flint winced as he thought of the Reynolds' television spot that had clinched the previous election. It was a family ad taped in Reynolds' living room. He had introduced his wife and his children to the television viewers. Then he reached for his two year old daughter, who toddled before the cameras to be lifted to her father's lap. As Reynolds lifted her, the pink ruffled bottom of the child's underwear was revealed to the television audience. It had been subtle, but the message had a sensational impact during the final week of the campaign. This good looking young man with the pretty wife and children, especially the adorable toddler, was a fine father who would bring good old American family values to the governor's mansion.

Louisiana knew virtually nothing about this man's political views, ability or personal character when he oecame governor.

Reynolds was a media product and the invention in large measure of Neill Moulard, who now served as his executive counsel and political mentor. Moulard was a former law partner of Reynolds' father. He had been a major figure in Louisiana politics for many years. Although never a candidate himself, he was a master strategist and political infighter who had been a confidante and advisor to many previous governors. Moulard had carefully managed Reynolds' relations with legislators and other political leaders, using his endless contacts to help elect Reynolds, then consolidate the governor's power during this first term.

Reynolds was surrounded with political high rollers. His financial campaign reports were peppered with many individual contributions over $100 thousand. These same people, along with an endless list of new names, continued to contribute even more generously in anticipation of the next term. Reynolds had quickly learned to exercise the prerogatives of his power.

His supporters were rewarded by various forms of gubernatorial blessings. Tens of millions of dollars of public contracts had been made available to his political friends .... professional service contracts, planning contracts, consultant contracts, construction contracts, equipment contracts, material supply contracts, office leases, warehouse leases were only a few among many, many others.

The power of the governorship could make bank charters and hospital permits suddenly materialize. It was done often and selectively. In turn, new business opportunities were made available to Reynolds and his family. His lawyer friends received lucrative contracts to represent state oil interests. The best way for the family of an imprisoned criminal to obtain a parole or pardon was to be represented by a law firm properly blessed by Governor Reynolds.

Everything from janitorial contracts for cleaning state buildings, to rental by the state of office space; from awarding state insurance contracts to contracts with auto dealers for supplying state automobiles were forms of political patronage under the Reynolds regime. There were subtle ways of overcoming contract law procedure obstacles in order to be certain the right bidder got the contract.

Cronyism was rampant. Favoritism brought contributions and money making opportunities for the governor. It was not an atmosphere in which real progress could be made for the state. But it was politically sound and solidified the strongest political machine the state had seen in fifty years.

Reynolds was strong with black leadership, labor leadership and enjoyed strong regional support along the Mississippi River Parishes below Baton Rouge where his hometown, in Iberville Parish, was located. Reynolds maintained a respectable amount of business support, despite the large tax increases he had pushed through the Legislature during the first year of his term. Business support was insured by the opportunities he could provide influential people to do business with the state.

The Reynolds bandwagon was full with no real difficulties in sight.

The qualifying date for the October 22nd elections would be in late July, only forty-five days away. No opponent had surfaced to run against Reynolds. Even the president of the Louisiana Business League had acknowledged the virtual certainty of Reynolds' re-election by declaring that the League would not oppose Reynolds but would concentrate instead on electing more pro-business legislators. A strong gubernatorial campaign took two years to organize. Unopposed re- election would be an overwhelming mandate to continue business as usual for another four years.

Early in Flint's career, a reform movement had gotten underway. It blossomed in the early seventies. The Legislature had tried its new political wings of independence. But a retrenchment had occurred in the early 1980's. The new breed of legislator was politically pragmatic, with little sense of idealism, independence or respect for the hard-earned reforms of the prior decade. "Good government" ideas were hooted as silly and impractical. Exceptions to these reforms became manifold. Public bid laws, central purchasing laws, public contract laws, Code of Ethics laws, budgeting procedures, review of agency rules, highway construction standards and priority spending .... all were watered down and politically manipulated by the Reynolds regime.

The preoccupation of the public with labor-business controversies overshadowed and obscured from notice the destruction of the reforms people like Flint had worked so hard to accomplish.

The moment of truth had arrived for Darin Flint. The frustration and anguish of further service in the Senate would be almost a punishment for him. Retirement to his private grocery store business and family life in New Orleans would have its rewards. His wife and family would welcome his retirement from politics with open arms. But retirement by such people as Flint would leave the power and responsibility of governing in the hands of those he felt would worst abuse it.

Alternatively, Flint could remain in the Senate and do his best to awaken the people to the political catharsis mixed with borderline corruption that existed in Baton Rouge. He wanted to run for governor. But the governorship was a fading dream for him.

"Hell", Flint muttered to himself, "I'm too old to start kidding myself again."

THREE

"It seems that somewhere in the legendary past of louse history, an offspring of a living form, not unlike our book louse, found that life could be infinitely simplified, if instead of having to grub for food in straw, under tree bank, in moss, on lichen, in decaying cereals and vegetables, it could attach itself to some food-supplying host and sit tight."

Hans Zinsser
(1878-1940)
American bacteriologist
Rats, Lice and History

Governor René Reynolds stretched his jaw to allow his private barber to get a closer shave of his face. It was part of his morning regimen. He liked the luxury of a private barber's service each morning at the governor's mansion. The daily attention of the barber kept Reynolds' blond hair perpetually at moderate length, styled with a traditional part and the hair brushed in a well trained manner across his forehead. Reynolds took pride in his appearance.

As a youngster, Reynolds had been very chubby and overweight. He had overcome it. He was proud of the fact he was successfully fighting the battle of the bulge. At five feet ten inches and one hundred and eight-five pounds, he was stocky but not fat. Nevertheless, his jaws, cheekbones and brows were softly rounded, a hint of his tendency to gain weight. The light complexion of Reynolds' skin was matched well by his greenish-blue eyes, which often seemed preoccupied and inattentive. The mouth was small and without expression. Although Reynolds was famous for his humor and gift for comedy, he rarely grinned. His jokes were delivered before audiences with a straight face, or at best a slight smile. Perhaps he was self-conscious because a full grin revealed gaps between several of his upper line of teeth, the only flaw in a face that was unusually handsome.

"Neil, tell whoever helped you with my speech that I like it," said Reynolds. "But I'm making some changes so I'll need part of it retyped."

"O.K." answered Neil Moulard, Reynolds' executive counsel and chief political troubleshooter. Moulard was an intensely serious, pragmatic politician who understood the power of the governorship perhaps better than anyone in the Reynolds camp. His dark complexion and reserved demeanor contrasted sharply with his style of dress. He liked bright colored bowties. Today's tie was an orangish-red with a blue paisley design. His suits were expensive, usually silk and fashionably cut. Today's suit was no exception, a beige Brooks Brothers suit with a blue pinstriped shirt and gold cufflinks matching his gold rolex watch. He was well groomed and presented an impression of being well organized and successful. His bad habits were chain-smoking and occasionally drinking too much alcohol. Moulard was a workaholic who slept little, seldom going to bed before two o'clock in the morning. He never failed to arrive at the mansion by six o'clock each morning. His lifestyle was taking its toll. He was fifty-two years old yet suffered from numerous minor physical ailments. His bald head and large stomach made him look much older.

Moulard gazed over his lifted coffee cup as he sat in a lounge chair in Reynolds' bedroom in the mansion. Reynolds' wife, Felicia, was not present as she occupied a separate bedroom adjoining this one. "You want to talk about the changes?"

"It's simple enough," said Reynolds. "You mention the agency shop bill in the speech. I don't want ᴐ mention it."

Moulard looked at him with a slight smile. "What are the union boys going to think when you ignore their biggest proposal of the session when you're speaking to a joint meeting of the House and Senate. They'll hit the roof and I wouldn't blame them."

"That's tough," responded Reynolds. "But they'll get over it. Don't forget, they supported the man who signed the Right to Work law. Remember? So they should be able to put up with me. After all, they've got me for another four years." He paused, looked away from the mirror and said, "Christ, Neill, if that bill passes then I've got to decide whether to sign it. It's a no win situation and this is an election year."

"You don't have to decide whether to sign it. You must sign it and you know it," replied Moulard. "You are totally committed. Besides, you don't even have an opponent so why worry about the fall-out?"

"I need to be strong here at home when I go to the national convention next year."

Reynolds buttoned his collar and began combing his hair as the barber collected his supplies and left.

"Yes, I'll sign the bill if it passes," he said. "But that's a big if. I don't want that damn thing to land on my desk. I'm sure as hell not going to ask people to vote for it in my speech."

"O.K. What else? What other changes," asked Moulard as he mashed his cigarette in the ashtray.

"That's all. The rest is O.K. It'll be fine."

René Reynolds finished dressing, then he and Moulard went downstairs to face an assortment of political friends scheduled for breakfast at the governor's mansion. Reynolds had already had his daily light breakfast of toast and poached eggs served upstairs. He liked to be awakened with his food. Now he was free to think and speak while the others ate.

"Good morning." Reynolds greeted the visitors one by one then settled in his chair at the head of the breakfast table. The service of food began as Reynolds glanced out the window to the manicured lawn of the mansion premises.

Moulard leaned against the doorway sipping his coffee and casually took inventory of the politicians gathered at the table. Senator Colbert Freeman, ambitious and a hard-core union man was gobbling his food, his fork repeatedly jabbing like a lizard's tongue at the food on his plate. Senate President Sonny Stokes, the master of the Senate's give and take clubhouse politics nodded his big, shaggy head to greet Moulard. Moulard noticed the shiny lizard skin cowboy boots on Stokes' feet, with silver tips on the toe and heels, and speculated on how many pairs of boots this man must own. Moulard had made a game of taking inventory of Stokes' boots because he never seemed to wear the same boots twice. Stokes used downhome humor along with his country boy common sense to keep things in the Senate under control.

Ross Chandler, the governor's former law partner who had his finger in everything that meant money in the Reynolds' administration, was there. Jackson Wells, the New Orleans black leader-businessman whose support and political organization had been valued at one million dollars (the price Reynolds had paid the Wells organization) in the last gubernatorial campaign, sat at the opposite end of the table.

These men had been successful these past four years in gaining control of key executive positions and top legislative posts. Wells virtually controlled black patronage in state government, including the state contracts secured by black businesses which totaled many millions of dollars each year. If one of these men wanted a permit granted or job filled then that wish was generally granted. If they wanted certain state bonds or tax free bonds issued, the bonds were usually issued.

Nevertheless they felt frustrated far too often by the Legislature. Too often they were forced to compromise their desires in order to gain legislative approval. The budget was now tight as new tax proposals had failed for two long years. The revenues from the tax increases three years earlier had long ago been consumed.

In the Reynolds political machine, an ample public works budget and a heavy emphasis on the welfare administrative budget kept the troops happy. The Welfare Department had dozens of offices for its hundreds of programs statewide. Its thousands of employees represented an extremely influential, if informal, political force.

The public works budget kept the other side of the economic spectrum happy. Every new project had to undergo feasibility studies; cost estimates; engineering; design; acquisition of concrete, steel, gravel, sand, equipment, fuels, etc.; acquisition of rights of way; actual construction. Many public and private jobs and contracts were involved in every project. Millions were to be made and enormous political power was at hand. Whether one distributed gasoline, sold insurance, typewriters, paper or computers or brokered real estate.... state government contracts could potentially make you wealthy.

But without the lubricant of sufficient tax revenues, the joints of the political machine would grow rusty and grind to a halt.

Reynolds had pressed for enormous tax increases the first year of his term and had succeeded in passing the great bulk of it. But the political appetite of Reynolds and the Legislature had more than matched the size of the new taxes. Sudden growth in state spending occurred in the wake of the new taxes. As Reynolds faced re-election, the new revenues were now exhausted and the fiscal experts were hard pressed to find methods to balance the state budget.

The troops were getting restless with the talk of spending cuts, lay offs and postponements of bonds for new public projects.

The smoke drifted from Moulard's nostrils and mouth in a smooth stream as he considered how effectively he had guided Reynolds' fortunes to this moment. Reynolds was unopposed and it was simply too late for a serious opponent to run. He would continue to raise funds for Reynolds during the forty- five days that remained before qualifying. They would put up billboards to scare off any last minute opponent, then turn full attention to defeating the small cadry of legislators who had stood in their way of complete control of the Legislature. The constitutional requirement of a two-thirds vote of both Houses for new taxes and for bond authorizations had grown more and more difficult to obtain.

After qualifying, their hands would be free to defeat Reynolds' opponents and re-elect those legislators who were in trouble due to their pro-tax votes. These were the people he could best count on to help him with next year's inevitable tax program.

The machinery had to be greased.

FOUR

*"Wes Brot ich ess, des L ied ich sing." (Whose bread
I eat, his song I sing.)*

Middle High German saying

"Self-preservation is the law of nature"

Samuel Butler
(1612-1680)
English poet, satirist

Neil Moulard's thoughts were interrupted by the discussion at the breakfast table.

"If we can knock off Flint then the best possible example will be set. He's outspoken, he motivates opposition and he's a pain in the ass," said Senator Colbert Freeman, the governor's top floor leader in the Senate. "Flint educates the others. His staff does the advance work and he can usually arouse opposition on short notice."

"No," came Reynolds' firm answer. "I've got no problem with Flint. So he doesn't always agree with you people. Problem is, all of you are doing dozens of things in my name that I don't know anything about. I'm sick of it. Most of the things Flint nails you on I have nothing to do with anyway. I don't know what's worse, the occasional embarassment caused by Flint or the things my so called friends are doing behind my back. I'm probably getting the worst of both worlds because Flint's only catching you ten percent of the time."

Moulard had been momentarily caught off guard by the governor's outburst. Christ, what's wrong with him today, he wondered.

Freeman jumped back in without hesitation. "Don't blame that on me Governor. I take more heat for you than anyone. When I hear from someone in your office, I presume it's with your blessing," he replied.

"Well, you've had a pretty good agenda of your own for the nursing home owners," said Reynolds. "How much have they given you in contributions? And what about the sheriffs and assessors? You've handled all their payraises, expense accounts and retirement bills so they've pretty well lined up for your next race. And how are you doing with the cable television people and their exclusive franchise bill; and the Beer League bill to keep new beer labels from being distributed in Louisiana. You've handled the new licensure laws for everyone from beauticians to used auto parts dealers. Imagine not being able to sell a car part unless you get a state license. But all your bills have grandfather clauses, don't they Colbert?"

Reynolds glared angrily across the room at Freeman.

"How many of those bills do you think you could have passed if you were not my floorleader, Colbert?" asked Reynolds. "Do you think you could have passed them without everyone assuming these were administration bills?"

"I didn't hear you complain," Freeman replied lamely.

"No, and I haven't complained about all the projects you've loaded down the capital outlay bill with either," said Reynolds. "But I also won't complain if Flint beats you on some of those bills. I'd be happy if somehow he beat you on every one of them."

Freeman got up. Moulard thought he was going to walk out in a fury. But after a moment, Freeman looked at the others hesitantly and sat back down.

Sonny Stokes spoke up in his best country boy style, a broad smile spreading his red jowls. "Governor, I know how you feel. But Colbert earns his keep. Like getting those taxes passed. Voting for taxes and spending the money is two different things."

Then Stokes smiled even more broadly and took a bite of chewing tobacco before dropping one of his "good ole boy" one liners on the group.

"Voting for taxes is like pulling down your pants," he said. "It may be embarrassing but you've got to do it to make love, don't you see. Ole Colbert here has learned his job well. Maybe too well at times (he winked at Colbert Freeman). But he's been valuable to us in the Senate. Over the years, he's talked a lot of those boys over and over again into pulling down their pants on taxes so we can all make love spending money."

Stokes leaned back and spit a large wad of brown saliva into his waterglass in obvious satisfaction with the outburst of laughter from his colleagues.

"We shouldn't blame Colbert for wanting to get ahead spending some of that tax money," he added.

Stokes let that settle in for a moment. Then he looked at Reynolds and continued in his drawl.

"Now we don't mean to pick on Flint. I like him all right. But I'd like him a lot better if he were back in New Orleans tending to his grocery store and let'n somebody else sit up here in the Senate. Flint's like that leader duck. You shoot him down and the other ducks scatter. Flint has earned his retirement, so let's retire him."

Stokes finished with a smile as his last remark brought another round of chuckles from everyone, even Freeman who was still smarting from the governor's harsh words.

Moulard spoke for the first time. "Sonny's right, René. The press loves Flint. They hit you on twenty things at a press conference, you try to answer them, then who do they go see for the other side of the story? Hell, Flint probably feeds them a lot of those questions to begin with."

Reynolds took a long sip from his coffee then looked at Jackson Wells. "What do you think? What do they think of Flint in New Orleans?"

Jackson Wells looked around at the others. He had been unconsciously scratching the back of his head, the fingers of his right hand penetrating the neat semi-afro haircut. Wells was nattily attired in pleated slacks and a casual open collar shirt. His right hand left the back of his scalp and moved to his moustache where his thumb and forefinger twirled the long whiskers at the right corner of his pursed mouth, a large diamond mounted in the thick, gold ring worn on his ring finger gleaming in the morning sun. "Flint's a white fiscal conservative in a district with a pretty heavy black vote. But the blacks like him despite all of his budget cut proposals. He was advocating integration and voting rights when the rest of the Legislature advocated Jim Crow laws. He's the one who fought for fair black representation during the reapportionment fight. It was his bill that gave homebound sick people the right to absentee vote. It was his bill that allowed voter registrars to set up temporary offices around parishes, even in churches or shopping centers to register people to vote. He's always been good on black issues when you other white boys were running off and hiding."

Wells smiled broadly at them. He enjoyed digging at his white political friends.

"But he's also got opposition," Wells observed. "Those votes against the taxes offended the teachers' union, who will tell their people he must have been against their pay raises. The welfare people would surely like to burn him for a lot of those spending cuts. Of course, Colbert's special interest friends would love to kick Flint's ass too."

Wells looked at them again and summarized his thoughts, "It wouldn't be easy to beat Flint. You would need to get a candidate who could split the whites, then spend a hell of a lot of money with the blacks." Wells' right hand dropped casually to the table top as if to punctuate his final statement.

Moulard had wondered when Wells would get around to talking money. But he agreed with Wells' evaluation. Flint would be hard to beat and it would be expensive.

"What about all the Republican legislators and the tax opponents? Do you plan the same kind of effort against them?" asked Reynolds of no one in particular.

Freeman spoke up again. "Why don't we just let nature take its course with the ones who are strong. No use wasting our time against a popular Republican in a conservative district. We'll see who runs against them and perhaps help the opponents. Labor will oppose a bunch of them. If it looks as though someone who is vulnerable might slip past qualifying without an opponent, then we'll try to find a candidate. So basically we'll low key it."

"O.K.," Reynolds replied. "If you can find a strong opponent for Flint, then go for it. Don't get me publicly involved in any of these races. Let's just keep things quiet until qualifying is over. I don't want an opponent."

FIVE

*All great reforms, great movements, come from the
bottom and not the top...Whenever there is a wrong,
point it out to all the world, and you can trust the people to fight it.*

John Peter Altgeld
(1847-1902)
Governor of Illinois

(One Month Later)

Flint opened his eyes as the morning light filtered through the
blinds of his Baton Rouge hotel room window. He rolled over to
check the time. 5:45 a.m. He closed his eyes and remembered
the bitter battle on the Senate floor last night. Thank God the session was ending today. He had never seen Colbert Freeman blow
his cool so entirely. It had been a typical Freeman bill .... creating
a statewide bond authority to approve tax-exempt bonds for private
businesses. The new authority would be exempt from public bid
laws, Code of Ethics, legislative rules review, the open meetings
law and public records law.

In effect, this new authority would be able to give virtually
unlimited amounts of loan money to businessmen at two points
lower than the prime interest rate, and do so with impunity, privately without public scrutiny. The potential for favoritism, abuse and
self-enrichment were absurdly apparent.

Flint had failed to kill the bill because of the weight of the governorship. Freeman argued it was an essential part of the governor's
"economic development program". But Flint had been successful
with amendments to subject this new bond commission to the open
meetings law and the public records law although Freeman had
opposed both amendments. His other amendments had failed.

Flint smiled at the memory of Freeman taking the mike on personal privilege after debate to excoriate and angrily attack Flint
because he believed Flint had intentionally embarrassed him during debate.

22

It had been another defeat for Flint. His amendments had improved the bill but still the new law was another step backwards.

Flint got out of bed and slipped into his running shorts, shirt and shoes. If he could not sleep maybe he could lose a little weight. He took the elevator downstairs and walked to the top of the nearby levee of the Mississippi River. He gazed at the State Capitol rising thirty-seven stories above the skyline of Baton Rouge. Then he went through some quick calisthenics before beginning his two mile run along the top of the Mississippi River levee.

Flint felt a love-hate relationship with this town and the Legislature. He had spent most of his adult life as a state senator. He had achieved little recognition outside of New Orleans and Baton Rouge except among the state's politicians and press. Flint was not particularly popular among legislators although he was not really disliked either. He had made them too uncomfortable too many times when hard decisions were to be made. Many did not want to know (and they certainly did not want their constituents to know) what they were about to unknowingly do wrong, especially when they were already committed on a vote. That only made a tough decision even tougher.

But the years had softened Flint. He was far less abrasive than in his earlier days. He had become adept at resolving most issues that concerned him privately before they ever reached the Senate floor. He found that the great majority of legislators did not want to pass a bad law and, equally important, most wanted to vote for good, progressive ideas. But politics ruled their minds. He learned that his efforts of persuasion had the highest degree of success when exercised in the privacy of a quiet conversation. A floor fight inevitably made people choose political sides, instead of deciding the merits of the issue. So a floor fight was a last resort.

Last night's floor fight had been unavoidable. Freeman, Stokes and the others knew that it was to their advantage to push the issue to a head. Each senator had to deal with the governor on everything from drainage problems in their districts to their own legislation. Flint could not win against such influence.

The cool morning air felt good in his lungs. It was therapeutic to gaze over the tiny tugs and the ocean vessels moving over the water as he jogged along. As he made his turn after ten minutes of jogging and started back, his gaze again fell on the Capitol building. Although much frustration and discouragement had been experienced in that building during his career, there had been many good times too.

After all, twenty-seven years ago there had been no public bid laws, central purchasing laws, highway priority program, dual office holding law, Code of Ethics, contractual review law, open meetings law or public records law available for Freeman and his cohorts to try to destroy. Racial justice had been established in this southern state during his political life. Many good improvements had been made over the years.

He did not know whether the summers away from Susan and the kids attending legislative sessions had been worth it. While the kids were growing up, they had spent portions of each session with Flint. But Susan and the kids would usually grow weary of it quickly after a couple of weeks and return home.

It seemed strange to be ending his last session of the Legislature. How quickly the years had passed. He felt no older, no wiser. Only more aware of his mortality, his limitations, his shortcomings. He had been unable to share his retirement plans with anyone but Susan. He would tell the rest of his family tomorrow. His colleagues would find his personal letter waiting for them when they arrived home from Baton Rouge, and he planned a press conference next week.

It would be a low-key withdrawal with no fuss.

The message light was blinking on the phone when he returned to his hotel room. It was 6:45 a.m., still early for a call. The desk gave him a long-distance number for Jeffrey Bordelon. He dialed for the operator. Bordelon was a highly respected, retired congressman from the Third Congressional District. Now a youthful, vigorous seventy-five years old, Bordelon conducted a highly successful law practice in New Iberia while maintaining his role as the elder statesman of Louisiana politics.

"Congressman Bordelon, this is Darin Flint returning your call."

"Hello, Darin. Good to hear your voice. You're kind of late getting in, aren't you? You must have been out all night celebrating the end of the session." Flint could hear the older man's chuckle in the phone.

"No sir. I just got back from a little early morning exercise on the levee. Sorry I missed your call. Is there a problem?" Flint asked.

"I don't have a problem, but we do. Darin, I gave most of my life to public service in this state. I had a lot of fun, don't get me wrong. But there were plenty of sacrifices. I don't want to see it all go down the drain. I don't like what's happening in Baton Rouge," said Bordelon.

"I understand your feelings. I don't like it either."

"Well, what are you going to do about it?"

"Well, I've done what I can in the Legislature," answered Flint, feeling a bit annoyed with the question.

"I know you have, Darin. I appreciate it. But it's not enough," said Bordelon, echoing Flint's own feelings. "We need to organize a campaign against René Reynolds. That's what elections are for, you know. What do you think?"

"Frankly, I don't see anyone on the horizon with any chance at all, especially at this late date," Flint answered quickly. "Best thing to do is to concentrate on House and Senate races, and try to improve the people we have there."

After a moment, Bordelon said, "Well, sometimes it's better late than never. You realize Reynolds will be deeply involved in legislative races if he doesn't have a race of his own."

There was another pause.

"Listen, Darin, a bunch of us will be meeting at Jon Douglas' home at noon in Baton Rouge to talk about all this. Will you come?"

"Yes, sir, I'll come."

"Good, see you at noon."

SIX

"Sometimes people call me an idealist. Well, that is the way I know I am an American. America is the only idealist nation in the world."

Woodrow Wilson
(1856-1924)
28th President of the United States
Speech, Sioux Falls, September 8, 1919

Darin Flint pulled his '81 Olds to a stop across the street from Jon Douglas' home. He had come early in hopes of having a talk with Jon before the meeting. But he could see from the five cars in the driveway that several people had already arrived.

Jon Douglas was an old friend he had gotten to know early in his legislative career. As a professor at L.S.U. and a statistics expert, Jon had been on contract with the Legislature to prepare computer programs for legal research, legislative bill drafting and bill tracking during sessions. Jon was in private business now and had a growing reputation as an expert in polling and political consulting. He was energetic, humorous and a pleasure to work with.

"Hello, Darin. You're early," said Jon Douglas at the front door of his home. "How've you been?"

"Well, the session is ending and I'm heading home tonight. So I guess I'm doing pretty well," said Flint with a smile as they walked toward the dining room.

Flint felt like he was interrupting a meeting instead of arriving at the beginning of one. The smoke was thick and there was a half empty dish of cookies on the table.

"I believe you know everyone," said Jon. "Congressman Bordelon, Eric McKay, Barbara Durham from my office, Rodney Libscomb, Carey Jefferson, Jane Baldwin, Terrell Franks, and Joel Whitney."

Flint greeted them one by one. McKay had been deeply involved in the multi-parish banking controversy and had spent much time lobbying Flint. Libscomb of Shreveport had formerly served in the House of Representatives and had been one those renegade

"Young Turks" who had started the reform movement almost twenty years ago. Carey Jefferson was a lobbyist representing several different business clients but Flint only knew him casually.

Jane Baldwin was a veteran member of the City Council in New Orleans and was well known for her ascerbic wit, political savvy and her blunt honesty. She was in her forties, thin and bespeckled, with a warm, friendly smile.

Terrell Franks and Joel Whitney were close friends of Jon Douglas. Franks was the only black at the meeting. Whitney was a well respected business attorney and civic leader in Baton Rouge. Flint did not know Whitney very well.

"I thought I was early but it appears I'm late," said Flint with a laugh.

"No, you're right on time," answered Jon. "I hope you like Popeye's fried chicken. We're informal today."

Jon brought several bags of chicken to the table along with paper plates. The group exchanged small talk while they ate lunch. The conversation turned to politics.

Flint gazed across the room at Bordelon's features. He remembered this little man as a fiery, demonstrative, articulate stumpfighter during his prime in politics. Bordelon's outspoken style had been vintage Louisiana. Bordelon's common touch and gregarius nature had made him a favorite with local politicians. He enjoyed a good party and understood well the give and take necessary for success in Louisiana's political world. But he had also been very different from others in his generation of politicians. Although he played the political game where necessary to survive, he felt hypocritical in the process. He clung to a high ideal of simple honesty, frank talk and genuine belief in statesmanship. Bordelon felt genuine guilt whenever practical politics led to a compromise of these ideals. His fun-loving nature was balanced by an almost studious approach to legislation. He spoke several languages, aside from English and French, with precision. His Cajun upbringing among a family where hard work and little money was a way of life had instilled in his character a gutsy and fiesty will to succeed.

Bordelon had held only one office during his long career. Congressman from the Third Congressional District of Louisiana. His career in Washington spanned thirty years, the last twelve as Chairman of the powerful House Rules Committee. His retirement five years ago had surprised everyone. He had explained his retirement from Congress in typical Bordelon fashion, "I'm seventy years old. Nobody should own a seat in Congress. It's time for new blood to take over."

But retirement did not mean inactivity. Bordelon had moved home to New Iberia, opened his new law practice and built a solid reputation in the legal community.

Jeffrey Bordelon was small, slight and dapper in his attire. A well-organized man. He had a full head of white hair, contrasting comfortably with the slightly red tint of his face. His demeanor was calm. Only his bright, alert blue eyes betrayed the intense energy packaged in that small body.

Flint had never known Bordelon well. But he had always admired him.

"Darin, have you given our conversation this morning any more thought," asked Jeffrey Bordelon.

"Not really. I've been preoccupied all morning," answered Flint to the older man's question. "But, really, my opinion is the same. You can harass Reynolds with an opponent but you cannot beat him."

"Well, let me ask you a different question," Bordelon persisted. "What would you do if you were the governor of this state?"

Startled, Flint stared back at Bordelon for several moments, gained control of his poise and said, "Well, if you really want to know, I'll tell you. But I'm sure you don't want to sit here and listen to me critique a dozen issues."

"Humor me, Darin. Tell me what you'd do about highways for instance," Bordelon requested.

"O.K." Flint looked at the others for some clue as to what this was about. He could not read their faces. "Well, I think we need a five year plan to four-lane the eight or ten essential highways linking regions of the state. The highways chosen would compliment, not duplicate, the interstate highways. Several of these most essential roads are already four laned but need upgrading and better maintenance. Part of this plan would be designating another ten or twelve routes for constructing passing lanes. We'd finance construction and maintenance by dedicating a portion of our special fuels tax, which is already dedicated generally to the highway program. These essential highways would be designated as a separate program and removed from our highway priority program. Otherwise, I would insist on strict adherance to the priority program."

Flint stopped. "Shall I go on?"

"What about government operations and education?" asked Bordelon.

"All right. I'd enforce those portions of the capital outlay law that require every project be evaluated for cost and benefits before presentation to the Legislature. I'd stop the assault on the reforms we enacted over the past fifteen or twenty years. In public education, we'd have a new career teacher salary plan. Salaries would be higher. But for one to move up the ladder each year, their supervisor must certify the teacher met certain fundamental standards of competency in her teaching effort. I favor a practical merit plan. As in civil service, an appeal plan would have to be put in place for teachers who feel they've been evaluated too low. I'd also like to initate a system of sixth grade centers in urban centers statewide. In higher education, I'd resurrect the old masterplan of the Board of Regents to define the role of each state college and eliminate duplication."

"How much would a teachers pay plan cost?" asked Lipscomb.

"Depends on how high you want to raise the salaries. Roughly, we'd spend $100 million to $160 million for a meaningful payraise. Some dedication of new offshore oil revenues may be appropriate. But the fact is that at least $100 million of payraise money must come from spending reductions. If you eliminate just those new programs or program expansions created since Reynolds' last round of new taxes, you'd have more than that $100 million of savings. We proposed almost $200 million of spending cuts this summer during budget debates. Some of the cuts would bring political complaints but no serious loss of services would occur."

"Anything else fundamental," asked Libscomb.

Flint stood up. "Yes, civil service needs a complete overhaul. We've developed a sound plan on how to do it. We can reduce 2500 classifications to under one thousand. Eliminate inequities. We can change the step pay plan to put merit in the system as its supposed to be. We can expand our executive training program. We can release our upper echelon positions from specific salary scales. It's called a modified open range payscale. We can save millions by eliminating many of the unclassified, political job positions in state government."

Flint hesitated for a moment, then added, "I think we need much better environmental protection, especially in the wetlands and the Mississippi River."

"Well, Darin, you're certainly not short on issues," laughed Jon Douglas.

Flint smiled, "I've been accumulating them for twenty- seven years. But, really, there are some more broad questions that trouble me. The annual labor-management battles kill our economic development efforts. The fighting never stops. I would do my best to push them into compromise on the most controversial issues. Perhaps business could make concessions to labor on workers' compensation and safety issues if labor would agree to a long moratorium on Right to Work or agency shop legislation. We need to reduce unemployment compensation expenses. Our business image is terrible compared to other southern states."

Flint thought a moment, then continued, "And we need to outgrow the mentality that favoritism and sweetheart contracts are normal political practices....that contributing to a candidate so you can double your money later is some kind of legitimate game. I'm no prude but this marginal corruption is killing us. Do you realize we are spending way over $100 million this year just on consultant study contracts? Many of those contracts were let for just one reason and that's to line someone's pocket. Why do you think so many of the governor's friends and ex-employees have opened consultant firms?"

Flint caught his breath. "Hell, they'll study anything. I read one thirty page report last week that was little more than a high school research project. The state paid sixty thousand dollars for it."

Flint stared into his coffee then looked at Congressman Bordelon.

"You know, Congressman, the vicious cycle of political contributions and reward by favoritism can be broken. But to do it, it must be proven it doesn't have to cost millions of dollars to be elected governor. If we can ever control contributions, then maybe we can control the pressure for abuse."

"Are you willing to be that candidate to try to prove it?" asked Bordelon. "You know state government, you're a good campaigner, you're qualified and you have a good record."

Flint sat silent and looked down at his hands, gathering his thoughts. Then he looked back at Bordelon.

"There's nothing I'd like better. But it's never been a realistic goal for me. To be frank with you, I've decided to retire from politics altogether. I'm not running for re-election to the Senate."

Now it was everyone else's turn to sit silent, in surprise, for a few moments.

SEVEN

"There are plenty of political problems with my record," Darin Flint said to the group as they watched him intently. "I'm vulnerable and I've alienated plenty of groups. I have few sources of funds and no organization. I'd be a disaster."

Jane Baldwin interrupted him. "Darin, I'd like you to listen to some information Jon has been explaining to us."

The attention turned to Jon Douglas who was wiping clean a large blackboard in a corner of the room.

"Darin, we've been doing some pretty intense studies of Reynolds over the past three months. His name identity is virtually one hundred percent. His approval rating is only mediocre and actually dropping. It was sixty-eight percent in April but now its dropped to sixty-one percent in July. Among blacks, his approval rating is at seventy percent. Among whites, its only fifty-six percent."

Jon paused. "Any questions yet?"

Jon looked at them then turned back to the board.

"Reynolds has always been strong among the poor. Whites with income under fifteen thousand dollars give him sixty percent approval. That certainly isn't overwhelming. Ofcourse, the black ratings are much better but that's to be expected. But again, blacks overall approval is seventy percent. I've seen him much stronger in the past. His greatest weakness is in college educated whites where his approval actually falls to fifty-four percent among white women. Among college educated blacks, his approval drops to sixty-four percent."

"What about your geographic results?" asked Flint.

Jon reached for a separate file.

"Mostly, its what you'd expect. Reynolds' best ratings are in the river parishes, in Acadiana and in New Orleans. But his Acadiana score is not overwhelming. Among whites, it is sixty-four percent. In Lafayette, his white approval is only fifty-five percent. Across north and central Louisiana, Reynolds has always been vulnerable and he still is. In Jefferson Parish and St. Tammany Parish, Reynolds' negative rating is over thirty percent. Of course, those are big Republican areas."

"What's his overall negative rating?" asked Flint.

"Eighteen percent."

Flint studied the figures Jon had been putting on the blackboard.

"Jon, I don't know much about polls. I've seldom used them. Why don't you consider Reynolds' sixty-one percent approval as being good?"

"Well, it is pretty good," Jon explained. "But its not great or spectacular as Reynolds' ratings have often been before. Remember, only three months ago his approval rating was sixty-eight percent. A drop of seven percent means something is happening out there."

"Like what?"

"I'm not sure," Jon replied. "I think a lot of incumbant legislators can be beaten this fall. Reynolds is not immune to the same discontent."

"What's the bottom line?" asked Jane Baldwin. "How do you see Reynolds' strength for re-election?"

"He's strong but has noticeable cracks in his armor. Time is on his side. A short campaign doesn't give an opponent much chance to attain name recognition, develop organization, raise funds and create a following. Reynolds will probably be reelected no matter who runs."

Jon stopped and smiled at Flint. "I've been polling you too. In fact, we matched a lot of people against Reynolds. The results on you would be valid only in the Orleans metropolitan area and the Baton Rouge area where you have some name recognition. The people who've heard of you like you very much. After twenty-seven years in office, that's quite an accomplishment. You've been around a long time but you're only fifty-seven years old. You look younger. In the poll, people like your maturity and your independence."

"Tell me about the Orleans area," Flint requested.

"Well, your name recognition is seventy-five percent. Of those who know you, you have a seventy-eight percent approval rating. Blacks and whites rate you about the same. Your negative is less than five percent which is negligible. It gives you a real jump in a statewide race to have a substantial name recognition in the Orleans metro area to build on."

Jon stopped to thumb through his papers, then looked up when he found what he was searching for. He wiped the blackboard clean.

"Now look at this. I put you head up with Reynolds in your legislative district. We asked six hundred of your constituents who they would vote for. You narrowly won thirty-six to thirty-five percent with the rest undecided. Your district is over thirty-five percent black. I think that is a remarkable showing."

"But it's my own district. Why is that so remarkable?"

"Because the people who know you also know Reynolds. His approval rating is seventy percent in your district. His name recognition is one-hundred percent. He's the governor. Our poll shows your people think you could be governor too. If your campaign could sell to the rest of the state what you've sold in your district, then you're a winner. Most importantly, that poll result shows you can run with Reynolds among black voters."

"Jon, I think you're reading way too much into that," protested Flint.

"Hold on, Darin. We also polled you head up with Reynolds in the four parish Orleans region. Now among all voters, you are stomped fifty-nine percent to twenty-five percent, the remainder undecided. Actually that's pretty damn good for someone who is not even a candidate. But among those who recognize your name, Reynolds gets less than fifty percent. He beat you forty-eight percent to thirty-two percent with the rest undecided among that group. That's a most impressive statistic."

"O.K.," interrupted Congressman Bordelon. "What are Flint's chances to win if he runs?"

"With the short time remaining, Flint would be considered very successful if he won forty percent of the statewide vote. It is very unlikely he could do better than that. For him to win would take a major political miracle. It would take a great campaign and a lot of luck."

Flint had stopped believing in miracles a long time ago. But if there was a chance to win, even if remote, then he was interested. A long silence prevailed as another round of coffee was poured and everyone collected their thoughts.

"Well, some of you have done a lot of listening and no talking," said Congressman Bordelon, interrupting the silence. "Eric, tell Darin what you think"

"Congressman, you know how I feel. I want to mount a campaign against Reynolds and his bunch. Darin, I've admired you for a long time. So have others who may not always agree with you. I would be very excited about your candidacy and you could count on my complete and deep involvement."

McKay dabbed his mouth with his napkin, then continued, "There's more good news than bad news in those polls. To me, those statistics say you have a decent shot."

Joel Whitney entered the conversation. "Reynolds may not be possible to beat but I'd like to find out. Here in Baton Rouge I think he's beatable. He's Labor's boy but they haven't appreciated the way he's ducked their issues. Don't get me wrong. They'll stick with Reynolds. But they don't see you as an enemy. They might enjoy watching Reynolds on the hot seat for awhile. That might give you an opening to maybe halfway neutralize Labor. We can raise money for you in Baton Rouge and organize a good volunteer headquarters."

"Thank you, Joel. I appreciate your offer," said Flint. "Jane, what do you think?"

"I think Reynolds needs an opponent, a strong opponent. I just hate to see you give up your senate seat for a campaign that is unlikely to succeed. But you can count on my complete support if you do it. In New Orleans, I think you can beat him among whites. You have always had good black support but, frankly, I don't think you can expect them to support you over Reynolds. You'd do well to get twenty-five percent of the black vote. With that, you'd split or lose Orleans by a small margin. But you can win in Jefferson, St. Bernard and St. Tammany."

Jane Baldwin took a drag from her cigarette then completed her thoughts. "So, in the four parish Orleans area, its doable."

"Anybody else? Terrell?" asked Bordelon.

Terrell Franks had been completely quiet throughout the discussion. The former newspaperman sat up in his chair and looked at Flint. "Darin, when I first began as a reporter covering the Legislature, I noticed you and wrote about you in the Advocate. You reacted to issues from the gut, you were outspoken and always in a floorfight of some sort. You were good copy. But I figured you wouldn't last much longer. You'd either get beat for re-election or you'd rapidly run for some higher office. The Legislature was just not big enough for you. Instead, you've spent twenty-seven years there. To me, you are the perfect picture of political frustration. You can't be happy spending more time in the Senate. But you shouldn't retire. My advice? I say roll the dice. Go for it. Even if you lose, you can make a tremendous impact. If you win, you can permanently change Louisiana politics."

"Carey, you want to add anything?" asked Bordelon.

Carey Jefferson put down his coffee cup then spoke, "Just this. I lobby for a lot of clients and business associations before the Legislature. If we offend the governor, then my job as a lobbyist gets much tougher. And my clients suffer. But my people will help as much as they can within limits. Why? Dammit, the independent oil producers are good citizens of this state. We're not like 'Big Oil'. We live and work here."

Jefferson was interrupted by laughter from everyone at his last comment. He persisted with his line of thought. "Same thing with the Retailer's Association. They are offended and embarrassed by the politics in Baton Rouge. We can gather a lot of small contributions from individual members. But no formal endorsement or support can come until we can see more clearly how the campaign is developing. Personally, I'd like to see you run and I'll do all I can to a point. I draw the line when my involvement would hurt my clients."

"How much will you raise immediately," Congressman Bordelon asked abruptly.

"I can commit fifty thousand dollars for the campaign. I'll raise twenty-five thousand dollars by qualifying."

The week of qualifying would begin on July 23rd, two weeks away.

"After that, it depends on whether Darin is turning them on," Jefferson added. "I'd like to have Darin speak to the convention of both the retailers and LAIPRO this summer. It might be interesting because Reynolds will also speak to each group. I could also arrange private meetings with my key members."

Flint felt his heartbeat quicken in his chest as a rush of excitement and anticipation went through him. The thought of head to head confrontations with Reynolds so early in the campaign got his competitive juices flowing.

Darin turned to Rodney Libscomb, his friend from the early reform battles. "Rodney, I'd like your advice."

"Darin, I wouldn't be here if I didn't want you to do it. It's never easy to sell a New Orleans boy in north Louisiana. But I think they'll like your message. You've been too damned liberal for me like I've always told you. Too much civil rights in your blood, and it won't do you any good. Reynolds and Jackson Wells will buy up every black organization in the state. But you know better than I do what your chances are with blacks. I can organize a good headquarters effort in Shreveport. I can get deeply involved in statewide fundraising if you wish. Reynolds support in north Louisiana is skin deep and I think people would welcome a good alternative. I'm ready to start tomorrow morning."

"Well Darin, I guess that leaves only me," said Congressman Bordelon. "I organized this little meeting. Jon Douglas and his people started polling last spring at my request. I've had a growing feeling about Reynolds. He's not as strong as he seems. I have a feeling about you too. You've persevered for almost three decades doing what's necessary to survive but remaining independent. You're an idealist. That's what Louisiana desperately needs right now. There's a thirst for it. I urge you to run and not waste another day. I think you should let Jon's people start arranging your calendar right now for organizational meetings in each section of the state."

Bordelon paused and looked down at his fingers, which were lightly tapping the table top. Then Bordelon's dancing blue eyes rose quickly to meet Flint's.

"In Acadiana, we'll surprise the hell out of Reynolds. He's not the only Cajun boy who knows his politics and I want to remind him of that. Let's make the decision, decide who's going to do what, have some quick meetings around the state then announce your candidacy within ten days. What do you say?"

For the first time since the meeting began, Flint relaxed and smiled broadly.

"Frankly, I'm speechless. I'm willing to give it hell if you are. Jon, I need to make a telephone call to my wife Susan. I've got to stop some letters announcing my retirement from politics from being mailed. Where's your phone?"

EIGHT

"Poor man's candidate and rich man's friend."

American Political Formula

René Reynolds watched the pretty girl walk from the bed where he was lying beneath the covers toward the bathroom of his suite in the Baton Rouge Hilton. Her long dark hair fell across her bare shoulders. His eyes surveyed the slim back, the rounded hips and her well proportioned legs. Reynolds suppressed his rising desire to pull her back into bed for another round of lovemaking.

He needed to get to the Mansion by seven o'clock.

"Honey, open the curtains," Reynolds asked her. He watched her naked body walk across the room and silently obey. She was about twenty-three he guessed. Perfect breasts, Reynolds thought to himself as she again crossed the room and entered the bathroom. He had noticed her in the Capitol last week and learned she was a secretary in the Attorney General's office. Reynolds reflected on the fact that she was married. He wondered what she had told her husband to stay out all night.

Reynolds gazed out the broad glass window at the early morning light falling over Interstate 10 and the smaller buildings fifteen floors below. Reynolds liked young, attractive, married women. They were sexually experienced and knew how to keep their mouths shut. He had enjoyed this girl more than most. She had seemed hesitant, even innocent, but she had become very passionate as the evening progressed. This one would be promoted next week.

The bathroom door opened and the girl stepped out. She had dressed and was ready to leave.

"Should I have one of my men drive you somewhere?"

She shook her head side to side.

The girl did not look up at him. She moved quickly for the door.

"You're beautiful," Reynolds said. "I'll keep in touch."

Reynolds did not notice the girl's hand tremble as she reached for the doorknob. He did not see the tears on her face.

She left without a word.

Reynolds stared at the door the girl had closed behind her. He thought about his wife. As he lay back on the pillow, his mind wandered back to the early days of his relationship with her. Reynolds had met Felicia during their college days and married her before either of them had graduated. The marriage had been a spontaneous unannounced decision. They had been hopelessly in love. Reynolds' parents had been furious and even threatened to cut off his financial support. But it worked out. Felicia graduated the next year and taught school while Reynolds entered and finally graduated with honors from the Loyola Law School in New Orleans.

Seven years passed before they had children. By that time, Reynolds was independently wealthy. Reynolds had proven to be an aggressive lawyer with keen business instincts. It had been easy to build on his father's successful law practice and business connections. Neil Moulard was his father's law partner and it was during this period that Moulard began guiding his career, expecially after the death of Reynolds' father.

But those lucrative years had taken a toll on his relationship with Felicia. Maybe he had been wrong to insist that she stop teaching after his graduation from law school. But he did not want her working. After all, they had not needed the money. Reynolds had planned a political career early on. He wanted Felicia to join civic organizations, charity drives and community activities. He had been insistant that she cultivate friendships and social connections. It would be beneficial later on.

Their marriage deteriorated. Reynolds was consumed by his career. Felicia was unhappy and rebellious. She had become distant and resentful. In retrospect, Reynolds did not blame her for her feelings. He realized he had neglected her badly. But at the time, Felicia's attitude had infuriated him. He remembered the ugly, loud arguments that had almost ended their marriage.

Then their first child had arrived. Then another. Then after a few years, the third child. All three were girls, Celine, Elise and Sarah. They were ten, nine, and five years of age respectively. The children had immediately filled the void he had created in Felicia's life.

She was a devoted, full time mother. More accurately, she was both mother and father to the children, he thought to himself with a deep feeling of self-reproach. He sincerely loved his children. But politics was a jealous mistress. René Reynolds had not been around much for family activities during the past ten years.

He had hoped the advent of children would rebuild his relationship with Felicia. It had not. The children replaced him. Reynolds gradually had become the resentful partner in the marriage. From the meteoric beginning of his political career, he found many opportunities for discreet affairs with other women. As time passed, he had begun accepting and finally often seeking such incidents with an almost detached attitude. Now it was commonplace.

If Felicia knew, she kept it to herself. They got along well enough these days. Felicia no longer objected to his politics or the long absences necessitated by his career. In fact, Reynolds' wife and his young children were very attractive and valuable parts of his political image.

The many stories of the Reynolds children playfully appearing from under a table or desk during an important governmental or political meeting at the mansion were manifold. It was reminiscent of the John Kennedy toddlers in the White House. Neil Moulard had recognized the public relations value of such stories and had made certain the press always picked up on these items.

Suddenly aware he was dozing, Reynolds pushed his thoughts of Felicia and the children from his mind. He got up and dressed. One half hour later, Reynolds was back in the mansion having his shave while Moulard brought him up to date on the morning news.

"We've got a problem in New Orleans," said Moulard. "A School Board member named Jerry Giaccia announced yesterday to run for the Senate in Darin Flint's district."

"Why is that a problem? I thought you were looking for opponents for Flint."

"We are. But Giaccia is a very close friend of Flint's. He's like an adopted son to him."

Reynolds quietly pondered this piece of news while the barber wiped the last of the shaving cream from Reynolds face with a hot towel. "Well, do you figure Flint is retiring and put this guy in the race."

"That may be it. But Flint never struck me as the retiring type. I've got people checking with Flint and Giaccia today to see what's going on."

Reynolds nodded, adjusted his tie and started for the doorway. "Are we all set on the fundraiser?" he asked as he left the room.

Moulard walked with Reynolds across the hallway to the staircase and answered in a matter of fact manner.

"It's going well. The receipts are over $850 thousand and we're still hitting it hard. The heavyhitters' midnight breakfast will probably be another $400 thousand." Moulard's monotone concealed his pleasure with the success of his efforts.

Moulard took pride in being the best money raiser and organizer in Louisiana history. He and the members of Reynolds' large and experienced finance committee had directly "solicited" every contractor, consultant, textbook company, nursing home owner, office equipment supplier, building lessor, real estate broker, oil and gas firm (in exploration, pipelines, refining, distribution), utility companies, political appointees and anyone else their computer revealed doing business with the state to buy at least a table of tickets.

Local political leaders were mobilized in every community to do the same thing.

It was a black tie affair at the Monteleone Hotel in the heart of the French Quarter, with tickets priced at one thousand dollars per couple. Al Hirt and Sammy Davis, Jr. would supply the entertainment while hors d'oeuvres were by La Louisiane Restaurant. The midnight breakfast would be in the Plimsoll Club high above the New Orleans skyline in the International Trade Mart Building. The food would be served by Commander's Palace Restaurant. Al Hirt and Sammy Davis, Jr. would offer an encore at this late night affair. The price was five thousand dollars a couple. This was the heavyhitter's function.

Moulard's fundraising wizardry over the past three years had Reynolds' campaign treasury flush with over four and a half million dollars. Tonight's events would push that close to six million dollars. If an opponent surfaced, even a minor opponent, Moulard could more than double that amount for Reynolds during the next three months.

"Who's here for breakfast?" Reynolds asked as he finished dressing. He had dressed casually in slacks, an open collared, short sleeve shirt with a light summer sports coat.

"Danny is here with the video tapes, radio ads and the newspaper insert. He also brought you the final color layout of the billboards. Unless you say no, they go up this week."

Breakfast was to be served on the patio under a slowly revolving fan. It was seven o'clock and still cool. Reynolds' active evening had left him more hungry and thirsty than usual. He requested a full breakfast.

Danny Ross greeted him with a smile. Ross was not only a talented ad man, he was also married to Reynolds' youngest sister. He was thirty-three years old, slim and olive skinned, articulate and personable. Danny Ross appreciated his brother-in-law's confidence in him, but he felt somewhat smothered by Reynolds and embarrassed by the easy success his marriage had brought him.

Ross never knew what to call Reynolds ....Governor, René or what.

"Let's get down to business, Danny. Let's see what you've got."

Danny reached for his folder and produced the billboard layout which Reynolds reviewed, then approved. Over one thousand full size billboards would appear across the state before the end of the week.

Julie Ross, Reynolds' sister, arrived during breakfast with the ten page newspaper insert that Ross and Associates had been perfecting for two months. Reynolds had told Danny and Julie to charge him the highest fee they could possibly justify for their public relations work, then double it. It was a good way to get campaign funds into a family business, and Reynolds was not concerned about ever running short of campaign funds.

The timing of the insert was finalized. It would be in every Louisiana daily newspaper on the Sunday morning before qualifying began. All these expenditures would justify his fundraising in the public eye while also discouraging last minute opponents.

Next, Danny turned on the oversized television set his crew had set up and inserted the video cartridge. "We've prepared four sixty second spots from the shooting we did during the session. We've incorporated the script changes you suggested last week," Danny explained. "We really could use only two, or we could rotate three of them....or all four if you want."

They watched and studied each tape several times. Reynolds enjoyed this work. He liked seeing himself on television. He knew he was effective. The ads portrayed him as a very energetic, strong leader. One ad included tape of him being sworn in as governor....then conducting a cabinet meeting....finally speaking directly to the television viewer about his accomplishments and hopes for Louisiana. In another, Reynolds was shown with his horses, playing with his children on the lawn in front of the mansion, then shaking hands on a busy street with constituents, finally concluding with a emotional face to face statement to the television audience as he held his wife of eighteen years near him.

They decided to rotate these first two spots for the next week on prime time on every television station. They would decide later whether to use the other two spots during the week of qualifying. Similar decisions were made on his radio spots and newspaper advertisements. Final approval was also given by Reynolds to a two hundred thousand piece mailing that would be dropped eight days before qualifying began.

The expenditures of the Reynolds campaign would run over one million dollars by the time he submitted his qualifying papers to the Secretary of State.

By nine a.m., Reynolds was in his office hearing veto or approval recommendations from his staff on new laws just enacted by the Legislature. Moulard walked in and interrupted the meeting around eleven o'clock.

"René, I need to talk with you for a minute."

Reynolds asked the others to leave them alone. When they were alone, Moulard said, "I just spoke to Jackson Wells on this Jerry Giaccia and Darin Flint. If the rumors we're hearing are true, Flint's not retiring. Hell, the sonofabitch is running for governor."

NINE

"I hold a little rebellion now and then is a good thing, and as necessary in the political world as storms in the physical."

Thomas Jefferson
(1743-1826)
Third President of the United States

Events moved fast that week for Darin Flint. Flint's wife, Susan, had been Flint's campaign manager in two of his Senate campaigns. She and the family responded to Flint's decision to run with enthusiasm. John, his oldest, was thirty-seven years old and had grown up in the swirl of Flint's politics. John had gotten an accounting degree, then his law degree. He was a tax attorney. Flint's daughter, Jenny, was also a campaign veteran and had just graduated from L.S.U. with a business degree. At twenty-two years of age, she was a replica of her mother...slim, medium height, long brown hair and brown eyes. Also like her mother, Jenny was outgoing, well-liked and level headed.

Each family member accepted heavy responsibility in the campaign. John would be Flint's campaign treasurer, thereby accepting the task of filing all financial reports, administering all bank accounts, deposits and expenditures. Jenny would be in charge of Flint's scheduling and would work in concert with Barbara Durham of Jon Douglas' office in this capacity. Susan Flint would initially be in charge of organizing the volunteers in New Orleans until a permanent replacement could be found. As the candidate's wife, Susan would be needed on the campaign trail with Flint as soon as possible.

Flint had decided he would name Congressman Bordelon as his campaign manager. Bordelon had already assumed that role anyway. But Flint would wait to announce the appointment later to gain another wave of free media coverage after he had qualified as a candidate. Bordelon would bring instant recognition and credibility to his campaign on a statewide basis. But first, Flint would establish his own independence. Flint wanted no suggestions that he was anybody's candidate but his own.

Finance Chairman would be Joel Whitney. His informal finance committee of Carey Jefferson, Eric McKay, Joel Whitney and Rodney Libscomb was already hard at work. The first set of checks would be deposited when Flint formally announced his candidacy on July 18th, the Wednesday before qualifying would begin.

Jane Baldwin was already serving as his Orleans Parish campaign manager but that formal announcement would also come later.

Flint had slightly less than twelve thousand dollars still in his Senate campaign fund, which he had planned to donate to good legislative candidates around the state. Now he placed it in the "Flint for Governor" treasury to cover his initial expenses prior to his announcement.

Their meetings had produced a long list of things to do. Flint purchased three thousand plywood sign boards. A simple logo was designed in Jon Douglas' office; a silk screen team of students and friends of John and Jenny Flint were mobilized behind Flint's Grocery Store. They worked long shifts for seven straight days painting signs. This effort would continue throughout the campaign.

Flint's hope was to have six hundred signs erected state wide by the day after his announcement on July 18th in order to coincide with press coverage.

The organizational meetings that Flint, Congressman Bordelon and the others hastily arranged during those first three days had produced a small, enthusiastic group of organizers in each area of Louisiana. Congressman Bordelon's contacts all over the state had gotten him off to a fast start. The sign project was a test of their willingness. The hurried effort was carried out in a controlled panic. But by July 16th, reports from every district indicated they were ready to start erecting signs.

Two other important projects were underway. A pamphlet needed to be printed; Flint's announcement had to be planned and arranged. Flint secured copies of his old campaign materials, advertisements and pamphlets. He wrote a five page biographical sketch of his life. He updated his synopsis of his major legislative accomplishments, along with his past awards and honors. Then he prepared a list of his goals for Louisiana. All of this was placed in Jon Douglas' hands so appropriate material could be chosen for production of a pamphlet.

46

A series of photographs were taken of Flint and his family in different activities for use in the pamphlet. Flint turned over his file of old photographs to Jon.

Terrell Franks was designated by Flint to be his press coordinator. Franks needed the pamphlet printed in time for the July 18th press conference. He became deeply involved in its immediate production. Within five days, the pamphlet had been designed, approved by Flint and taken to the printer.

Franks, Barbara Durham and his daughter, Jenny, took charge of organizing the announcement. There would be a ten a.m. press conference in Baton Rouge in the senate briefing room. Joel Whitney, Jane Baldwin and Susan were making certain all of Flint's friends and political supporters were invited. Jane and John worked on young people and students to attend the press conference. They put their volunteers and friends to work assuring an enthusiastic crowd.

Flint personally took charge of another aspect of the press conference. He spent hours on the phone selectively speaking to close friends in government, colleagues in the Legislature and other public figures to ask them to attend either the Baton Rouge press conference or the one to be held in their region of the state.

Another important element was the blacks. Flint telephoned his most reliable friends in the black community and asked them to take responsiblities in his campaign. Most discouraged him or were non-commital. He gave Susan a list of key black supporters from his previous campaigns and had her call each one. Flint figured that whether they agreed to support him or not, they would appreciate being personally informed of his decision to run for governor.

Terrell Franks had close contacts with key black citizens statewide. Every black media person, including radio and newspaper owners and reporters, were contacted by Franks and asked to attend as a personal favor. In Baton Rouge, Franks secured the promise of key organizational leaders to at least attend and see what Flint had to say.

By July 17th, the day before his planned announcement, speculation about Darin Flint was surfacing in the newspaper. Curious television and radio reporters sought brief interviews with Flint and included him in news programs statewide. When asked if he was running, Flint's answer was simply that he would make an announcement of his decision on Wednesday.

During those hectic two weeks, Flint did one more thing. He convinced his good friend Jerry Giaccia, a young Italian serving on the Orleans School Board (who Flint had virtually raised from childhood as a part time employee in his grocery store), to run for the Senate seat Flint was leaving vacant.

Jerry Giaccia had announced his candidacy on July 12th.

TEN

There was a soft knock on the door. Flint looked up from the papers on his desk in his bedroom. "Come on in."

Susan pushed open the door. "I thought you could use a refreshment break." She carried a tray with two cups of coffee and a plate of cookies, and placed it on a table beside him. She pulled up a chair.

"Hey, you must be reading my mind," Flint said as he began munching on a cookie. "What's going on downstairs?"

"Jenny and Greg are handling all the calls and trying to get next weeks' schedule finalized," Susan answered. "How's it coming?" Greg Hawkins was Flint's legislative aide.

"I've got it down to eight minutes."

"Darin, I think you've got it short enough. You're too worried about boring the press. All the points you're covering are important."

Flint had been working on his announcement speech at every opportunity. He had finished his first draft yesterday morning and read it to Susan. After revisions, she had listened to it again last night and timed it at ten minutes. Flint wanted it hard hitting, thorough but short enough to leave plenty of time for questions from the press.

Jon Douglas wanted the typed speech delivered to his office by nine a.m. tomorrow so it could be copied and included in the five hundred press kits being prepared for Wednesday's press conference. After the ten a.m. press conference, there would be a one-thirty p.m. press conference in New Orleans held in Flint's front yard. Following the New Orleans press conference, Flint would spend thirty minutes knocking on doors in the Fountainebleau Drive neighborhood of New Orleans, then drive across town to a Ninth Ward black neighborhood party that had been arranged at the home of Reverend Roland Copeland, an old friend and an effective political organizer in the black community. He was to be there by three-thirty, give a short speech to the party then walk door to door in the black neighborhood until six o'clock.

Terrell Franks was arranging intense press coverage of all these activities. Press releases describing each activity would be disbursed at the morning press conference.

Flint would then have two hours to change his clothes, eat and return telephone calls. Former Speaker of the Louisiana House of Representatives Thomas Ramsey, a very close friend from Flint's early days in the Legislature, was hosting a large reception for him in his westbank home that evening. Ramsey was strongly anti-Reynolds and would be Flint's first major endorsement.

The following day, press conferences at the homes of supporters were scheduled in Houma, Lafayette and Lake Charles. Then on Friday, a private plane would fly him to press conferences in Alexandria, Shreveport, and Monroe. After the weekend, Flint would start the grind of his daily campaign schedule.

"I agree the speech is short enough, but I need to improve my delivery. Also, I'm trying to anticipate every question the press might ask so I'll be ready with my answer. That's why Terrell Franks and Jane Baldwin are coming by for breakfast tomorrow morning. They're preparing questions on everything they can think of and we'll work through them in the morning."

Flint watched Susan as she reached for another cookie. She was more beautiful to him now than she had been on that first day he had seen her in a Catholic Church in San Diego, California so many years ago. Flint had been in the Navy, only twenty years old and stationed on the west coast. He was an usher at church that memorable Sunday morning when Susan had entered church with several girlfriends. Flint had ushered them to a front pew near the altar. She had caught his eye immediately. The long dark hair, the skin deeply tanned by the California sun led him to speculate she might be Latin American. Actually, she was a college student from New Orleans. But she was not impressed by him and even thought him rude when he tried to introduce himself after church.

For the next month, Flint had been certain to appear as an usher each Sunday in hopes of getting to know this girl. Even now, years later, Susan would kid him about his clumsy efforts to impress her during those early days. Flint sipped his coffee for a moment then looked at his wife. "Do you think I'm nuts? What have I gotten us into?"

"Darin, it scared me to death at first to think about running. But I'm glad you're doing it. You've had this in you from the start. It's your dream come true. And in three months it will all be over, win, lose or draw. I think you would be a fantastic, wonderful governor."

"You're prejudiced," he said with a smile.

"No, I'm just really excited about you and your campaign. Jenny and John are excited about how involved you've got them. I'm so proud of you."

"Well, let's win first then be proud," Flint laughed. "You know, it's really amazing. Two weeks ago I was retiring from the Senate and perfectly happy with the thought of growing old with you and the store. Now look at me."

"I don't know if you were really that happy with the idea of retiring. I think you had just gotten used to it because you had reached a dead end in the Senate. It was time for a change."

Susan thought for a moment. "You were retiring from the Senate but I don't think your retirement from politics would have lasted very long. Politics is in your blood."

Darin watched Susan as he finished his coffee. He was well aware of the sacrifices and the upheavels in her life that she was accepting. Then he asked, "Are you ready for these next three months? Are you ready for the emotions, the ups and downs, the criticism, the time apart, the demands on you? We may not have another chance to just sit, talk and share a cup of coffee for a long time."

"Don't worry about me. I'll let you know when I have a complaint."

She stood up and started for the door with the tray.

"Susan, have I told you lately how much I love you?" Flint stood and kissed her, gently guiding her chin with his hands.

"Thank you," he whispered to her.

ELEVEN

"When you have no basis for an argument, abuse the plaintiff."

Marcus Tullius Cicero
(106-43 B.C.)
Roman orator, statesman

Neil Moulard sat down in his Baton Rouge law office and looked across his desk at James Harriford, a tall, white haired man wearing a creme colored suit.

"I guess you know why I called you," Moulard began.

"Darin Flint," Harriford answered. "I heard a couple of days ago he might run. When I got your message, I knew it must be true."

James Harriford had worked both for and against Moulard's candidates in previous elections. Moulard had learned that Harriford was a very valuable man to have on your side and a bad one to have against you.

Four years ago, Harriford's analysis of the record of Reynolds' opponent had been thorough. His ideas to distort that record had been imaginative and effective, with sufficient accuracy to avoid any adverse backlash. Harriford's work had been a telling factor in the campaign. His investigative work had turned up several minor skeletons in the opponent's closet which Moulard had been able to successfully exploit and exaggerate to Reynolds' benefit.

Unfortunately, Harriford was also a potential liability to any candidate. A decade earlier, while an investigator with the State Police, he had been in the middle of an ugly scandal involving drug trafficking and blackmail. The affair had been kept quiet and finally resolved internally as numerous political figures were the blackmail targets. No charges had been filed against Harriford, but he was quietly expelled from the state police with loss of all benefits and retirement rights. He had been very lucky to avoid a long jail sentence.

Moulard was meeting with Harriford at his private law office, not the State Capitol, as a precaution. Harriford was not known generally to the press or the public, but Moulard wanted no risks.

Harriford's association with the Reynolds' campaign had not been publicly known four years ago and the same precautions would be taken this year. Moulard would not allow Harriford to get anywhere near René Reynolds. He simply wanted the valuable benefit of Harriford's extremely capable services.

"I want to know everything there is to know about Darin Flint, especially things he doesn't want anyone else to know. That includes votes that would make important groups angry. It includes contradictory votes. I want to know his worst votes on farm issues, on labor issues, on welfare and the poor, on budget cuts and amendments to the appropriations bill or the capital outlay bill. If he voted against a project in Lafayette, for instance, tell me about it. Especially if the project did not pass. You get the point?"

Of course this man got the point. Harriford would think of things to check that would never occur to Moulard in a hundred years. He was a pro, the best in the business, and Moulard knew it.

"I want to know Flint's politics. Who his friends are, his neighbors. His enemies. Who he does business with. What real estate does he own? Who his wife's friends are. Has she ever had any boyfriends. I want to know about their kids. Does he have any problems with his children? Have they ever been involved in drugs or any other types of problems."

Moulard stood up and loosened his tie. "I want insurance, James. Flint's getting in this race too late to win. But I don't want to take any chances. I need something in reserve just in case he gets too close. Check his military record, his police record, school records, his health records, people that knew him growing up, his family, everything."

"My fee has gone up. I'll have to drop everything else to take this job."

"You be reasonable with me, then I'll be reasonable with you."

"Give me two weeks and we should have a first report for you." Harriford stood to leave. "You'll hear from me." He walked from the office without another word.

Moulard reached for his watts phone and dialed Jackson Wells number in New Orleans.

"Hello." Jackson Wells' voice came on the line.

"Hey, Jackson. Anything new on Flint?"

"Yes. His son opened a campaign account at Second Security Bank. They're making signs in a warehouse behind Flint's store.

He's got Jon Douglas involved. We've spotted his people at Flint's home. Flint's making calls to blacks and he's told the press he'd have an announcement on Wednesday."

Moulard's mind was moving fast. Second Security had over ten million dollars in state deposits that could be moved in a moment at the governor's whim. It should not be hard to keep track of every deposit and expenditure from Flint's account. He made a note to learn from the bank each day whose checks were being deposited in Flint's account.

"Jackson, stay on top of it. Find out more about his Wednesday announcement. Is there a press conference? When, where and anything else you can learn. And let's start contacting every black businessman, politician and minister to make certain everyone knows the governor is watching them."

"O.K."

"Keep me posted. Bye."

Moulard telephoned Clyde Flowers, the governor's press secretary, and asked him to check around with media people to try to learn more about Flint's plans for an announcement on Wednesday. If it was a press conference, Moulard wanted to make sure some good questions were asked.

Moulard leaned back and took inventory. Precautions were going well. The Sheriff's Association was touching base with the sheriffs, the Assessor's Association with the assessors, the Clerks of Court Association with the clerks. The School Board Association, the Municipal Association and Police Jury Association had also been put to work for Reynolds. Moulard had his office contacting friendly legislators. The governor was making the calls to the congressional delegation, key legislators and political leaders statewide.

If things went well, the door would be slammed on Flint's campaign before he even announced his candidacy.

The Reynolds fundraiser and midnight breakfast had netted over $1.5 million. Since Flint had surfaced as a candidate, Moulard had given the go ahead for ten more fundraisers around the state to be organized over the next seven weeks. Their polls indicated good response to the media campaign and billboards. The ten page newspaper insert would be in next Sunday's morning paper. Two hundred thousand letters would be mailed tonight to voters statewide.

An overall media strategy and schedule had been developed, then approved months ago on the assumption there would be an opponent for Reynolds. Moulard had directed that the plan be reevaluated and adjusted in light of the Flint candidacy. A strategy session would begin shortly in Moulard's conference room to hear Danny Ross' recommendations.

Moulard would discuss the changes in campaign strategy with Reynolds when he was satisfied a good, final plan had been perfected.

A call came through on Moulard's private phone. It was from the executive director of the Sheriff's Association.

"Neil, we're making the calls but there have been a few problems."

"What problems?"

"Most of them have been called by someone for Flint."

"Been called by who?"

"Some by Flint. A lot of them by Congressman Jeffrey Bordelon."

"O.K. Keep me posted." Moulard said instinctively and hung up the telephone. What is that old goat doing for Flint, he asked himself. When he looked up, Clyde Flowers, the governor's press secretary, was standing in the doorway.

"Neil, I picked up some news. Flint's on the agenda with Governor Reynolds at both the Independent Oil Producer's convention and the Retailer's Association convention."

"Damn!" muttered Moulard.

TWELVE

"I want to do away with everything behind man, so that there is nothing to see when he looks back. I want to take him by the scruff of his neck and turn his face toward the future!

Leonid Andreyev
(1871-1919)
Russian writer

Greg Hawkins, Flint's legislative aide, drove Flint and his family to the State Capitol. They went directly to Flint's office in the sub-basement to avoid being prematurely sidetracked by friends and supporters. Flint wanted a few minutes alone to collect his thoughts before the press conference.

Volunteers were decorating the senate briefing room under the direction of Terrell Franks. A simple table with a rostrum was in place for Flint and his family. A parallel table was placed in front for the press. The press kits stacked on the press table contained a news release, a copy of Flint's speech, a biography, his new pamphlet, a glossy print of Flint, and one of Flint and his family. A plethora of microphones had been attached to the rostrum by the electronic media. Television camera people and photographers from around the state were setting up their equipment.

Of course, Jon Douglas had his own microphones and video cameras in place because the news conference would provide good video and photographic material for their advertising campaign.

As ten o'clock approached, the room became packed and the reporters took their seats. Terrell Franks was relieved to see that the crowd was a good mixture. Aside from personal friends he had called upon, even black leaders who were employed in the Reynolds administration were there out of a mixture of curiosity and respect. A handful of Flint's colleagues and former colleagues from the House and Senate had come. Terrell smiled as he noticed Jackson Wells by the doorway watching the proceedings.

Flint banners decorated the room. Many of the volunteers were wearing Flint t-shirts they had silk-screened locally. Two of Flint's plywood signs were mounted side by side on the wall behind the rostrum. Terrell Franks had planned the decorations and seating to insure that the television cameras would pick up both the banner and the crowd for the six o'clock news.

In his office, Darin Flint tried to concentrate. The events of the past week kept flooding his thoughts.

Joel Whitney had raised over twelve thousand dollars in Baton Rouge. He was organizing a Baton Rouge finance committee to raise more money. Flint had managed to raise another eleven thousand dollars through his own telephone calls. Carey Jefferson had quietly worked his lobbying clients and raised the initial twenty-five thousand dollars he had promised. Congressman Bordelon, Rodney Libscomb, Eric McKay and Flint's personal friends in New Orleans had also raised money. Fundraisers were being scheduled in New Orleans and Baton Rouge for August. Plans were tentative elsewhere.

It was a decent start. He was hoping a campaign budget of one million dollars was realistic. But he realized he may have to do with much less. Much depended on the initial impact produced by his signs and the free media from his press conferences.

Flint forced his mind to concentrate on the task at hand. He reviewed the outline of his speech, then reviewed the facts and figures he would need in answering questions. He remembered Congressman Bordelon's warning that there would be questions planted by Reynolds aimed at embarrassing or angering him. He must maintain his poise.

Flint's time was up. He gathered his file and stepped into the reception area where his family waited with Greg Hawkins, Joel Whitney and Jon Douglas.

"All set?" Douglas asked.

"All set."

"Then let's go," said Douglas. "When we get outside the door I'll give the signal to Terrell. He'll announce you, then its all yours."

Moments later, Flint heard Terrell Franks calling for quiet then announcing, "Ladies and Gentlemen, I give you the next governor of the state of Louisiana, Senator Darin D. Flint."

Flint and his family walked into the packed room of cheering supporters and glaring lights, then he took his place behind the mass of microphones.

"Ladies and gentlemen, thank you for your kind reception. I have called this press conference to announce formally my candidacy for governor."

Flint was immediately interrupted by a standing, sustained ovation from the cheering audience.

"We know the future of Louisiana can be far better than her past. No longer can we tolerate the power of government being used for self enrichment. We offer a better alternative. A plan for Louisiana to progress in transportation, in education, in law enforcement, in industry.

"Our highway system has progressed under the Highway Priority Act. But we still have one of the worst safety records in the nation. Political interference too often causes our highway budget to be squandered on low priority projects. As a result, too often Louisiana travelers are riding on crumbling highways, their lives and their family's lives endangered. Last year we had over eighty thousand people maimed or killed in traffic accidents on our Louisiana highways. Our highways rank among the most dangerous in America.

"Upon election, I will initiate a Highway Masterplan to establish a fundamental system of four lane highways connecting the major geographical regions of the state. The purpose and concept is to complement and supplement, not duplicate, our federal interstate highway system."

Flint turned to his right and pointed to a Louisiana map which Greg Hawkins had mounted on a stand beside the podium.

"Here's a map depicting in green our existing federal interstate highways. The eight proposed four lane highways are depicted in red, then a system of twelve major rural highways, which we've colored in blue, we would improve with passing lanes. Many of these four lane highways already exist but are in deplorable condition. The cost of new contracts and improvements will be two hundred and fifty million dollars over a five year period. We will finance the construction and permanent upkeep of these highways by dedicating four cents of our special fuels tax to this purpose.

"Our purpose with the Highway Masterplan is to assure that fundamental, major, heavily used roadways are good and safe highways. It will also help us attract new businesses to areas of our state isolated by narrow, dangerous roads."

Flint paused, then turned his thoughts to the field of education.

"Politics has also penalized Louisiana for decades in the field of education. Louisiana's public school system is a wasteland of political patronage. Huge portions of our education dollar goes to hire non-classroom personnel instead of putting our money to use reducing the teacher-pupil ratio. We tell the public we are budgeting one teacher for every twenty- three students. But in our minimum foundation formula that distributes the money, we only provide for a twenty-nine to one ratio. In every parish, classrooms with 37 or 38 kids are common.

"As governor, I will emphasize the use of teacher funds for in-classroom teachers as opposed to non-classroom personnel. We will reduce the bureaucracy and patronage in the Department of Education thereby freeing funds to help reduce the teacher-pupil ratio.

"The fundamental reform of providing a favorable teacher- pupil ratio will be our first educational reform. It will open the door for others.

"We need to establish a dual diploma system in education similar to the pioneer plan that has worked so well in Winn Parish. If a student does not desire to be in the pre-college curriculum, but wants an academic diploma with vocational training in a certain business, trade or skilled crafts, then this alternative high school curriculum should be available to that student. Our high school graduates must be prepared to make a living in the real world. A dual diploma system will help us accomplish this goal.

"We must deal with the excessive numbers of student dropouts. Evidence abounds that dropouts are not very employable. A dual diploma system will also help us stimulate students to gain a useful education in high school to meet the practical career goals in the Louisiana job market.

"There is a great need to reform Louisiana's teacher salary scale. Efforts have been defeated year after year. I will implement a generous career system of step increases for teachers based in part on seniority, in part on the level of academic achievement by the teacher and in part on a teacher being certified as being competent in the classroom. Every student must be guaranteed that their teacher is prepared and competent. So I favor this form of merit pay for teachers.

"I favor the concept of student testing as a factor in promoting students to a higher grade level. Remedial summer courses must be available for those whose grades or testing don't justify promotion in order to help that student be promoted with his class. I favor supporting new academic requirements necessary to earn a high school diploma. I favor these prerequisites being phased in over several years so that those who are already far along in their high school years will not be penalized unfairly. I will not abandon the concept of thorough testing of new teachers as a prerequisite to getting a Louisiana Teacher's certificate.

"We have seen demonstrations in several cities that the concept of sixth grade centers provides dramatic improvements in education. Alexandria is perhaps the best example. The sixth grade is a transition from grammar school to junior high school. It is our last chance to be certain the student has a firm educational foundation before leaving grammar school. As governor, we would initiate through pilot programs the implementation of sixth grade center programs in all metropolitan areas throughout the state.

"In higher education, we are troubled by mediocrity and duplication because we have so many state colleges offering essentially the same curriculum. Back in the 1970's, the Board of Regents proposed a plan specifically defining certain academic roles and specialization for each college so that excellence could be achieved and expensive duplication avoided. As governor, I will propose establishing an updated version of the Board of Regent's plan.

"Every person who becomes governor wants to attract new business, industry and jobs to Louisiana. So do I. I believe my Highway Masterplan and education reforms will help us do that. But there is another step necessary to make Louisiana truly attractive for new businesses.

"We must end the chronic political war between organized labor and business in this State. The Legislature has been the annual battleground for bitter, divisive struggles between these two political giants over right-to-work, unemployment insurance, workers compensation, agency shop, prevailing wage law, so-called labor violence laws, right-to-strike legislation, compulsory arbitration, public employee unions and other less infamous battlegrounds.

"Instability has resulted. Whichever side loses one year may well reverse the tables the next year. An attitude of extremism has prevailed. Neither considers the opposition's point of view. Efforts to find a middle ground .... a lasting and enduring compromise .... simply never occur.

"To attract industry, jobs and investment, we must resolve this bitter stalemate. An era of understanding and mutual effort toward progress must occur. We must reduce the high costs of workers compensation and unemployment insurance. I envision a day when labor can accept at least a moratorium on its struggle to repeal Right to Work. Its become clear that we have no hope of attracting new manufacturing firms to our state as long as Right to Work is under attack. We must push our congressional delegation to secure a federal forgiveness of our huge unemployment insurance debt. This would enable us to reduce our taxes, attract new business and create new jobs.

"I envision a day when the strategy sessions in the Department of Commerce to attract industry include both the chief of the AFL-CIO and the chief of the Louisiana Business League. A time when our two giants will seek jointly to bring new businesses to this state. To offer new investors an assurance that our laws will not be changed on them after they arrive here; that an understanding and partnership between business and labor will exist that assures the investor of a well-trained, free work force while assuring the worker of clearly defined safety, salary and benefit standards.

"The death struggle between the AFL-CIO and LBL must end. It is the duty of the governor to bring common sense and patience to bear, to establish this new era of harmony. As governor, no task will be more important to me.

"Let me conclude with this thought.

"I have great respect for the office of governor. I seek this high office with a sense of humility but also a sense of confidence and hope. I love this great state of ours. I've wearied of watching persons temporarily in power abuse her great assets. We must clean up our Louisiana politics once and for all. With the strength of your support behind me, our election victory will be only the first step in building a better future for Louisiana.

"THANK YOU."

A thunder of applause fell upon Flint and surprised him. The audience was on it's feet clapping, stomping and finally falling into a long refrain of "We want Flint, We want Flint, We want Flint."

The demonstration of enthusiastic, emotional support had even swept up most of the reporters and security officers.

The demonstration continued for several minutes before Flint's requests for order gradually had affect. When quiet was restored, Flint introduced each member of his family and began fielding questions.

Initially, the questions centered on Flint's highway masterplan proposal. Was Flint abandoning the Highway Priority Act reform which he had so jealousy guarded as a legislator? This reform had been aimed at highway dollars being spent where need was greatest, not where political muscle was strongest. Flint answered that the Highway Priority Act would govern all highway and bridge construction and maintenance beyond the masterplan dedication of funds.

Flint was asked whether he envisioned any changes in government operations. Flint declared that a primary theme of his campaign would be to advocate far reaching civil service reforms. He explained in detail the modified open range classification and pay plan he would support to eliminate inequities in the present plan, while establishing a significant element of merit for payraises and promotion at the management level.

"Would you oppose Sonny Stokes' re-election as Senate President?"

"I've gotten along well enough with Sonny for a long time," Flint answered diplomatically. "We'll sit down together when the time comes and see if there are any problems. I would insist that he learn to conserve money in the future as well as he's spent it in the past. If he can't agree to change his bad spending habits, we will have problems."

Then Flint recognized Gordon Twilley of the Associated Press who had raised his hand for a question. "Senator Flint, what is your position on the Right to Work and agency shop issues?"

It was a question Flint and Terrell Franks had expected Reynolds to plant since Reynolds himself was so uncomfortable and uncertain with his alignment with labor on both issues.

"I favor Right to Work and oppose agency shop," Flint quickly answered. "My record in the Senate already reflects that. But more than anything else, I favor stability. Potential investors must be assured such fundamental laws as Right to Work will not be changed. Otherwise, Louisiana will remain at the bottom in the south in manufacturing jobs for our residents.

Shortly thereafter, the press conference ended with another ovation. As the newspapers reported to their readers the following day, Flint had been interrupted seventeen times by the applause of his audience.

One of the few quiet observers had been the tall, thin, white haired man in the back of the room. James Harriford slipped out just ahead of the crowd.

THIRTEEN

"This world is a comedy to those that think, a tragedy to those that feel."

Horace Walpole

"At bottom the world isn't a joke. We only joke about it to avoid an issue.... Humor is the most engaging cowardice. With it myself I have been able to hold some of my enemy in play far out of gunshot."

Robert Frost,
"Selected Letters"

The four luxury automobiles were being escorted by state troopers from Esler Field where Governor Reynolds had just arrived, to the convention hall in downtown Alexandria. They rounded the final corner and parked outside the entrance to the building. A trooper opened the car door. Reynolds stepped out and entered the building surrounded by a mixture of key local supporters, press personnel and his traveling companions. He was greeted in the hallway by a black woman who was his black coordinator in the area.

Inside, the ceremonies to honor Reverend Ralph Fredricks had already begun. Reverend Fredricks was an elderly black minister and political leader who had been an outspoken, persistent civil rights advocate for fifty years.

As Reynolds groped in his mind for the black woman's name, his eye was distracted by three people walking out of exit doors at the opposite end of the building. He recognized Darin Flint immediately.

"Flint's been here?" he asked.

"Yes, he's been here for about forty-five minutes," she responded. "He just introduced himself to people at the tables and left his pamphlets. They let him speak for a minute and he introduced his daughter. Not much to it. There are a lot of candidates here for various offices doing the same thing."

"How'd he do?"

"It didn't do him any good, Governor. This is your crowd."

As they entered the rear of the auditorium, he was recognized immediately by the speaker and greeted with the traditional standing ovation given to governors. Reynolds worked the crowd. He seemed taller than his five feet ten inch frame as he shook hands and worked his way to the front. It was an impressive entrance and reception.

He greeted Reverend Fredricks personally when he reached the stage. The two men spoke for a few moments while the black crowd resettled in their seats. The master of ceremonies immediately launched into a long introduction of the governor, then Reynolds went to the microphone after another standing ovation.

Reynolds started his presentation with a steady stream of jokes and one liners. He told a couple of cajun jokes, then a couple of jokes about himself and his political problems. It was vintage Reynolds, displaying the kind of quick wit and stand up humor that had been an important key to his political success. He could make people laugh and forget about the serious accusations that often surfaced against him or his friends.

"I know all of you have read the rumors in the newspapers that some of my friends have mafia connections. That we are not cracking down on their illegal gambling business in New Orleans. That there may even be indictments. But like I told the newspaper publishers in Baton Rouge last week, there's nothing to it. I don't like my friends to gamble. It's morally wrong and I'm against it in New Orleans or anywhere else." Reynolds paused a moment, then added with a grin, "in fact, I offered them two to one odds I'd never be indicted and no one took the bet."

The crowd roared their approval.

"I was really impressed by the Baton Rouge Morning Advocate. They've been criticizing me and the Legislature for three years for the tax increases. They say instead we should have cut spending, fired some employees, eliminated some programs for the poor. The Advocate says its wrong to put new taxes on people. Of course, yesterday when I went to purchase a newspaper, lo and behold, the Morning Advocate had raised their price from a quarter to forty cents."

At this remark, Reynolds was lifting his arms and shaking his head in exasperation, then resting his forehead on the microphone in mock surrender.

His audience loved it.

Then Reynolds pointed to Reverend Fredricks. He traced Fredrick's career with words of high praise. He spoke of Fredrick's instrumental role in the civil rights movement and in the church ministry. He congratulated the audience for bestowing honors on the deserving minister. The Governor then asked Reverend Fredricks to step up to the microphone.

Fredricks was a small, slightly stocky, light skinned black man with a small, gray, pencil moustache, a balding head and eyes that were narrow slits. With this much shorter man beside him, Reynolds told the audience, "Besides, if you had not sponsored this very special day for Reverend Fredricks, I would never have known he was a black man. I always thought he was a Chinaman."

The crowd exploded in laughter and so did Reverend Fredricks. Reynolds had successfully made a joke of the honoree's appearance, an unlikely trick few other politicians could have gotten away with.

Reynolds gradually allowed the humor to recede. He further congratulated Reverend Fredricks for his career of accomplishments then awarded him the Governor's Medal for Outstanding Citizenship.

In closing, Reynolds reminded the crowd that it was election time and he needed their vote. Again joking, he told the crowd, "I don't know what that man Senator Flint told you earlier today, but whatever it was don't believe a word of it."

Reynolds left the building with his cadre of friends, again shaking hands as he made his way thru the crowd to the exit door and to his limousine.

A reporter for the Alexandria Daily Town Talk had observed the speech with two members of the New Orleans press who were traveling with Reynolds. He offered them a ride in his car back to the airport. The two reporters jumped in the car and they quickly fell in line behind the motorcade.

"It never fails to amaze me what Reynolds can do in front of a crowd," said one of the reporters from New Orleans. "Those people are paying more sales tax and gasoline tax and the budget still isn't balanced. Reynolds makes them laugh about it."

"That's politics," said the other. "Reynolds is damn good at it. Humor is an essential part of his style, especially on the issues where he's most vulnerable. It helps him dodge political bullets and distract the public."

"Do you guys see this governor's race as being any kind of contest?" asked the Alexandria reporter.

"Maybe in the Orleans area. Flint's well known and popular in Orleans parish with both the blacks and whites," explained the first man. "And his no-nonsense approach and opposition to many of those taxes will get him support in conservative areas around Orleans. Flint is well known in the Baton Rouge area and could pull a good vote there too. But I see no chance of Flint winning or really pushing Reynolds elsewhere."

They drove along in silence for a few moments.

The first reporter then asked, "How do you see it around the Alexandria area?"

"I believe a lot of people are not very happy with Reynolds. Not many have ever heard of Darin Flint but if he proves to be a reasonable alternative, I think he'll find considerable support here."

"Does Flint have a central Louisiana organization?"

"Well, he's gotten a lot of these plywood signs up." The local reporter pointed to one of Flint's blue and white signs standing in a pasture they happened to be passing at that moment. "He has a young attorney heading up his Rapides Parish organization who's only twenty-four years old. But they're opening a little headquarters and getting volunteers. So they're long on enthusiasm but short on experience."

"Did Flint have a press conference in Alexandria when he announced?"

"Yes, and it went over well. He had Rodney Libscomb, who used to be a state senator from Shreveport, introduce him and endorse him. They held the conference in the front yard of the home of that young lawyer I mentioned. They had an advance press release inviting the public. They rounded up a good crowd, they decorated the place with signs and staged a pretty good media event. I had never met Senator Flint before but I was very favorably impressed by him."

"He's a good man and would be a good governor," added the

first reporter. "How did Flint do with that black group tonight before Reynolds got there."

"He was just the opposite from Reynolds but he did well. No jokes. He was introduced by Reverend Fredricks. Seems that Flint was a young state senator back in the early sixties when the Legislature passed all the Jim Crow Laws. Fredricks told them Flint was the only friend the blacks had in state government back then. He said Flint fought the poll tax, the literacy test of voters, the anti-demonstration laws. He said Flint had even favored integration of the schools back then. The old man got a little emotional about Flint. Of course, that was long before René Reynolds got into politics."

"It sounds like Flint did damn well. Can you wire me a copy of your story on Flint so I can include that in my story."

"Sure, no problem."

FOURTEEN

"Genius is one per cent inspiration and ninety-nine per cent perspiration."

Thomas Alva Edison
(1847-1931)
American inventor

The Flint campaign seemed to take on a life of its own. The scheduling of one event led inevitably to another campaign stop in a nearby area. In each community, there were certain persons to be seen .... a sheriff, a mayor, a newspaper editor, a certain businessman among many, many others. A visit for a speech or party at someone's home inevitably led to scheduling appointments with the local radio station, the newspaper or perhaps one or more potential contributors. If Flint didn't see those key people while in that particular town on that occasion, it might be weeks or much longer before he would be back for a second chance.

So his schedule was full wherever he went. Many things Flint needed to do simply could not be scheduled. Time was his enemy. October 22nd was election day, less than three months away. It was virtually impossible to visit individually so many key people in a community, to attend certain events, and to cover effectively more than two communities in a single day. Too much time was lost driving between towns.

After the first ten days, the overloaded schedule seemed impossible to sustain. Flint pressed on without complaint, but his daughter Jenny (who was traveling with him) and Jon Douglas realized the missed meals, the early mornings, the late nights, the late arrivals and early departures would soon tire him out and hurt his effectiveness.

Jon Douglas decided to personally oversee the advance scheduling until Barbara Durham developed a better feel for what was doable on a sustained basis in a twenty-four hour day. He insisted a minimum of seven hours must always be set aside for Flint's sleep. Flint must always be given thirty minutes to eat each meal. One hour each evening must be set aside for return of telephone calls.

69

This list of calls would be prepared during the day at the Baton Rouge headquarters, carefully screened, then given to Jenny or Flint each night for the one hour of telephone calls. Douglas, Bordelon or others would tend to the many other telephone calls. Flint must be allowed sleep without interruption while traveling between towns.

It was a good, organized plan to establish a reasonable, effective schedule and pace.

But the plan never had a chance. Flint's persistent determination to make every possible visit to every town continued unchanged. By shaking every available hand, making every possible personal visit, never missing a radio station or newspaper office and always, without fail, walking main street, a shopping center or a neighborhood in every large or small community, Flint established a standard of campaigning that became infectious among his organizers and volunteer workers.

There was a mountain to be climbed. Political seeds to be planted throughout the state. Election day was less than three months away. Flint's message was clear. He, and those who were helping him, had a great deal of lost time to make up. That meant missed meals, lost sleep, clogged schedules, and maddening levels of disorganization. He was in a hurry and could not wait for the fine details of his schedule to be perfected. Telephone calls were received and made at virtually any time of day....during tea parties, while attending church, while trying to bathe or while cramming a fast food hamburger down his throat.

He stuck with it. Then got used to it. After a few weeks, Flint even learned to enjoy it. He was getting results.

The articles in the small town weekly newspapers, the reactions to local radio interviews, the growing level of small donation checks people were pressing in his hands, the satisfaction of five or ten bumper stickers or yard sign locations in a neighborhood he had just walked....these results nourished, renewed and motivated Flint to more determined efforts each succeeding day.

He learned to laugh at bad jokes he did not understand. He learned to tell a few himself. A natural listener, Flint also learned to carry a conversation where others were quiet or perhaps uncomfortable meeting a candidate.

Flint discovered within himself a determination to succeed, to win, that he had never realized he possessed. He was not just making a stand, raising an issue, or going down fighting in a losing cause. He found fertile ground among these voters. They were responsive to him and he to them. It was as true in French Vermillion Parish as it was in Ouachita Parish at the opposite end of the state. Outworking, outcampaigning, and outlasting his overconfident opponent was the path he decided to follow. He did not have time to discuss any other strategy with Jon Douglas.

In time, even Jon abandoned his efforts to moderate the tempo of Flint's campaigning.

They all accepted Flint's philosophy. In a long campaign, his pace perhaps would be impossible. But they could push themselves to the limit in a hard, short campaign.

Although the campaign seemed fast and furious to Flint and his fellow workers, few in Louisiana were even aware a campaign was underway. There was sporadic media attention. No paid media could be afforded. It was August. Families were vacationing, engaged in summer baseball programs, preparing for the beginning of school. Politics was of secondary interest to most. And the great mass of Louisiana's four million people had no idea anyone named Darin Flint even existed. Yet he persistently pushed his way forward.

FIFTEEN

"Crime is contagious. If the government becomes a law-breaker, it breeds contempt for the law."

Louis D. Brandeis
(1856-1941)
U.S. Supreme Court Justice

Congressman Jeffrey Bordelon had the Flint campaign well prepared for the Retailers Convention in Shreveport. He had spoken to the editors of the Shreveport Times and the Shreveport Journal, making them aware of the potential significance of this first confrontation between the two candidates. He made the same efforts with the management of the Shreveport television and radio stations.

Carey Jefferson distributed press releases statewide for the Retailers Association emphasizing this first joint appearance of the candidates would highlight the convention. The local press gave the meeting thorough and prominent advance coverage.

Terrell Franks made certain the statewide wire services and daily newspapers covered the event. Good friends on the staffs of local newspapers assured him they would report Flint's speech.

When the time came, the press was on hand in full force.

Governor Reynolds was to be the principal speaker for the Saturday evening dinner. Flint would speak at midday. The conventioneers had been attending various small meetings and seminars at the hotel all Saturday morning. The noon luncheon would bring them together in the large banquet hall for Flint's speech. Flint and Reynolds would not actually meet. Their confrontation would be in the minds of the convention goers and the observing press who would witness their speeches six hours apart.

Flint arrived in Shreveport Friday evening for a cocktail party hosted by Rodney Lipscomb at the hotel. An invitation had been in the convention packet of every convention registrant. The party was well attended, giving Flint the opportunity to meet many of the people who would be in his audience the next day.

When Flint arrived for his noon speech, he had already put in a full morning of campaigning in Bossier City. He was warmed up, eager and confident. His audience was a business group. He talked about the economy and labor. He talked about excessive spending and the new taxes.

"Where has the money gone?" Flint asked repeatedly, as he described each new consumer tax that had been enacted. He spoke of the budget reductions that had been rejected. He reminded the audience that the state budget was not balanced. He compared the Louisiana state budget to the spending of other states to demonstrate that virtually no other state Louisiana's size was able to match her spending habits. The Louisiana budget was larger than other states, yet achieved less results in education, highways and law enforcement. He described his Highway Master Plan, his sixth grade center concept for public education, and his hopes to repeal some of the Reynolds taxes.

With his right hand reaching forward to emphasize every point, Flint declared war on Louisiana politics.

"For twenty-seven years I've watched in frustration as political parasites have followed successive governors into power. After a term or two at the public trough, another governor and another group of similar people replace their predecessors. Politics has been another way of saying 'favoritism'.

"More than any other single reason, that is why I am running for governor. To do my very best to clean up the mess. To let the word NO be heard for the first time in our State Capitol. To say NO to the spending of tax dollars for unscheduled, unplanned, unnecessary, and undeserving public projects. To make decisions based on priority, merit, qualifications and need, not on political muscle and favoritism.

"As governor, my office will be open to all groups. My political friends will be and are those who want me, as governor, to clean the dirty face of Louisiana politics forever. Not those who would ask me to pervert the authority of the governorship into sweetheart contracts for unnecessary and unneeded public contracts or similar activities."

Flint straightened up and looked out across the auditorium. "Frankly, I want to clean house in Baton Rouge. No more rip offs. Money spent on consultant contracts will be drastically reduced. New public buildings will be standardized when practical so we can save on engineering and design expenses. Cost controls will be put on medicaid matching fund programs. We will build fewer new roads and, instead, concentrate on improving the ones we already have.

"There will be no connection between contributions to me and grants of permits, licenses, pardons, paroles, certificates of need, attorney contracts, public works contracts or the like. Where possible, I will use diplomacy, tact, thoughtfulness, and persuasion to accomplish legislative goals. I will not tolerate the ugly, petty politics of old. It has penalized this state and our economy. It has held us back long enough."

He finished his speech. Silence followed Flint back to his seat on the dais. It was as if the last words he had expressed in his speech were still being consumed and digested by every person in the room. But as he sat down, the silence was shattered by enormous applause from the audience. In the middle of this commotion Carey Jefferson, who was master of ceremonies, motioned for Flint to again stand. When he stood, the applause heightened a second time. Jefferson walked over and shook Flint's hand, then began motioning for quiet.

Flint was elated by the response, but grateful when the applause finally receded allowing him to again be seated and for the attention to return to the master of ceremonies.

Terrell Franks stood in the back of the auditorium enjoying the spectacle. He had been clapping louder than anyone. The old man was giving them hell straight from the heart. Let Reynolds try to top that, he thought to himself.

. . . .

"I don't like it," said Governor René Reynolds as he walked across the kitchen of Frank Anthony's home in Shreveport and dropped on the table a copy of both yesterday's and that morning's editions of the Shreveport Times.

"The press is trying to help Flint with all this bull so they'll have something to write about all fall. Everytime the man farts, it makes headlines," Reynolds spat out the words in frustration.

Frank Anthony, a friend and supporter of Reynolds, pushed the remains of his breakfast aside and picked up the newspapers. He was a heavyset man with thick arms, thick neck, thick girth ....everything about Frank Anthony seemed large, thick and ponderous. Curly black hair covered Anthony's scalp. It also covered his arms and flowed above the collar of his short sleeved shirt. He had begun his own tire business thirty years earlier after dropping out of school. Through dedication, hard work and a friendly nature, he had built this business into a highly profitable chain of automotive service centers statewide. Anthony was no politician. But he had made himself a very wealthy man. René Reynolds was the first politician he had ever had close contact with. But Frank Anthony had proven to be a gold mine for Reynolds as Anthony applied his traits of hard work and persistance to fund-raising. Anthony almost idolized Reynolds. He was honored to have the governor of the state in his home overnight.

Anthony read the headline from the previous day. "Reynolds, Flint Arrive For First Debate". Large photos of both candidates were on page two. Then he looked at this morning's paper. "Governor's Race Highlights Retailers Convention".

There were two articles, one emphasizing the content of the speech Flint had given and the other describing Reynolds' speech. The lead editorial on the editorial page summarized the differences between the candidates and the major features of each man's program. Flint had received equal billing in the press reports of their speeches.

"Hell, they treat Flint like a major candidate even though he hardly makes a bleep in statewide polls," Reynolds observed in an annoyed voice.

"Governor, you wiped him out last night," Anthony said. "The article about your speech is good. You had them laughing, then really serious. I thought you tore up his highway master plan idea. And when these people around here read that Flint's from New Orleans, that's all it'll take to turn them off."

Despite his annoyance with the newspaper articles, Reynolds managed to grin at Frank Anthony from across the room. "Thanks, Frank. But you're not too objective. You'd think I gave a great speech if I sat on an egg in front of those people. Don't worry. Flint's no problem. But the press is going to try to help him make the race serious. But its too little, too late."

Within five minutes, Reynolds had left Anthony's home and was on his way to the airport. He would fly to Baton Rouge on the state airplane.

At that same moment in Baton Rouge, Neil Moulard was mashing his fifth cigarette of the day in the ashtray on his office desk. It was 7:15 a.m. The eyes of James Harriford studied Moulard's face as Moulard worked his way through the final pages of Harriford's typed report. The silence had endured without a word being spoken for almost ten minutes.

Three weeks had passed since their first meeting in July. Flint had made a splash statewide for several days with his initial announcement and press conferences. Flint had continued to get decent press sporadically around the state as he campaigned. But the polls showed only minor progress of Darin Flint and his campaign for governor. Without a sustained public relations campaign, Moulard had felt secure that Flint's campaign was destined to remain obscure.

However, the intense press coverage of Flint's speech before the Retailer's Association now renewed Moulard's concern.

Moulard had reached the conclusion earlier that this background check on Flint might be an overreaction and unnecessary. But the Flint-Reynolds speeches in Shreveport had made front page news statewide. Flint's persistence was an irritant. Harriford's new report now peeked his interest.

"Do you have proof of this stock ownership in Noble Airlines?"

"Yes".

"You are certain of this conflict of interest."

"It's a little tenuous and it was several years ago. But I think I can get the information to make it stick long enough to use at the end of the campaign. I hope to get a copy of the actual stock certificate."

"How much more time do you need to nail down these possibilities on Flint's personal affairs?"

"I can't answer that. In fact, I don't know if we can find anything damaging in his personal life. We have a theory based on some fairly reliable hearsay. It goes back to his Navy days. Could be pretty ugly. I can push it or drop it. Makes no difference to me," Harriford explained.

Moulard decided to play it safe. "Push it."

Harriford got up, picked up his briefcase and left. Moulard placed the report in his desk drawer. He looked at his watch, then left his office hurriedly to meet Reynolds' plane at the airport.

Thirty minutes later Neil Moulard watched from his car as the plane carrying Reynolds arrived at the Baton Rouge Airport and taxied down the runway to the hangar housing a variety of private planes. The governor joined him in his car.

"We had a pretty fair trip to Alexandria and Shreveport Neil. What have I missed around here?"

"Not much. Have you seen the papers this morning?"

"Only the Shreveport Times. What have you got?"

"The Picayune, the Advocate, and Lafayette Advertiser. The coverage is basically the same as the Times except for some feature articles. They have all played up the Retailers Convention as some kind of confrontation. The Advocate and Picayune are already talking about the LAIPRO meeting in Lafayette as a second debate," observed Moulard.

Moulard drove without saying a word while Reynolds read quickly through the newspapers.

"Look at this shit!" Reynolds suddenly exclaimed. "This Picayune article on the Reverend Fredricks meeting in Alexandria makes it sound like Flint was the hero of the day up there. They've even got a wire photo of him with Fredricks. That's complete bullshit. We got there just as he was leaving. He had no impact at all and spoke for only a minute. I got several standing ovations and had them eating out of my hands by the time I left. It was one of the best events I've had lately."

Reynolds looked to his left at Moulard and held up the picture of Flint with Reverend Fredricks. "Did you see this article?"

"Yes, I saw it," Moulard answered. "That was one of the feature articles I mentioned. I imagine the same photo of Flint must be in the Alexandria Town Talk."

They drove along in silence for several more minutes while Reynolds continued to dig through the pile of newspapers.

Moulard steered the car off the interstate highway toward the governor's mansion as Reynolds finally put the newspapers aside.

"Neil, I know we have a full schedule for today and tomorrow. But I want to have a strategy meeting with every district coordinator, with Danny Ross, our finance people and whoever else you think should be there. Over-confidence is hurting us. Our people are not working. I want thorough polls initiated immediately so I'll have the results within forty-eight hours. Any problem with that?"

Moulard shook his head side to side as he stopped the car for a red light in front of the Department of Transportation building. "No problem."

"Appearing at the Retailer's convention the same day as Flint just gave him too much publicity," Reynolds continued. "We've got to avoid doing the same thing at the LAIPRO Convention. Seems to me, we need to cancel or get them to cancel him."

Moulard looked straight ahead for a moment without a word. The light changed to green and he drove forward.

"René, I really think that would be a mistake. It's too late. The press has already picked up on it. If you cancel, they'll have a ball with it. If he's canceled, then it'll be even worse. Hell, we'd be suppressing free speech as well as dodging him."

"We could put up with that for a few days," Reynolds replied. "It couldn't be any worse than another round of this debate crap I've been reading about. What debate? We each gave a speech. We never even saw each other in Shreveport."

After a moment of thought, Reynolds asked, "What'll be the format at the LAIPRO meeting?"

"You speak at the opening luncheon as the principal speaker of the convention. They'll be hearing speakers in the morning then all afternoon. Flint speaks at the first session after lunch."

"So he speaks right after me?"

"Right."

"So he'll inherit my crowd, my media and I speak first so I'm at his mercy. I get no reply if he drops something new. God, Neil, who in the hell set this thing up?"

"You've been scheduled for months, long before Flint got in the race," Moulard explained.

"You think I should go through with it?" asked Reynolds.

"Yes, I do." Moulard drove the car into the underground garage of the mansion and turned off the ignition. "But I have an idea. Let's put a little pressure on LAIPRO to rearrange that schedule. Maybe Flint could speak at eight that morning instead of after lunch."

Reynolds considered the suggestion for a moment, then laughed out loud as he opened the car door. "Hey, that's good. Who's going to get up to attend a Saturday morning convention speech? I like it." He laughed again. "Give it a try and see if you can arrange it."

Three days later the phone on Congressman Jeffrey Bordelon's desk in his New Iberia home rang at precisely seven in the evening. Jon Douglas was seated beside him discussing the campaign. Bordelon answered the phone. "Hello, this is Jeffrey Bordelon."

"Congressman. This is Carey Jefferson. We've got a problem for the LAIPRO convention."

"Let me guess, Carey. They want Darin off the agenda."

"Well, that's almost correct. They want him to speak at eight a.m., not one-thirty," said Jefferson.

Bordelon was silent for a few moments as he considered this development. "I guess they figure to embarrass Flint by having him speak to an empty room." Bordelon pondered for a few more moments. "Can you just tell them no, that the agenda is locked in and final?"

"No way," said Jefferson. "They've gone over my head. There are board members who want to help Flint but they can't afford to let Reynolds know that. There are others who'd probably be willing to tell Reynolds to jump, but I cannot recommend that. Besides, Reynolds has his friends in LAIPRO. Good friends. I've been told to make some changes."

"May I make a suggestion?" asked Bordelon.

"That's why I called."

"I suggest you cooperate with them," advised Bordelon. "Or at least seem to. That way Reynolds will quit worrying about it and the pressure will be off. Don't make a big deal of changing the agenda. Don't complain about political pressure, Reynolds or anything. Just tell them Flint is being offered another time slot and being told one-thirty is impossible due to a conflict. Be helpful to Reynolds people. Don't argue for Flint."

"I don't get it? Very few people will attend an eight o'clock speaking slot. Its going to defeat Flint's purpose entirely."

"I know. Flint's going to take your eight o'clock offer under consideration," said Bordelon. "Meanwhile, you'll need another speaker after lunch to fill that empty slot. Just quietly place me on the agenda at one-thirty. I'm your one- thirty speaker. O.K.?"

Bordelon could hear Jefferson chuckling. "O.K., Congressman. You're our speaker."

"And Carey, delay notifying the press as long as possible. Tell your people Flint's been removed and leave it at that."

The telephone conference ended and Bordelon hung up the phone. He turned to Jon Douglas with his face more red than usual and his blue eyes bright with the challange of overcoming a new problem. "Reynolds is more worried than I thought."

Jon Douglas nodded his agreement. "Flint is making an impact and maybe its showing up in Reynolds' polls. It's still August. Reynolds is so far ahead, there's only one way for him to go. Down."

SIXTEEN

"If capitalism is fair then unionism must be. If men have a right to capitalize their ideas and the resources of their country, then that implies the right of men to capitalize their labor."

Frank Lloyd Wright
(1869-1959)
American architect

Darin Flint arrived with Jenny at the AFL-CIO union offices in Baton Rouge at seven in the morning. Flint had spoken with Vernon Looper by telephone briefly prior to his announcement as a courtesy. But it was not enough. A more frank discussion and understanding between them was needed. He decided to face the labor leader directly and personally arranged an early morning meeting. Joe Randall, a labor lobbyist for over twenty years, was pouring coffee when Flint entered with his daughter.

"Hello, Joe. Good to see you. Do you know my daughter Jenny?"

"Sure. Hello. Had coffee yet?"

They poured coffee and headed for Vernon Looper's office.

"Good morning, Darin," Vernon Looper said with a smile as he rose from behind his desk to shake hands. "I appreciate you wanting to talk and coming down so early." Looper took a cup of the coffee and sat back down. "I've been hoping we'd get a chance to talk."

Flint again introduced Jenny and explained she was helping him with his daily schedule.

Flint and Vernon Looper's relationship had begun twenty- seven years ago when Flint arrived in Baton Rouge for his first session of the Legislature. They had not started off well. Flint had been unpredictable from the start, fiercely independent in the legislative debates. Looper was then the top labor lobbyist in the Senate. His rise to the presidency had been a natural ascendancy after thirty-five years as a union officer and lobbyist. Looper was now in his third year as the Louisiana AFL-CIO president. From the beginning he had been distrustful of Flint's independence. But gradually, over two decades, their attitudes had relaxed. Looper's formal, icy demeanor had been transformed into friendliness. A mutual respect and genuine friendship now existed between them.

Looper was not by nature a friendly person. His temper was volatile and his manner abrupt. He was of medium height with heavy, thick limbs developed initially from his early years as a construction worker and softened with outer layers of flesh accumulated during his decades in the AFL-CIO offices. The scalp of Looper's round head was covered by a short, grey haired crewcut. He had a large, dimpled chin supporting a full, wide mouth. Looper's harsh, gruff voice, and the political power he could assert, had intimidated many politicians over the years into acquiescence to union views. The political influence of organized labor was stronger in Louisiana than any other southern state, but its dominance had been eroded by the emergence of the Louisiana Business League as a power since the mid-seventies. Yet Looper, as the personification of the labor union movement, remained the essential base of support of such politicians as René Reynolds. Such politicians could not, without gravely endangering their political careers, venture far from the labor union's liberal positions on issues ranging from education, welfare, and the equal rights amendment to the traditional labor issues of right to work and worker's compensation as otherwise their public careers would rapidly collapse.

There might be brief flings occasionally by such officeholders at independence like a horse chomping at a bit, but inevitably the restraint of the labor union bridle was finally, albeit reluctantly, accepted. Looper had long ago accepted the fact that Darin Flint was an exception to that rule.

"How is your campaign?" Looper asked.

"It's good. One step at a time. Our organization is good. The fundraising is on schedule. Press is good. We have an important message and people are responding."

"You know we are with Reynolds. We have to be," said Looper.

"The political rules are changing Vernon. You don't 'have' to be with Reynolds," said Flint with emphasis. "You're an honest man. I don't believe you approve of the people around Reynolds and the way they do business. And labor has nothing to gain or lose in this election."

"Reynolds has been a friend. He's done what we wanted, when we want. We must support a sitting governor who has been a friend. You knew that before you walked in here. Besides, we're not too thrilled with your moratorium idea on Right to Work."

Flint poured a second cup of coffee. "Well, what are you going to do to help Reynolds and to hurt me?"

"We have phone banks and direct mail to our members. We are raising money for Reynolds. We'll provide manpower if he needs it. Most of all, we can help him with the blacks," said Looper.

"And what will you do to hurt me?"

"What do you mean," asked Looper.

"I've seen labor really go after opponents before. Will I be denounced as anti-working man? As an enemy of organized labor? Will I be called callous, unfeeling, lacking sympathy for the unemployed and the poor? Will you tell rank and file that I've got a bad labor record? If it gets close, will labor start slinging mud at me? What will you do to hurt me?"

Flint saw Looper's jaws tighten. Perhaps he'd gone too far.

"Now wait a minute, Darin. Labor is fair and...."

Flint interrupted. "Labor is determined to win elections. All I want to know is how determined is labor to win this election for Reynolds and to defeat me."

Flint saw Looper glance at Joe Randall who was sitting in the corner. Looper rubbed the short hair on the crown of his scalp then picked up a pen on his desk and patted it unconsciously on a tablet.

"Darin, what do you expect?" he asked.

"Only what you said a moment ago," answered Flint. "Fairness." Flint paused then continued, "That's what I've given to both you and business for twenty-seven years and that's what I ask in return. If you say nothing more, nothing less than that to your members and to the press, then I'll have no complaints either now or after the election."

"After the election?" Looper inquired with a smile, eyebrows arched.

"After I win," said Flint with finality. There was no smile on his face. "Do we have an agreement?"

Looper again glanced at Randall then exhaled. His eyes moved back to Flint. "Yes, I think we do."

Following the meeting with Vernon Looper, Jenny and Flint began the drive across town to Jon Douglas' house for an 8:00 a.m. strategy session.

It was raining and very overcast. Flint watched the rain splashing on the windshield, briefly dripping over the glass before being wiped suddenly away by the sweep of the wipers. The rain was a welcome change from the weeks of intense, humid heat of that summer. Flint felt refreshed and a sense of elation. Susan and John had driven into Baton Rouge last night and spent the night. It had been a pleasurable respite from the campaign to have the family together for the evening.

Flint had learned that Reynolds' greatest weakness was among middle income, professional people. He was surprised to discover Reynolds also had problems with conservative, working people, even rank and file labor union members, who resented his new taxes and spending policies. These were working people who could contribute quietly to a campaign with a little money, their time and talent. Young people, college age students and housewives could be stimulated by the idealism of Flint's message and the determined flavor of his underdog candidacy.

These anti-Reynolds groups had given sustenance to Flint's growing volunteer organization. Now the problem was to continue building and expanding the campaign while bringing efficiency and direction to their efforts.

Flint closed his eyes and lay his head back against the headrest of the passenger seat. The first phase of the campaign had been successful, he believed, because of the initial surprise element and the natural reluctance of the governor to acknowledge his shoestring campaign. Reynolds probably had no choice but to try to ignore him. But that strategy had played right into Flint's hands. Reynolds' overconfidence had allowed Flint to take the offensive. Flint realized it would not be so easy from now on. He had gained significant public attention but his foothold could just as quickly be lost and forgotten.

It was time to shift to a higher gear.

Congressman Bordelon, Barbara Durham, Terrell Franks, Joel Whitney, Carey Jefferson, John and Flint were at Jon Douglas' home seated around the big table when Flint and Jenny arrived.

"How did it go with Looper?" asked Bordelon.

Flint smiled and glanced at his daughter. "I don't know. What did you think Jenny?"

"I didn't know what to think for awhile," Jenny laughed. "I thought they were going to have a fight."

"Looper made it clear labor will be one hundred percent for Reynolds," Flint said as he sat down beside Douglas. "He says he'll tell rank and file that I've always been at least fair to labor, but they'll stick with Reynolds."

"Do you really think he'll treat you that well?"

"Well, I guess it doesn't matter what I think. Looper feels certain I can't win so he doesn't envision ever having to really fight me. If he'll give me credit for being a reasonable man on labor issues, that's the best we can hope for."

He accepted a doughnut and orange juice from Jon Douglas. Flint looked toward his son. "John, how's our money look?"

"Not good. We've paid for statewide saturation television for the last five days of the campaign," John answered. "We've paid for a portion of the art, design, photography, and production expenses of the eight page newspaper insert we'll use in two weeks in the Sunday newspapers statewide. We still owe another $50 thousand. But that's only a fraction of the cost. The newspaper charges for that tabloid insert and the printing bill will be another $80 thousand. I don't see how we can get the bill paid in time. We may have to postpone the insert."

Flint had decided to devote their limited funds to paying for a media blitz the last three weeks of the campaign. He wanted to make absolutely sure he would not come up short of money at the end of the campaign; then either limp across the finish line or be forced to borrow large sums of money. He believed a good finishing kick was essential. Flint wanted his campaign to reach a peak of public awareness and approval during that final week. So they were paying for media one day at a time, from election Saturday backward. The eight page, newspaper tabloid section he wanted to publish early in September was the only exception to that strategy.

"What about television and newspaper advertising?" Flint asked.

"We've paid for saturation television the final five days of the campaign. We've also deposited enough to cover three one-quarter page ads in each daily newspaper in the state except the

Picayune. We haven't set aside anything for the Picayune yet or for any of the state's weekly newspapers," answered John.

"How much do the Picayune ads cost?"

"Two-thousand dollars for a one-quarter page ad," John said.

Flint shook his head in disbelief and took a bite from the doughnut. After a few moments of silence, Flint again asked for more information.

"How much did we pay for those five days of statewide television?"

Jon Douglas explained the media buys. "We purchased a six o'clock news spot, a ten o'clock news spot, a prime time evening spot and four wildcard spots during each of those final five days on every t.v. station. Most of those wildcard ads will fall during soap operas, the early morning shows and the Johnny Carson show after the news. Everything is in thirty second spots."

"So how much have we spent?"

"We have paid $148 thousand for those five days," answered John Flint. "It'll cost us over $320 thousand to purchase two more weeks."

Flint made a note of those figures on his legal pad. "Now break down the figures for me on the tabloid. Why is it so expensive?"

"The production and printing of the eight page tabloid insert, in color and if using slick paper is approximately $130 thousand," explained Douglas. "We must print 900 thousand copies. The newspapers will charge another $50 thousand. So a first class job has a total price tag of $180 thousand. We've paid $50 thousand so far."

Jon Douglas took a sip of his coffee, then summarized. "So the insert will cost us another $130 thousand."

Flint made a few notes and did some figuring. "What about radio and newspaper?"

Jon Douglas again explained the buys. "Our people are looking at market statistics to decide which radio stations to use in each area of the state. I believe we can pretty well cover radio statewide for approximately $25 thousand per week. If we plan four one-quarter page ads per week in each daily, and one ad per week in each weekly paper, then we are looking at a $100 thousand newspaper budget for three weeks."

Flint added up the figures that Douglas and John had been explaining to the group. "According to my math, that presents me with a $615 thousand bill," said Flint.

"No," said Jeffrey Bordelon. "It presents all of us with that bill. How much money do we have on hand?"

"The count stands at precisely $31,646.40," answered John Flint, reading from his accounting sheets. "We need to keep a steady reserve of approximately twenty thousand dollars to make sure our monthly bills stay current. We will have ten regional headquarters in operation by September first. The start-up costs, telephone deposits and utility deposits are expensive. We've had to pay for stamps, envelopes, stationary, staplers, xerox machines, pens and voter registration lists to supply each headquarters. Our rental expenses are fairly low because most of the offices have been donated. But that money we have in the account is needed to cover our daily expenses in all the headquarters and get us through the first of September."

"How is our supply of campaign pamphlets?" asked Jon Douglas.

"We took an inventory of every headquarters last night," answered Barbara Durham. "There's a shortage everywhere because we've been organizing the rural parishes. Each headquarters divided their supplies with surrounding parishes. We ordered and paid for a forty-five thousand piece order last week which we hope to get in today. But when you divide that up among ten headquarters and the rural parishes, it won't last long. We need to order another forty or fifty thousand so we can use them in local mailouts and door to door efforts. So far, we've made good use of our xerox machines to make copies of good newspaper articles to hand out, but we need those pamphlets."

"What about posters and billboards?" asked Joel Whitney.

"I doubt we'll have any billboards," answered Flint. "They're expensive. It would cost us $120 thousand for thirty days of strong billboard coverage statewide. Jon's people have designed a very nice yardsign poster but it also has a very hefty price tag."

Jon Douglas then further explained their yard sign plans. "If we decide to have posters, we will only order enough to use the last two weeks or ten days of the campaign. That's the most we can afford."

Terrell Franks had been quietly listening to the growing list of needs and expenses. "Folks, its obvious we have serious money problems. Even if we had a million dollars to spend during the next two months, we would still be running a very limited advertising and media campaign."

Franks stopped speaking for a moment, stood and shook his head in exasperation, "We haven't even discussed direct mail to voters' homes, election day expenses, polling expenses, the money its going to take to compete for organizational support in the black community. Hell, man, Reynolds spent over a million dollars in Orleans Parish in the black community during the last three days of his last campaign."

Franks paused, then asked the group, "Do you people understand what I'm saying? Reynolds' billboards are already up. You've been seeing his television spots in waves since early spring. He's already had one tabloid section in the newspaper. He had over five million dollars in the bank before qualifying last month. Now he's squeezing everyone who does business with the state because suddenly he has an opponent. We're helping him make money because now he has an excuse to go back for more. He's capable of spending eleven, twelve, or thirteen million dollars in this campaign."

"Terrell, what's your point?" asked Congressman Bordelon.

"Come on, Congressman. I've already made my point. Three weeks of our low budget media versus Reynolds one hundred percent name recognition, months of media, incumbancy and his unlimited supply of funds to keep the big name black organizations happy and working. And we haven't even figured out a way to pay for our measly three weeks of media!" Terrell Franks ended his speech with both hands reaching out toward Bordelon, fingers outstretched for emphasis. His look of desperation was almost comical.

Flint's burst of laughter broke the tension in the room. "I think Terrell makes a very good point. He's a media man. Our media is important but it will never match the complete saturation Reynolds is producing. Our campaign must be different or somehow unique if we're going to win."

"That's right," said Franks. "Our public relations campaign sure isn't going to win it for us."

"One thing we can do is make an issue of the money he's spending," said Bordelon. "That's a big reason we're in this campaign. To stop the vicious cycle of huge donations and favoritism."

"It would be interesting to see how the black voters would respond if they knew how much money was being given to the so-called leaders," Franks wondered out loud.

"Aw come on, Terrell," said Carey Jefferson. "Everyone knows your friend Jackson Wells and his organization in New Orleans has made millions off politics. No one seems too offended by it. His group keeps winning elections."

"Maybe we haven't really pursued the issue. I'm a black. Jackson is my friend. But he's forgotten why we got into politics. He's not working for our people anymore. He's working for himself," Franks declared.

Flint interrupted the conversation, "I think Terrell is right. I think a lot of black voters resent big money politicians just as much as white voters do. It's a good issue and I'll start using it. But we need to get better organized within the black community."

"O.K. Darin", Franks answered. "We'll start getting you more opportunities to give speeches to black audiences. I've followed up on every black contact you've made so far, just like you suggested. Maybe we need to invite everyone we've gotten involved so far to Baton Rouge for a meeting with all of us. We can develop the strategy, appoint spokesmen, and go to work."

Franks stopped and thought for a moment. "What do we do when they want money to work?"

"We'll tell them the truth." Flint said matter of factly. "We have no money. They're either with us or not. We have no money."

"Dad, you'll be attending ten headquarters openings over the next two weeks. That'll take you to every section of the state," Jenny pointed out. "I'll give Terrell the dates and places. We'll see if there are events in the black community you can cover in those areas."

Franks nodded. "And I can also help your local leaders be certain there are plenty of black faces at your grand openings. We could even set up local black organizational meetings at the various headquarters either before or after the grand openings."

Flint nodded and looked at his watch. It was almost time to leave. "Time is a little short so lets cover some things quickly. Can we get a quick report on fundraising?"

"Jane Baldwin reports that preparations for the fundraiser Wednesday in New Orleans are going well," reported Joel Whitney.

"She wants to schedule another fundraiser in early October and hold it at her home. The Shreveport fundraiser is next Tuesday. Rodney Libscomb tells me he expects to clear over thirty thousand dollars. Carey and I have scheduled a meeting of the Finance Committee for this afternoon. Virtually every member has assured me they would bring a number of donations with them. I'm expecting fifteen thousand dollars today anyway. We have five fundraisers scheduled in September around the state."

"Darin, the fundraising is going as well as can be expected," said Bordelon. "But we want to try a fundraising newspaper ad in Lafayette next week. If it works, then we will try it in other communities. We've also organized a fundraising letter in Baton Rouge directed at middle income people. If it works, then we'll also try it elsewhere."

"How are we set for the LAIPRO Convention?" Flint asked Carey Jefferson.

Bordelon interrupted. "Darin, when Reynolds first had you bumped from the agenda, it occurred to me to have Carey place me on the agenda in your place so I could later step aside for you," said Bordelon. "But that might look a little silly and contrived. Why don't we just make the best of it. You're on for eight-thirty a.m. Carey says he can go ahead and make it a full breakfast with all the trimmings, invite members and their wives. We could advertise this convention as a second debate despite your early morning time slot. We could highlight the breakfast as having equal status with the luncheon meeting. We can get volunteers there in force to make sure its packed. We can have plenty of signs, posters, Flint T-shirts and a strong show of support. We could turn it into a Flint media event."

"That's right," said Carey. "We're going to print the programs tomorrow and we'll then issue the final agenda to the press. We can feature you and the governor on the program cover. How about it?"

"O.K. Let's do the breakfast," Flint said with finality. "Terrell, you should also schedule a press conference for that afternoon immediately following Congressman Bordelon's speech to the convention. Let the press know Congressman Bordelon will have a very special announcement."

Flint looked across the table at Bordelon. "Congressman," he said. "It's time for you to make your endorsement and assume the title of campaign manager. It'll be in Lafayette in your own backyard."

"I like it," Bordelon declared as he nodded with approval. "Maybe I'll even declare you the winner of the second debate."

Flint turned to Greg Hawkins. "What about the position papers?"

Hawkins leaned forward to give his report to the group. "We'll start our weekly position papers at a press conference next week. It's up to every local headquarters to get our position papers distributed in each area. We are asking each parish organization to put up the money to publish a copy of the position papers distributed in each area. We are asking each parish organization to put up the money to publish a copy of the position paper, with Senator Flint's picture, in their local paper each week. That will be a weekly item."

"I will write the position paper each week," added Flint. "Congressman Bordelon and Terrell will help me. Hopefully, they'll be no longer than one short page, uncomplicated, direct and hard hitting."

"Darin, will you do me a favor," asked Congressman Bordelon.

Flint looked at him quizzically.

"Please don't call me congressman anymore. If you don't call me congressman, then I won't call you senator."

The two men stood, laughed and shook hands. "One more thing, Darin. Jane Baldwin called and told me she's discussed with the League of Women Voters the possibility of a television debate between you and Reynolds. Her idea is to have the League of Women Voters demand the debate instead of you. That should put Reynolds on the spot. And of course, the League would offer to sponsor it."

"Good idea. Reynolds can ridicule and ignore any challenge from me to publicly debate. But it will be more difficult for him to ridicule and ignore the League of Women Voters."

Bordelon nodded in agreement. "Then I'll give her the green light."

Later that day, Flint and Susan took steps to borrow $50 thousand from a New Orleans bank, placing a mortgage on their home to cover it. The funds were used as another partial payment for the eight page statewide newspaper insert, which Flint felt was an essential expense to achieve better name recognition.

In making this loan, both were breaking a rule they had always followed throughout Flint's career .... never allow politics to endanger the security of their personal finances. But it had been Flint who had made the rule almost thirty years ago; now it was Flint who proposed breaking it. "We are asking others to invest their time, money and efforts in our campaign. It may hurt a bit but we can afford the $50 thousand. It's our investment in the campaign."

Susan listened quietly then said, "I won't say no but I want you to know that I don't like it. Everybody knows you've been knocking yourself out and making every sacrifice for this campaign. We shouldn't be expected by anyone to borrow thousands of dollars."

Flint paused thoughtfully, then answered his wife. "Whether we like it or not, in the final analysis, Susan, this campaign is our battle. It's true I was urged to run by others but I'm not their candidate or their responsibility. You and I actually made the decision to run. We knew the campaign would be expensive. Now we must face our share of the music. I won't suggest borrowing more than this unless we're near the end with a clear chance to win. Even then, I won't go too far. Trust me."

Susan agreed and the loan was made.

SEVENTEEN

"Get your facts first, and then you can distort them as much as you please."

Mark Twain
(Samuel Langhorne Clemens)
(1835-1910)
American novelist, essayist

James Harriford sat in his suspenders and watched the face of Governor Reynolds speaking to him from the television set.

"My father was a share cropper. He was poor. I look today at my mother and I remember the sacrifices she made so that we kids could go to school. My father picked himself up by the bootstraps to become a lawyer. I've known since my early days we must continue our commitment to the poor, the halt, the lame, the dispossessed and the unfortunate. We must not allow others to take away medical care or close nursing homes, stop hot meals at school and cut other vital services. It may not be popular for me to fight for those programs but doing what's right is more important then being popular. That's the price of leadership."

The camera froze on Reynold's concerned face. A deep voice stated, "Let's keep bold leadership. Governor René Reynolds for Louisiana."

"Bullshit," Harriford muttered as he reached for the knob of the television and turned it off.

He placed his briefcase on the desk top and removed a stack of documents and a photograph. He placed a copy of each document and the photograph in a large manila envelope and wrote Neil Moulard across the front.

Moulard will love this, he thought to himself.

He pulled the photo out of the envelope and looked at it again.

I've never seen a more perfect job, he thought as he mentally congratulated himself for his photographic handiwork. He looked it over and decided on his course of action. The black and white photograph was grainy and taken in poor light. It depicted two young men, halfdressed, in an embrace. The face of only one was

93

visible. His hair was very dark, not at all unlike the black hair of Darin Flint. The eyes, the nose, the mouth were also close enough.

The photo was placed in a second envelope. Harriford picked up the phone and quickly dialed the telephone number of the governor's office.

"I'd like to speak to Neil Moulard, please."

He waited for the connection with Moulard's secretary. A pleasant female voice asked, "May I say who is calling?"

"James Harriford."

A moment later Moulard was on the line.

"What's up?"

"I've got something for you. But its going to cost twenty thousand dollars."

"It had better be good, Harriford."

"It's very good."

"I'll have to discuss it with Reynolds."

"Fine. You know how to reach me."

Harriford hung up the phone, smiled at himself in the mirror over the dresser, then flipped the television back on. He ordered room service for dinner.

At that same moment, across town in the capitol, Neil Moulard entered the governor's office. Reynolds was conducting much of his current campaign work from his office. This seemed a safe way to avoid bringing undue publicity to the campaign and to his opponent. His traveling primarily involved appearances as a speaker and at fundraisers. His staff had a succession of key persons on his rotating telephone lines all day. He was personally speaking to one hundred and fifty to two hundred persons a day.

Moulard waited patiently as Reynolds engaged in a telephone conversation with a key political operative with Texon Oil Company. Reynolds had carefully cultivated "big oil". The oil industry had contributed millions in his prior campaign simply because they knew he was going to win. They had been rewarded when Reynolds' package of tax increases carefully sidestepped and avoided any new levy on the oil and gas industry. Instead, the tax package was composed entirely of consumer taxes....sales taxes, gasoline taxes, personal income taxes, special fuels taxes, liquor and beer taxes, cigarette taxes, corporate taxes that would be passed on to the consumer.

Reynolds had argued that Louisiana had been too reliant on oil and gas taxes in the past. But he did nothing to reduce that reliance. The new consumer tax revenues were quickly eaten up by new spending in construction projects, new education bureaucracies, new "economic development" programs and balancing the previous year's excessive budget. Reliance on energy revenues continued to pay for the pre-existing spending of state government.

"Look, Bill," Reynolds said to the Texon representative over the telephone. "You tell those guys that the Legislature's going to want some of those consumer taxes repealed and to go instead with a tax on offshore oil and gas. The state gets nothing from offshore production and you know how low our severance tax rate is compared to other oil states. I'm tired of fighting your battles for you."

Moulard watched Reynolds manipulate the oil representative on the telephone. He knew it had to be Bill Beeson of Texon. My gosh, it took gall to hit those guys up again for more donations, he thought to himself as he settled into the cushioned chair facing Reynolds' desk. He had taught Reynolds well.

Reynolds winked at him.

"O.K., Bill. I understand it is not easy for you. But our campaign's expensive and we're counting on you. And, by the way, Danny and Julie told me Texon's signed a contract with them for national advertising work. I want you to know I appreciate it."

Moulard thought about the millions this man, his family, his former law partners and friends had made. Reynolds had channeled many business people who came to his office to many businesses in which he had become a silent partner or stockholder....consultant firms, insurance companies, office buildings, oil and gas supply firms, real estate, oil exploration, pipelines, nursing homes, hospitals. Reynold's sister, Julie, had entered the public relations business only two years ago with her husband. They were now on retainer by dozens of businesses and were handling millions of dollars of political work for candidates wanting to identify with Reynolds. Texon had now become a client.

Moulard's thoughts were interrupted when Reynolds hung up the phone.

"What's up, Neil?"

"Harriford called. He must really have something on Flint this time. He says it will cost twenty thousand dollars.

Reynolds rolled his eyes toward the ceiling, shook his head side to side to express his scepticism silently, then exhaled heavily.

"Exactly what does he have?"

"You know how he operates. He never gives you the whole picture til he's got it finished. But his early reports were following several leads. One dealt with someone in Flint's family having stock in Noble Airlines. Flint may have had a conflict of interest on some votes regarding special tax exemptions for the airline. Also, he was following some leads on Flint's wife's family. Seems there was a suicide some time back that he was checking out. The third lead he'd gotten was on Flint's military days. We've paid for three trips to California for Harriford in the past month so I presume he's doing something besides vacationing out there."

Reynolds' mind dwelled on Harriford while Moulard brought him up to date on the three reports he had gotten from Harriford so far. Reynolds remembered that Harriford had used his position as an undercover agent to accumulate and develop incriminating files, tapes and photographs on many among Louisiana's powerful, influential and wealthy. Blackmail in everything from drug use to public corruption. Marital infidelity had become his speciality. Only Harriford's extensive files and a smart criminal attorney had kept Harriford out of a long jail term. But Reynolds also remembered how valuable Harriford's investigative work had been in winning the governorship four years ago.

"Neil, let's keep Harriford away from here. Somebody might recognize him. His name should not even be mentioned to a secretary. If he calls, he needs to use some other name."

"No problem."

"Well, do you think his information is worth twenty thousand dollars? And do we need it?" asked Reynolds.

"I'm sure that's a bargaining figure. We'll try for five thousand now and more later if we're interested in the full story. Those early reports interest me," Moulard said. "It would be nice to have a little insurance in this campaign. Flint is a Mr. Clean. Like a man in a clean white suit. Just a speck of mud on him could look real messy."

A voice over Reynolds' intercom interrupted them and informed Reynolds that three key politicians were waiting to speak with him on the telephone.

Reynolds quickly closed their conference. "Let's give Harriford five thousand dollars and see what he's got."

As Moulard left the office, Reynolds was already absorbed in his next telephone conversation.

EIGHTEEN

*"On the loftiest throne in the world we are still sitting
only on our own rear."*

Michel de Montaigne
(1533-1592)
French philosopher

The Louisiana Association of Independent Petroleum and
Royalty Owners (LAIPRO) were holding their convention at the
Hilton Hotel in Lafayette. Normally their conventions were quiet,
dignified meetings of many of Louisiana's most successful energy
entrepreneurs, characterized by long, technical speeches by government bureaucrats, energy regulators and members of Congress
on pending energy legislation.

This year was obviously different. René Reynolds had perhaps
been correct when he observed that the media wanted a campaign
to write about. Jeffrey Bordelon, Carey Jefferson and Terrell Franks
had found fertile ground with the wire services, the newspapers,
the radio and television reporters as they reminded various media
people to cover the event. The response had been enthusiastic.

Neil Moulard stood in the Hilton lobby as the noon hour approached. He had not planned on attending. But news speculation the previous day in Louisiana's major newspapers had
convinced him to come to Lafayette early this Saturday morning
to hear Darin Flint's speech. No apparent effort had been made
that morning to limit Flint's audience to LAIPRO members. Moulard
had witnessed, with growing annoyance, the breakfast crowd packed to capacity with Flint supporters, who cheered him repeatedly
before an attentive press.

Moulard burned with the realization that Flint's speech had received a rousing response and made a deep impression on the media.
Flint would get good headlines tomorrow.

No similar preparations had been made with the governor's local
supporters to assure a favorable crowd reception. Moulard had
gotten on the phone after Flint's speech to put their forces to work
in Lafayette creating a crowd for Reynolds. It was too little too

late. Although Flint's speech had ended and Flint had left almost two hours earlier, the hotel lobby was still packed with Darin Flint supporters. Flint badges were on the lapels of many; there were even people carrying Flint signs and placards. They were waiting for a glimpse of René Reynolds.

The media milled with the crowd in the lobby near the front of the hotel in anticipation of Governor Reynolds' arrival. Inside the convention hall, the membership of LAIPRO had already filled the table spaces and the luncheon was getting underway.

As Moulard paced nervously then walked out the front doors of the hotel to wait in the parking lot away from the crowd, Jeffrey Bordelon quietly watched the turmoil and noise from a chair in a distant corner of the lobby. He could not quite restrain the smile that tugged at the corners of his mouth.

I don't know if it's possible for Flint to win this election, but we're certainly going to give it a hell of a run, he thought to himself.

At that moment, a ripple of movement passed through the crowd as attention, then movement, turned toward the front doors of the hotel. Outside, Moulard was opening the back door of a long, dark Oldsmobile with darkly tinted windows. Reynolds emerged from the car, obviously surprised by the crowd of people blocking the entrance. Reynolds started for the doorway behind two state policemen. Smiling and waving, he began shaking hands. Then he noticed "Flint for Governor" buttons on the shirts of several bystanders. Once in the hotel lobby, a rhythmic, repetitious chant from the crowd assaulted his brain.

"WE WANT FLINT! WE WANT FLINT! WE WANT FLINT! WE WANT FLINT!"

The cheer grew in intensity. Flint posters held overhead were being thrust up and down to the beat of the chant.

Reynolds stood absolutely still in the doorway, seemingly frozen for a moment, the constant, continuous chant ringing in his ears. The smile was gone, replaced by an expression of bewilderment. The red color of his neck and jowls revealed a mixture of anger and embarrassment rising within him. Moulard forged a path and lead Reynolds through the crowd, amidst Flint posters and the loud noise, toward the convention hall where the luncheon was underway.

As Reynolds approached the convention auditorium, a radio reporter moved beside him and extended a microphone toward his face. Instinctively, without hearing the reporter's question, Reynolds pushed the hand away, accidently causing the off balance reporter to stumble backwards into the crowd. This caused others to lose their balance. The chanting was interrupted by the shouts and shrieks of those who were falling. A chain reaction of collisions occurred within the crowd. Several people were knocked off their feet onto the floor.

The crowd responded with angry jeers, boos and taunts as Reynolds finally stepped past the crowd and entered the luncheon area.

The entire assemblage of LAIPRO members and press, seated for their meals, had heard the loud chanting. They watched Reynolds enter the room, accompanied by the enormous volume of noise belching through the double doors from the angry crowd. Reynolds hurried into the room and headed for the head table. Someone closed the doors leaving the crowd outside the auditorium, thereby muffling the volume of their voices.

Reynolds did his best to regain his composure and present the commanding posture of an incumbant governor. However, his usual reserve of humor and confidence were noticeably absent during his speech.

The day following the LAIPRO Convention in Lafayette, the lead article on the front page of the New Orleans Times Picayune recorded the speech and events that followed this way:

VIOLENCE ERUPTS IN SECOND REYNOLDS-FLINT MEETING
Jeffrey Bordelon Named
Flint Campaign Manager

(Lafayette, AP) The gubernatorial campaign of State Senator Darin Flint made a splash in Lafayette yesterday that left an upstaged Governor René Reynolds angry as a wet hen.

In what was billed across Louisiana as their second debate, each candidate addressed the Louisiana Association of Independent Petroleum Producers (LAIPRO) at the Lafayette Hilton Hotel. In a breakfast speech to a crowd packed with his enthusiastic, vocal supporters, Flint lashed out at "the white collar criminals who peddle Reynolds influence and enrich themselves by arrogantly dispensing political favoritism." Later in the day Flint received the endorsement of former Congressman Jeffrey Bordelon, whose popularity and influence in Acadiana is prodigious.

The same crowd booed and jeered Governor Reynolds as he arrived to address the convention during its noon luncheon. His speech was politely received by LAIPRO members and was laced with acidic, distainful remarks, regarding "the silly, juvenile behavior" of the Flint supporters.

While leaving, Reynolds accidentally collided with one of the Flint supporters whose sign was knocked to the ground. Reynolds then tripped on the sign as he walked away and almost fell down. The state police accompanying the governor cleared the way thereafter and prevented further incident. A similar melee had occurred when Reynolds arrived at the hotel and was entering the convention hall to give his speech.

An actual debate failed to develop as the candidates delivered their speeches several hours apart. Senator Flint's speech covered issues he has previously emphasized on the campaign trail. He explained his "Highway Master Plan", his proposal to reform the public school teacher pay system, a three point plan to improve civil service and a financial plan to balance Louisiana's budget without new taxes. But he saved his strongest comments for what he termed "the abuses of public trust" by Reynolds. He criticized excessive attorney fees allegedly paid to Reynolds friends, special insurance contracts and consultant fees, special public retirement benefits for political friends, favoritism in awarding bank charters, real estate licenses, oil and gas leases, pardons and paroles of criminals, hospital and nursing home permits. He criticized Reynolds' alleged efforts to pack the ethics commission and to politically influence investment of public retirement system funds.

Flint characterized Reynolds as "the champion of white collar crime" and "a specialist in influence peddling." Flint described his own campaign as a "no deals campaign".

Former Congressman Bordelon endorsed Senator Flint during an afternoon press conference following the speech of Governor Reynolds. Bordelon described Flint as "the most knowledgeable man in state government today".

Governor Reynolds speech was a detailed review of oil and gas statistics indicating the energy industry was on the upswing. He was critical of the federal government's intrusion into the energy market place and he called for the complete deregulation of natural gas. Reynolds explained his recent tax increases had been to reduce the state's reliance on oil and gas revenues. He reminded the audience that no new taxes had been imposed on the oil and gas industry in Louisiana while other energy states had implemented more energy taxes.

In a related matter, the New Orleans League of Women Voters invited both candidates to appear in two one hour televised debates to be sponsored by the League on statewide television in October. Senator Flint immediately accepted. Governor Reynolds stated he had not yet received his invitation.

Furthermore, the Governor said, "I do not feel the candidacy of my opponent is serious enough to merit a debate."

Other Louisiana newspapers published articles on the speeches, the Bordelon endorsement and the League of Women Voters proposal to hold gubernatorial debates. The Lafayette Advertiser ran on its front page separate articles on each candidates' speech and the Bordelon endorsement.

The Alexandria News Weekly, a black newspaper, ran a photograph of Flint campaigning in a black neighborhood. The headline of the feature article was "Flint Challenges the Money, Incumbancy of Reynolds". Terrell Franks had been a very busy man. Such articles appeared in black newspapers across the state that last week in August.

Flint had his best television, radio and newspaper coverage of the campaign in the wake of the Lafayette speech. The Baton Rouge Morning Advocate announced it would conduct a readership poll the following week on whether Governor Reynolds should accept the invitation to a televised debate in the gubernatorial campaign.

Meanwhile Flint began two weeks of "grand opening" rallies of his ten headquarters in the major cities of the state.

NINETEEN

"Let us have faith that Right makes Might, and in that faith, let us, to the end, dare to do our duty as we understand it.

Abraham Lincoln
Conclusion of the
"Cooper Institute Speech"
at New York City, February 27, 1960

Darin Flint stood on the haywagon in front of his Shreveport headquarters in a King's Highway shopping center. It was a bright, sunny Saturday morning and the crowd was enjoying the activities. Most were in short sleeves and casual attire. A caravan of decorated cars covered with Flint posters had intercepted Flint's car outside of town. They had paraded through busy shopping areas and residential neighborhoods on their way to the headquarters.

The media had been there for Flint's colorful arrival, political music ringing out over the public address system. A Coca Cola booth was selling Flint T-shirts and handing out free soft drinks. The crowd was a good mixture of young and old, black and white. On the haywagon, a microphone stand was in place with half a dozen other microphones taped to it by various media people. Tables were in place where people could sign up as volunteers for headquarters work, bumper stickers or give their address for a yard-sign.

A large "FLINT FOR GOVERNOR" sign had been erected over the headquarters entrance. It was immediately behind Flint's head as he stepped to the microphone and launched into his speech.

Few noticed a beige Ford stationwagon parked on the periphery of the shopping center parking lot during the speech. Two young men emerged from the car with a stack of handbills in their hands. They immediately began placing a handbill on each parked car. By the time Flint was concluding his short speech, every car in the area had a handbill on the windshield or door handle. The two men and the Ford stationwagon were gone, off to another shopping center to distribute their handbills.

Flint concluded his five minute speech with some fresh news for his supporters.

"Ladies and Gentlemen. The League of Women Voters has recently invited me to meet Governor Reynolds before statewide television in two debates. I'm for it. The people of Louisiana are entitled to a fair, public discussion of the issues. My opponent has so far been non-committal, insisting that we are not serious enough opposition to merit a debate.

"Last night, I received the final figures on a statewide poll conducted by Jon Douglas and Associates of Baton Rouge. The results are incredible when one considers this campaign is less than two months old and we're facing an opponent many thought to be unbeatable only six weeks ago. The poll indicates that we would receive the vote of twenty-one percent of the people of this state if the election were held today. That doesn't sound too good until you realize that the poll also shows that only thirty-eight percent of the people have ever heard of Darin Flint. Ofcourse, a month ago virtually no one had ever heard of us. And Governor Reynolds, who was claiming seventy to eighty percent of the vote in polls only two months ago, has fallen below fifty-five percent for the first time since becoming governor four years ago.

"What does this mean? It means we have an opportunity to plow new ground. To change forever the corrupt nature of Louisiana politics. Real progress is difficult to achieve. And the opportunity to reach for it is rare.

"Unexpectedly...Just when politicians least expect it...Just when my opponent least expects it...The chance suddenly exists. The Louisiana people have given us their attention. We must intelligently justify this confidence in the enthusiastic but determined way we campaign, in our position papers, and in our discussion of Louisiana's future."

The speech ended among cheers. After another fifteen minutes of handshaking, Flint walked through every store in the shopping center greeting patrons and employees alike. He spent another half an hour walking house to house in the adjacent neighborhoods. He was following this ritual after each "grand opening" in order to create an environment of support in the neighborhoods where each of his headquarters were located.

The television cameras followed him in the neighborhood for

the first few houses. Then he was again alone, campaigning with his hand cards.

The seeds are being planted, he thought to himself with satisfaction.

He returned to the headquarters where Rodney Libscomb was waiting to drive him to the town of Benton, north of Shreveport, where one of the town alderman was hosting a bar-b-que for him. As he walked through the headquarter's door, Libscomb looked up at him from a table where several campaign workers were gathered.

"Darin, you're not going to believe this. Look at this garbage they're spreading."

He handed Flint two colored handbills, one pink and one blue. Flint quickly read through the first one. It was entitled "A Bushel of Cotton?". It read as follows:

"Darin Flint has taken a few months away from his $200,000 New Orleans home to run for governor. For the first time since he entered the Legislature twenty-seven years ago, he's shown some interest in the rest of the state. Will he still be interested when the election is over?

Flint showed up at a Farm Bureau meeting in Evangeline Parish earlier this month dressed in new blue jeans to look like a farmer. Naturally, he wanted to give a speech so the meeting was interrupted to let him talk. It didn't take Flint long to show his ignorance.

He tried to answer a question on cotton farming and declared 'I believe you're entitled to get a fair price for every bushel of cotton you sell.'

Bushel of cotton? You'd think that even a New Orleans blue blood like Flint would know that cotton is marketed in bales not bushels.

Don't be fooled by a man who is only out for himself and the big city interests he represents. Agriculture is an essential part of our economy and we need a governor who cares about our farmers. Flint has never cared about agriculture. Don't let him fool you."

Flint shook his head. "Incredible," he muttered and looked over the other handbill. It declared that Flint favored establishing a high property tax on everyone's home and doing away with the homestead exemption.

"I guess we should expect this type of thing but it still comes as a surprise. Where did you get these?"

"A couple of guys were handing them out to the crowd during your speech," said Lipscomb. "I had a few questions from press people about it and they seemed satisfied when I told them it was trash."

"There's no name on these sheets, no organization, no nothing," said Flint. "There's no truth to any of it either. This Farm Bureau business is total fabrication. And I've never suggested doing away with the homestead exemption from property taxes."

Over the next thirty-six hours, a variety of similar handbills were found to be in circulation across the state. More would appear during the weeks ahead as the campaign intensified.

TWENTY

"I never did give anybody hell. I just told the truth and they thought it was hell."

Harry S. Truman
(1884-1972)
33rd President of the U.S.

"René, Flint's coming up next on channel two," said Moulard as he turned up the volume knob on the television set in the governor's office. The governor, Jackson Wells and Danny Ross all turned from their conversation to join Moulard in front of the set and listen to the newscast.

"State Senator Darin Flint took his gubernatorial campaign to an oil well in Satan's Swamp today to dramatize the release of his position paper dealing with big oil and our environment. Here's a report from Sandy Myer of WXTZ News at the scene."

Sandy Myer, dressed in outdoor garb, appeared on the screen. "From where Senator Darin Flint stood for his press conference today, one could observe the rusty remains of abandoned pipeline outcroppings in the water; the discolored, stagnant marsh water polluted by dumping of drilling mud and waste materials into the waters where fish and aquatic life once flourished. To get here, Senator Flint invited the press to join him on a commercial fishing boat which navigated a complex of canals dredged through these marshes by oil and gas companies to enable them to move their large drilling platforms into place. Such canals have allowed saltwater to intrude deep into the wetlands, resulting in destruction of wildlife habitat and aquatic life. Senator Flint had this to say."

Flint's face flicked onto the screen surrounded by newsmen. His words stung Reynolds as he listened.

"Over thirteen thousand miles of these canals criss-crossing our marshes have been dredged by oil companies. Aside from the obvious destruction you can observe, these canals are the greatest reason for the erosion and loss of over fifty square miles of Louisiana coastline each year. The levees alongside these canals were created thoughtlessly during the dredging. The dirt was just piled

107

alongside the canals. Unintentionally these mounds of dirt are blocking hundreds of thousands of acres of marshland from receiving fresh water and silt deposits from the Mississippi River. Vast cesspools now exist where wildlife, plantlife, cypress forests and aquatic life once existed. Yet Louisiana is still granting more dredging permits to oil companies. In fact, no applicant has ever been denied a dredging permit in Louisiana history.

"When I become governor, new permits will not be issued unless clearly justified by both economic and environmental standards. We will initiate a program to eliminate these levees and to prevent such costly negligence in the future. Oil companies and pipeline companies will not be allowed to create the kind of environmental destruction we are observing here today, and certainly the abandonment of .wells and pipelines in this condition will not be allowed."

Then Sandy Myer again appeared on the screen. "Senator Flint also stated that over thirteen thousand waste pits containing toxic waste materials have been abandoned in Louisiana by drilling companies where oil wells once stood. Drinking water is commonly found to be contaminated and cancer rates high in such areas. The dumping in the Mississippi River has endangered New Orleans' emergency drinking water, yet Louisiana has applied to the federal government to allow more fertilizer manufacturers and petrochemical plants to dump more wastes into the river. Senator Flint declared these proposals should be withdrawn."

Again, video tape of Flint flicked back on the screen. "A superfund should be established perhaps through dedication of a portion of our severence taxes, or by new fees on mineral leases, drilling permits, dredging permits, pipeline permits, and other appropriate industry permits. This superfund will give us money and means to start cleaning up the environmental mess and protecting public health."

Sandy Myer returned to the screen. "Tomorrow evening, we will present Governor Reynold's observations and responses to Darin Flint's environmental plan. This is Sandy Myer, Satan's Swamp, Louisiana."

Moulard began flipping the channel to other stations. As expected, he found Flint was getting good coverage on every station.

"Oh great," said Reynolds. "They want my response tomorrow. That just means another round of free publicity for Flint."

"The man's becoming a perfect pain in the ass," added Jackson Wells.

"Don't get excited," said Moulard. "The man's been in politics a long time. You shouldn't be surprised he's resourceful. We should expect it. We should plan accordingly. We can use Flint's environmental plan to scare the hell out of the oil people. It would cost them an arm and a leg to clean up all those waste dumps and to find other ways of waste disposal at new wells. And if you tell them they can't dredge anymore, then how are they going to drill new wells at new sites in the marshes?"

"They can't," said Reynolds. "What Flint is talking about is unrealistically expensive. He's proposing new fees on virtually every activity in the oil patch. Producers are in a slump. I wonder what his new friends among the independent producers think of him now."

"I don't know about the independents, but "big oil" ain't too thrilled," Moulard said. "Texon's already running the figures. Bill Beeson called at five o'clock and said Flint's proposal would cost billions. The cost for Texon to return to all its old sites for clean-up operations and to eliminate the water flow obstructions would be prohibitive. Texon would have to pack up and leave the state."

"Texon pays a lot of salaries in this state," observed Wells. "And they pay a lot of taxes."

Reynolds inserted his thoughts, "Let's not fool ourselves. Texon's not going anywhere. There's too much oil under the ground and their investment in leases, production and transportation will keep them here."

He was quiet for a moment, then pointed out. "But it gives us a good position. I'll take the environmentalist position when I answer the press, but I'll be just a little less radical than Flint and a bit more sensible. How about a partnership between oil and state government to clean up the mess?"

"Love, not war?" Wells laughed as he spoke.

"Precisely." Reynolds glanced at Moulard. "Call Beeson back and plan responses from the various oil companies. They need to start telling their employees, and their families, that Darin Flint would cost them their jobs. They must hit it hard. In their press statements, they must describe Flint as radical, anti-business, impractical, a demagogue and any similar term they can think of."

Moulard rose from his chair. Reynolds spoke again. "Oh, Neil, one more thing. Tell Beeson that Flint's costing us a lot of money. Our goal is to raise another three million dollars the remainder of the campaign. Tell him I expect a great deal of help from the energy industry."

Moulard smiled and turned toward the door. Then he stopped and looked back at the governor.

"René, the League of Women Voters has not given up on the idea of a statewide debate. Louise Harrison has telephoned for you repeatedly. She's been patient with my explanations so far but they are scheduling a date, arranging statewide media hookups and all the rest. She wants a yes or no from us. What do you want to do?"

"Goddamn it, Neil. Can't we just tell her I have no serious opponent and that a debate is not necessary."

"Yes, we can do that. We'll have to take the flak from the press all over again. But let's not drag it out. If the answer's no, then let's say no and get it over with."

"What do you recommend?"

"It's a no win situation. I'm afraid a refusal will become a campaign issue. We can accept with the condition that we dictate the format. If we say no because he's not a serious candidate, then we'd better be damn certain he's not a serious opponent. Public reaction could quickly make him a contender."

"O.K. Again, what do you recommend?"

"Frankly, I believe the safest thing is to agree to the debate. You look better on television. You are more articulate. You're handsome and you're younger. You've always done well in live t.v. We can insist that there be only one debate and that it occur quickly within the next two weeks. That way, we can avoid the media build up. We can work up a format that avoids direct dialogue between you."

"I disagree." Jackson Wells stood up and countered Moulard. "The last thing we want to do is help Flint get name recognition. Why make him an underdog with a chance to win? I believe the governor should just answer the press by saying it's to be expected that a weak candidate would want a debate. The governor would create a crowd for him. Tell the press that Flint's got no chance and that he's going to have to find his own audience."

"Danny, what do you think?" asked Reynolds of his brother-in-law.

"Seems to me you have everything to lose and nothing to gain in a debate. Say that to the press. It makes perfect sense. Its the truth. They'll buy it."

Reynolds pondered for a moment, then looked at Moulard.

"Neil, I don't want this debate. Call it bad vibs or whatever you want," said the governor. "Let's just use our money on the media and do our scheduled functions. The combination of the black organizations and labor keeps our base in tact. We're going to wipe Flint out in Acadiana. And the most influential people in business, real estate development, and banking have all been well taken care of by us. They've got a stake in our success. They'll keep getting us money and votes among middle and higher income people so we can split that vote. That's our winning combination, Neil. Let's take no chances. Tell the League the answer is no. I'll tell the press."

TWENTY-ONE

"The men the American people admire most extravagantly are the most daring liars; the men they detest most violently are those who try to tell them the truth."

H.C. Mencken
(1880-1956)
American editor, writer

Clyde Flowers, Governor Reynold's press secretary, gave the microphones in the press room a quick final check. The large, paneled room was crowded with reporters, photographers, cameramen and a variety of observers, politicians and employees of the governor's office. Vernon Looper was there with several associates from the AFL-CIO. Senate President Sonny Stokes was chatting with Gordon Twilley of the Associated Press as they waited for the arrival of the governor and the opening of the press conference.

A moment later, Governor Reynolds was in the room with State Senator Colbert Freeman and Neill Moulard immediately behind him. The room brightened with television camera lights as Reynolds went directly to the podium and stood behind a mass of microphones.

"I want to begin with two announcements. First, State Senator Colbert Freeman (he nodded toward his floor leader who was standing behind him beside the doorway) has a surprise announcement. He is declaring his endorsement of me today."

Everyone laughed. Freeman took his cue and bowed to the audience with a smile and a sweep of his arm.

"Second, we've taken a survey and we've learned all the mud, sludge and waste left by oil drilling has been cleaned up and taken out of the state. Therefore, no election is necessary because there are no longer any issues, so its been called off. We'll take a vacation instead on October 22nd."

The Governor's sarcasm got another laugh from the press corps.

"Seriously, I do have an announcement regarding the campaign. I am advised our most recent poll indicates the highest approval rating I've had since taking office four years ago. According to the poll, seventy-two percent of the voters approve of the work our administration is doing. We are in excellent shape for reelection next month."

"In a far more serious matter, our economic development plan has taken two big steps forward. Funding for the final phase of the North-South Interstate Highway has been approved. Mr. Flowers has press releases setting forth the details of funding and mileage. With this important step forward, I am elated to announce that Interstate 49 will be one-hundred percent complete and in use within twenty-four months. A motorist will be able to travel on an interstate highway from Shreveport to New Orleans. As much as this means to our economy, it will probably mean even more to highway safety."

"Secondly, our work to develop a joint effort with private industry to effectively regulate hazardous waste and its disposal, to limit dredging in the marshlands, to establish environmental rules for abandonment of old oil wells and to prohibit dumping of oil production waste has been successful. Texon, Tenneco and Exxon are formally working with the staff of our Department of Environmental Quality to establish the program which will begin on a voluntary basis, then be presented to the Legislature next spring to be enacted into law. The Secretary of the Department of Environmental Quality, Sylvia Rogers, will formally direct these joint efforts. Her staff has prepared a formal press release and Miss Rogers will schedule formal briefings on a periodic basis until the program is complete."

Reynolds paused for a moment, then began fielding questions from the press. The questions revolved around Flint's environmental statements of the previous day, which were described by Reynolds as a "foolish declaration of war on the oil and gas industry", as "radical" and "overreaction".

Questions were asked about eliminating the thirteen thousand waste pits abandoned over the past decades by drillers, about the contamination of water aquifers, about the high cancer rates in production areas.

He answered, "Nobody knows if there's any connection. The diet in those areas, the life style, all of those things could be the reasons and factors in the high cancer rate. Nobody knows. The way to clean up those areas is by joint efforts of government and industry through the type of effort we've initiated through our Department of Environmental Quality."

He was asked about the thirteen thousand miles of canals in the wetlands, the resulting saltwater intrusion into the fragile marsh areas, the erosion and disappearance of barrier islands and large chunks of coastline thereby leaving coastal communities with less protection against storms and hurricanes. He was asked what was to be done about the continuing loss of coastal lands bringing the destructive saltwater deeper and deeper into the wetlands.

Reynolds answered that "much of the erosion was caused by the necessary construction of flood prevention levees which have had the unfortunate effect of blocking accumulation of silt deposits from the Mississippi River. But the good outweighs the harm," he said.

Governor Reynolds stated that every state makes certain environmental sacrifices for economic development. "Colorado must strip its mountain sides to create ski resorts. Wyoming must allow strip mining to produce its coal. In Louisiana, we punch holes in the ground. But through a partnership between government and industry, we can make certain the drilling sites are repaired, cleaned up and all toxic waste properly disposed of. That's what we're working to accomplish."

In response to another question, Reynolds stated that no debate with Darin Flint was necessary and none would take place.

"Naturally, Mr. Flint wants a debate. He has no support and has everything to gain, nothing to lose. It would be foolishness for us to debate and I'm not foolish."

The press conference had gone well. It was time to stop. But Governor Reynolds had observed that his reliable friend Gordon Twilley of the Associated Press wanted to ask a question. So he allowed one more.

"Governor, isn't it true that your initiative on working jointly with private industry to develop an environmental plan in the oil patch is the first of its kind in Louisiana history?"

"I believe it is," Reynolds answered the gratuitous question. "And it's consistent with our administration's strong environmental record and our desire to protect public health."

Before he could turn away to leave, Ross Reed of the Times Picayune hollered another question.

"Then why did you wait until now, only five weeks before the election, to start this new effort? You've been governor for four years. Did you dream it up overnight because of the program Senator Flint announced yesterday?"

No one could get Reynold's goat like Reed, who had spent most of his time in recent years investigating and exposing those activities Reynolds most wanted to keep private.

"Frankly, Mr. Reed, I don't care what you think." Reynolds himself was surprised by the hostility of his reflexsive response. "We've been trying to bring these various groups together for sometime to cooperatively develop a comprehensive program. This is the culmination of that effort."

"Has Secretary Rogers been leading that effort in the past?"

"That's correct," answered Reynolds.

"That's not what Miss Rogers said only yesterday, Governor. I interviewed Sylvia Rogers yesterday after the Flint news conference. She agreed with Flint that a superfund should be created. She also agreed that the oil and gas giants had been guilty of neglect in the past. She said big oil had killed legislative efforts to have the hazardous waste law apply to oil field toxic waste. She said nothing was being done with old waste pits because there was no money. And the oil companies certainly are not going to pay for it. Miss Rogers said she was frustrated over new dredging permits that had been granted. Can you explain the conflict between her statements yesterday and yours today?"

"Undoubtedly, you are misquoting Miss Rogers like you do most other people," Reynolds hastily responded, then turned to leave.

But Reed persisted. "I've got it on tape if you want to hear it. Isn't it also true, Governor, that you receive over one hundred thousand dollars every year from your oil and gas holdings? Isn't it true that you were on a large retainer of fifty thousand dollars annually from Texon before becoming governor?"

Reynolds stopped in the doorway and looked back at Reed, the smile gone from his face. Reed's questions continued in rapid fire fashion.

"Isn't it true that several of your closest associates, such as Neil Moulard, are still holding royalty interests in state leases held by certain oil companies? Isn't it true that Senator Freeman standing over there beside you is an owner of a dredging company that was created and has thrived during your administration? Isn't it true that your former law partner Ross Chandler has represented virtually every giant oil company in this state including Texon. Yet when the state became embroiled in an oil royalty dispute with Texon involving hundreds of millions of dollars, you had the Attorney General hire your former partner as special counsel for Louisiana to work out a settlement with Texon? A classic example of the fox guarding the hen-house. Isn't it also true that the settlement was ridiculously low and the attorney fees outrageously high?"

Reed was still hollering questions long after the governor had left the room.

The next day the Reed interview with Sylvia Rogers was published verbatim in the New Orleans Times Picayune with a preamble noting its conflicts with the governor's statements. The spectacle of Reynolds' clash with Reed was on every television news program and newspaper front page. But news accounts also included heavy criticisms of Flint's "radical" and "irresponsible" attack on the energy industry.

Editorial comment in Louisiana newspapers that next week questioned most loudly the "radical" anti-oil stance of Darin Flint, far outweighing the attention given Reynolds' close ties to the oil and gas industry.

TWENTY-TWO

"Last night the moon, the stars and all the planets fell on me. If you fellows ever pray, pray for me."

Harry S. Truman
(1884-1972)
33rd President of the United States

Darin Flint was deep in thought as he drove his car along the narrow stretch of highway between Crowley and Eunice in the heart of Acadiana oil country. He looked ahead over the flat road surface baking under the blazing Louisiana sun. The road ahead of him extended as far as the eye could see, becoming thinner and thinner as it disappeared into the broad horizon, the rising heat shimmering above the pavement and distorting the landscape. He was scheduled to be in Eunice at six o'clock for a small party being given for him in the home of a city councilwoman, who was helping organize his campaign in that area. He was driving himself today because there had been requests for Jenny to spend a day campaigning in St. Mary Parish. This was happening more and more. All the family members were having to share their campaign duties with others so they could make appearances all over the state. Susan had made appearances with him at least once in each section of the state. Her own travel schedule was beginning next week and would continue through election day.

It had been a very difficult week. The reaction, and the reaction to the reaction, after his environmental news conference had left him with a helpless feeling. How many times he had relearned the same lesson over and over again during his political career. Every effort to manipulate the press is a roll of the dice. So often the effort backfires and you are worse off than when you started.

The critical newspaper editorials had hurt him. But Darin Flint knew he had no choice but to roll the dice. He was way behind and could not afford to purchase media time. If he did not make something happen every minute for the remaining month, then he would have no chance to win.

A number of newspapers were lying in disarray on the seat beside

Flint, all turned to the editorial pages. Flint was reminded of an old quote from Earl Long, the legendary folk hero of Louisiana politics. "No news is bad news as long as they spell your name correctly," Uncle Earl was credited with saying.

"I hope Earl knew what he was talking about," Flint muttered to himself.

The editorials were uniformly critical of Flint's environmental stand. It was said he had declared war on the oil and gas industry. It was said his radical stance would be disastrous if he became governor. It was said he was a threat to the tens of thousands of people whose livelihood was in some way reliant on the energy industry. Sure, they said, there had been careless and damaging exploitation of natural resources to the detriment of the environment, but that was in the past. The industry is more enlightened today. It now invests millions of dollars each year to prevent and clean up such things. The editorials pointed out that the energy industry had been in an enormous slump recently and needed help, not the new fees, expenses and environmental limitations Flint had suggested for his superfund. Some editorials had even gotten a little nasty, suggesting that Flint should have better informed himself of the facts regarding Louisiana's most vital industry before becoming a candidate. Others accused him of "shameless demagoguery".

It was of little solace that René Reynolds had also had a rough week. The news of Reynolds' embarrassing confrontation with Ross Reed, and the questions reporters were asking about conflicts of interest and sweetheart deals were still in the newspapers. But those news stories had receded to the back pages. Reynolds had recovered his equilibrium and wit, and was easily sidestepping and down playing the issue.

Flint was discouraged. What had seemed so successful, now seemed a disaster. He had had an underdog's sense that everyone was pulling for him and that, at least privately, the newspapers liked his candidacy. The momentum, the excitement and the encouragement seemed gone. The tidal wave of criticism left him uncertain, upset and badly discouraged.

The editorial pages and the oil patch businessmen, large and small, had been equally merciless toward Flint. Part of Flint's strategy was to win the north Louisiana anti-Reynolds vote and the support of middle income suburbia residents of population centers who were most offended and fed up with the Reynolds administration's history of sweetheart deals and influence peddling. Flint could gain much of this vote by simply not offending these voters. But when the press labels you as a radical, anti-business environmentalist, that strategy is badly damaged.

In Acadiana, the fallout was more direct. His contributors from LAIPRO were upset, his conservative friends among the oil field contractors were upset, and various oil field union officials were branding him as "a threat to their jobs and security."

But he had gone into it with his eyes wide open. To minimize reaction, Carey Jefferson, Jeffrey Bordelon, Joel Whitney and Rodney Libscomb had been on the phone to key supporters even before his news conference had reached the airwaves. All parish leaders had been briefed that same morning. Most were ecstatic with the initial impact of his news conference. But the plethora of criticisms from oil interests and newspaper editorials had sobering, then depressing, effects on Flint's troops.

The setback of adverse publicity, though not entirely unexpected, had also depressed Flint. Was it a mistake to ever believe it was possible to win? He wondered whether he was in way over his head. What a mess he had gotten himself into. Why am I putting myself and my family through all this? I should be back at work taking care of the grocery store in New Orleans, he thought to himself.

Flint watched the small country houses, the fields, the occasional stores fly by as he drove along. He noticed the litter along the roads. Old dilapidated bars. There were shanties, some long abandoned and some still occupied. Many times during those past two months, Flint had stopped and done door to door campaigning when there was some slack in his schedule. Forty-five minutes of door knocking usually meant some bumper stickers on cars and a little name recognition in an obscure area where no one would normally expect it.

But Flint did not feel like it today. The onslaught of bad publicity and criticism had damaged his motivation.

He noticed just ahead a small community of fifteen or twenty houses, and a small gasoline station and grocery store. Then Flint remembered a lesson he had taught himself in his first campaign twenty-seven years ago. Go back to basics. When everything goes wrong, when the campaign is getting off track, when you are discouraged and even distraught with the adversity....go back to basics. Do the type of thing that can only help, that you know makes progress (even if the progress is miniscule), that will get you moving in the right direction again.

Flint pulled his car off the highway and parked it among a clump of small wooden houses. He grabbed a thick stack of campaign pamphlets and some bumper stickers, then walked to the front door of the first house. No one was home so he wrote a note in red ink on the pamphlet and left it folded behind the doorknob.

He received a polite reception at the next house. At the third house, there was a man working on the engine of his car. He allowed Flint to put a bumper sticker on his car and agreed to a yard sign in his front yard. Flint wrote the man's address in his pocket-sized notebook. Flint stopped in a store and introduced himself to everyone there. He had a friendly discussion at the counter with the owner and two customers. The owner put a stack of the pamphlets by the cash register and told him he could put a poster in the window alongside a number of other political signs. A customer allowed him to put a sticker on her car.

Then Flint went to the front door of another house and knocked on the door. He was already feeling better, the positive door to door work was raising his spirits. It was good to get back to work. Maybe he had overreacted to those editorials.

"Hello, my name is Darin Flint. I'm running for governor," he said when the door was opened.

Flint looked at the elderly gray-haired black woman whose features he could scarcely make out behind the old screen door. She gave no reply and made no offer to introduce herself.

"I just wanted to introduce myself and leave you with some information. I'd sure appreciate your vote for governor."

Flint opened the door wide enough to hand her one of his campaign pamphlets. She said nothing.

"Thank you, M'am," he said.

Flint turned to leave. Then he turned back. "Oh, by the way, I have bumper stickers and yard signs in my car. If you'd like one, it'd sure help the campaign."

Finally the lady answered. "Ah don't have no car. And Ah rent this house. But Ah reckon it'd be allright to put your sign in the front there by the road," she pointed to the spot for the sign.

"Thank you, M'am. I'll have it up before the end of the day."
Flint wrote her address in his notebook.

"I wanted to write down your name and address so I can stay in touch with you." Finally the lady introduced herself. Flint wrote her name.

Flint noticed a small child peering curiously at him from behind the woman's right side, probably a grandchild.

"Hello there. Would you like a sticker?" The child moved forward, then looked up at the old woman's face for permission.

"Well, go 'head," she said to the child. She opened the screen door wide. By the time Flint gave the boy the bumper sticker, four more children of various ages had emerged from the house. All signs of shyness had disappeared with the discovery of bumper stickers.

"What's y'name?" asked one.

"That's Darin Flint," answered the oldest child, a pretty girl Flint judged to be fourteen or fifteen years old. "Don't you know nothing?" she said to the small child.

She looked back at Flint and smiled.

"We've seen you on television."

"Well, I'm glad to hear that," Flint responded. "I need all the help I can get."

Flint gave all the kids a bumper sticker. He watched one put it on a small rusted wagon he was pulling. Another put it on the bent fender of a bicycle.

The teen-aged girl spoke again. "We'll put a sticker on my father's car when he comes home from the hospital."

Flint left moments later and went on through the neighborhood.

During the next forty-five minutes, Flint left a message or visited every house in the small community. He returned to his car and drove to each house where he had permission to put up a yard sign. The signs, stakes, hammers and staple gun were in the trunk of his car.

As he finished stapling the last sign, the teen-aged black girl stepped out of her house.

"We saw you on television last week talking about the mess oil companies make. They say it causes cancer. My father has cancer. He's at Charity Hospital. That's why our grandmother lives with us. My father worked on an offshore oil rig before he got sick. Do you think he got cancer working?"

Flint looked at her for a moment. "I don't know. Nobody really knows what causes so much cancer in Louisiana."

"Ah've wondered about our water," said the girl.

"What do you mean?" he asked.

"It doesn't taste right. It's dirty. And our drain is real white."

"Why is that?"

"Ah don't know. Everybody round here has that," the girl said.

Flint's curiosity was aroused. "Can you show me?"

He followed her into the small house. The family had made the most of very little. The house was neat and clean with inexpensive furniture that had been heavily used, but well preserved, over the years. The sink was stained white just as the girl had said. Flint tasted the water but noticed nothing obvious.

"Where does your water come from?"

"There's a well."

"Are there any oil wells around here?" he asked.

"No."

The girl's grandmother then spoke at a table where she had been slicing potatoes. "There used to be an oil well near here. A dry hole. Nothing much there now. There's just an old pit that stinks to high heaven."

"Where?" Flint asked.

"You can look out yonder from the back door and see where that pit is."

Flint looked out of the back door and saw a small ring levee approximately one-half mile away. He stepped outside and looked at the water pipes under the house. He noticed more signs of the white discoloration.

Flint returned to the kitchen. "Do you have a jar I could use to take some of this water with me to be tested?"

The girl found a jar under the sink, filled it with water, placed the lid on it and handed it to Flint.

"What's your name," Flint asked the teenager.

"Marsha Vick."

"Marsha, I'm sure your water is probably fine. Tastes O.K. to me. But I want to have it checked out for you. How can I reach you or your grandmother or perhaps your mother by telephone."

"My mother's dead."

"I'm very sorry," said Flint. "How can I telephone you?"

"You can telephone the store next door. I clean up over there every day so they'll give me the message."

"O.K. I already have your address. I'll be back in touch."

Flint said goodbye, again thanked them for their kindness and left.

Flint arrived in Eunice thirty minutes late. But his depression and discouragement was gone. His own problems paled in significance in the face of Marsha's family difficulties.

TWENTY-THREE

"A great city is that which has the greatest men and women,
If it be a few ragged huts, it is still the greatest city in the world."

Walt Whitman
(1819-1892)
Song of the Broad-Axe

Councilwoman Jane Baldwin sat quietly and watched the performance of the persuasive black man at the witness table. The gruff voice of Mayor Edmund Lawrence filled the cavernous New Orleans City Council Chamber. As usual, the subject was money. Or the lack of it.

Mayor Lawrence was a veteran of two decades of the New Orleans political wars. He was a practical, hard-nosed politician whose personality was softened by a good humor and even better intentions. Over the past two decades, the population of New Orleans had spilled over into the surrounding parishes while inner city decay had claimed many old middle income neighborhoods. Property values in attractive neighborhoods of Orleans Parish were prohibitive. The population of adjoining Jefferson Parish had risen to over four hundred and fifty thousand people, with a great many of its residents commuting each day to their offices and businesses in downtown New Orleans.

Similarly, St. Bernard Parish, St. John the Baptist Parish and St. Tammany Parish had grown dramatically. The black population remained in Orleans, dramatically changing the face of New Orleans politics forever. Black voter registration had passed the fifty percent mark years ago. There had been a succession of black mayors. Aside from Mayor Lawrence, over half the Orleans legislative delegation was black. So was its Congressman.

As much of the Orleans Parish middle class had escaped the higher tax rates, the high property prices and the threatening crime rate of the big city by moving to less populous surrounding parishes, the Orleans tax base had been eroded. Financial woes were worsened by a slump in the vital tourism industry. The problems faced by the city were greater, more pressing, more desperate than ever before. And more expensive. Its population was larger, more densely quartered and more poor than ever before. City services, utilities, plumbing, transportation, law enforcement, maintenance of streets, drainage, and sanitation had become an impossible burden for the city budget. It's public school system was in poor shape and facing critical money problems. Ninety percent of its students were black.

Heavy political patronage had been a political tradition long before Mayor Lawrence or Jane Baldwin arrived on the scene. It was more than tradition, it was the lifeblood of any mayor who wanted to continue being mayor. But it was extremely expensive.

That's what Mayor Lawrence's speech was all about. He was advocating the unthinkable and probably the undoable. New beer, alcohol and cigarette taxes for New Orleans combined with dramatic employee reductions and spending reductions in virtually every city department. Salary reductions included high salaried political appointees as well as a reduction of his own salary. All salaries below the executive level would remain the same but heavy layoffs would occur. Numerous social programs would be terminated.

In one sweep, Edmund Lawrence had brought upon his head the opposition of the well-to-do (who opposed taxes) and most of the political establishment (who needed the patronage), both black and white. Jane Baldwin was possibly one of those exceptions who might be willing to help him.

The Mayor's speech was a preamble to the slashed budget he was presenting to the Council for approval. Although he could potentially resort to the line item veto to cut the budget if necessary, his speech made no suggestion of such a confrontation. Mayor Lawrence's technique was one of persuasion, based upon an enormous amount of unavoidable horsetrading and quiet dealing with Council members.

Jane Baldwin's vote and assistance would be essential.

As he closed and offered to answer questions, the mayor managed a friendly wink in her direction. Jane's concentration was interrupted by her executive assistant whispering to her that Congressman Jeffrey Bordelon had arrived for their appointment and was waiting in her office. Jane had agreed to give a fundraiser for Darin Flint in her home. Bordelon wanted to discuss it with her because a meeting of Flint's finance committee was planned for noon. They needed to finalize details. Minutes later, the mayor's testimony ended and Jane Baldwin hurried to her office.

"Hello Jeffrey. Sorry to keep you waiting," said Baldwin as she placed her files on the desk. "We started hearings this morning on the city budget and it took me a few moments to get away."

"No problem. Good to see you." He greeted her with a polite kiss on the cheek.

They chatted a few moments and began a cup of coffee before they got down to business.

"How do you feel Darin's campaign is going?" Bordelon asked her.

Jane Baldwin hesitated a moment, gathering her thoughts before answering. "I feel pretty good about it. Frankly, I've never been sure Darin even had a chance to win. And he probably will not win. But I think he now has a chance."

She stood up and looked out the window. "I got involved because I'm so sick and tired of Reynolds and his garbage politics. And I've always admired Darin Flint."

She turned and looked at Bordelon. "To win, he must get a decent black vote and he must heat up this campaign. It needs to be red hot by election day. That'll get him name recognition, contributions and votes."

"Any ideas?" he asked.

"A few." She smiled at him. "Try this one on. Louise Harrison is President of the Louisiana League of Women Voters. She's also a close friend of mine. Reynolds infuriated her and the entire executive board by snubbing them on the idea of a debate. He strung her on and on about the debate. Meanwhile, many preparations were made to set it up with t.v. and radio people. But she could never even talk to him on the phone. She could never get past Neil Moulard. Do you know how she learned the debate was off?"

"How?" he asked.

"On the six o'clock news. Reynolds announced there would be no debate at one of his press conferences and never called her."

"Are you thinking of an endorsement from the League?"

"What I'm really thinking about is resurrecting the debate idea. It's not Darin demanding the debate. It's the League of Women

Voters. They could take Darin's position papers and demand some answers. They could even hold the debate, leave the invitation to Reynolds open, but if he doesn't show up then go on with the debate anyway."

"With only Flint there?"

"That's right. Just let him answer the questions," said Baldwin.

Bordelon laughed out loud. "I think I'll have another cup of coffee on that one." He poured a second cup. "Do you think it can be done? Will they do it? There's not much time."

"I mentioned it to Louise a couple of days ago. She liked the idea. She said she'd discuss it with some board members and get back to me. We have two of the board members working as volunteers at the Flint headquarters every week and I've already discussed it with them. They like the idea too. They'll encourage Louise when she calls."

Jane Baldwin reached for the phone. "Why don't I give her a call now and see what she says."

Moments later she was talking to Louise Harrison on the telephone.

Bordelon listened to the progress of the conversation. Obviously, Louise Harrison had gotten a good response from the board. Apparently, the debate plans had never been cancelled but only put on hold. The decision had been made to announce to the press that the debate would not be cancelled.

The conversation ended and Jane Baldwin looked at him with an excited smile.

"Bingo. It's already happening. She's scheduled a press conference today to confirm that the debate will be held as originally scheduled. They'll announce the invitation to Reynolds is open and they hope he'll come. If not, the debate will proceed without him."

"Jane, you're a genius."

"Not me. Reynolds dropped this opportunity in our lap all by himself."

"Let me use your telephone to get the news to Darin."

Jane punched the intercom and asked her secretary to get Jon Douglas on the phone at the Baton Rouge headquarters. While they waited, Bordelon asked her how the ticket sales were going for the fundraiser.

"I guarantee you we'll clear fifty thousand dollars from New Orleans ticket sales. Maybe more. We've held the overhead down by having it at my home. More than one hundred and fifty volunteers are selling tickets and we've already collected slightly over twenty-five thousand dollars in ticket sales with a week to go. Usually most of the money comes in the last week. I think we'll have a very good crowd."

She was interrupted by the intercom bleeping and a voice announcing Jon Douglas was on the phone.

"Jeffrey. Before you get on the line, let me tell you this so I won't forget. We need to talk about the black vote. Darin needs to sit down for a long talk with Edmund Lawrence. As you know, Darin talked to the mayor before he announced he was running. The mayor tried to discourage Darin."

"I know. I've also talked to Edmund a couple of times," said Bordelon. "He likes Darin but he doesn't want to get involved."

"Well, its time to get them back together." She handed Bordelon the telephone. He explained to Jon Douglas the latest developments on the debate.

"Jon, we need to schedule considerable time with Darin for preparation for the debate. You and I, Carey Jefferson and Terrell Franks need to meet tonight and put together a topic list for more research this week. We need fresh statistics and information on everything from unemployment to public education achievement test scores," said Bordelon. "And we need to plan heavy advertising across the state to make sure the debate gets plenty of attention."

Before ending the conversation, Bordelon mentioned the need for Flint to meet with the New Orleans mayor. "Jane Baldwin will find out from the mayor's office some convenient times for them to meet. We'll need you to fit one of those times into Darin's calendar. Jane wants them to meet this next week."

Douglas agreed.

A short time later, Bordelon and Jane Baldwin were in his car headed for the noon finance committee meeting at a private room in Antoine's Restaurant in the French Quarter.

"Jeffrey, you asked me my opinion on Darin's chances. What's your opinion?" Jane asked as Bordelon patiently probed his way through the heavy noon traffic on Canal Street.

"We've made steady, and at times dramatic, progress since the beginning. And we've had good luck. I don't know how accurate our polls are because we're using volunteer workers out of our Baton Rouge headquarters to do the telephoning. But Jon Douglas feels he's trained them well. Anyway, the last poll was interesting."

Bordelon brought the car to a stop for a red light at the Royal Street intersection.

"For the first time, the poll showed Darin with a significant negative. Some people who didn't know him before apparently didn't care much for his environmental stand. But also for the first time, over thirty percent said they would vote for Darin if the election were held today. Darin's vote was thirty-four percent. That's a tremendous improvement from twenty-two percent two weeks ago. Obviously, a lot more people liked his environmental stand than disliked it. Reynolds remained at about fifty-five percent. There's a margin of error, so Reynolds lead is approximately twenty points with less than a month to go."

"Do you feel we can overcome that?" asked Jane.

"We have the incumbent governor almost down to fifty percent of the vote. He's got to be very worried about that. Darin's name recognition is still pretty low. We've had no paid media yet. Our roto section will finally be in the paper this Sunday morning and should give us another lift. Its been delayed three times because we didn't have the money to put it in. That may turn out to be a blessing. We've got a chance."

"Do you think the poll accurately reflects the black vote?"

"Probably not," said Bordelon. "A lot depends on whether money talks this time around. Reynolds has the political leadership with him and the money needed for them to really go to work that final week. Labor will also turn on the juice the last ten days. But it shouldn't be a block vote. Flint's record is good and the black leadership knows that."

"What if it is a block vote?"

"Then you can add another ten points to Reynolds vote. Reynolds wins with fifty-five to sixty percent of the vote if that happens."

Bordelon pulled the car into a public parking lot off Chartres Street. They stepped out and Bordelon handed the keys to an attendant.

The conversation continued as they walked the final block to Antoine's.

"I think we need twenty-five percent of the black vote to win. That's not going to be easy to do. If money talks, then Reynolds will do all the talking."

Jane laughed as they entered the restaurant to join Flint's other finance committee members.

"We'd better get Darin down here to see the mayor as soon as possible," she reminded him.

TWENTY-FOUR

"God knows, I'm not the thing I should be,
Nor am I even the thing I could be,
But twenty times I rather would be
    An atheist clean,
Than under gospel colours hid be
    Just for a screen."

Robert Burns
(1759-1796)
Scottish poet

The governor's limousine passed the cars parked on each side of the road and turned into the packed parking lot of the large fundamentalist church in DeRidder. Governor René Reynolds instructed his driver, a state trooper, to stay near the entrance. Reynolds planned to leave the church concert early, at least thirty minutes before it would be over.

Reynolds stepped into a friendly group of church members at the doorway of the church and started shaking hands. The church service had been underway for a half hour allowing Reynolds to make the grand entrance he had hoped for. By arriving a little late and leaving a little early, he would save time, yet fully participate in the function.

The exuberance of the gospel music seemed to rock the church. As always, Reynolds felt lifted by the music and the perfumed fragrance of the air he had come to identify as uniquely Pentecostal. The enthusiasm and warmth were contagious.

The "Giving For Christ Concert" was a special annual event at this Pentecostal Church. The music of the Church's spectacular choir and soloists attracted hundreds of observers to join the congregation in raising funds for the church's worldwide missionary program. It was a good place for politicians to go as honored guests but to also be gently and humorously put on the spot publicly to make a sizeable financial contribution. Traditionally, it was a happy, enjoyable and successful function.

René Reynolds knew how to steal the show on such an occasion. The congregation was already standing, clapping their hands and singing with the choir as he was guided by the ushers through the double doors at the rear of the church auditorium. Reynolds walked briskly down the center aisle and leaped up the alter steps two at a time. He was greeted with handshakes by the pastor, Reverend Jonas Esmond, as the choir stood singing before them. Reynolds turned and waved to the crowd. He sat in a large chair on the altar beside the Reverend Esmond and began clapping the palms of his hands to the beat of the music. Reynolds was the center of attention and he knew it.

Between songs, Reynolds was welcomed at the pulpit microphone by Reverend Esmond and given a standing ovation. He made requests for the choir to sing two of his favorite gospel songs. He made one thousand dollar contributions each time his request was fulfilled. When Reynolds returned to the microphone, he reminded the church of the serious purpose of this happy occasion. He wanted to interrupt the concert in order for everyone to pause in prayer and give thanks for their many blessings.

As everyone stood and bowed their heads, Reynolds launched into a beautiful prayer (without notes) that lasted a full five minutes without a stumble. By the end of the prayer an emotional roar was rising from the congregation that again erupted into music and song. Reynolds returned to his seat and to his hand clapping.

Watching the Reynolds performance from the third row of pews was an individual who was feeling particularly obscure and underwhelming at that moment. Darin Flint had been invited to the function by the pastor (as most of the state's politicians had been invited) and had been seated among the many other politicians who were in attendance. He had received a very kind introduction early in the program and been recognized as a candidate for governor. His three hundred dollar contribution had been acknowledged. But Flint was dwarfed and forgotten in the stir of Reynolds' presence. Reynolds probably did not even realize Flint was present.

Reynolds was again given the floor with various donation checks and contributions in his hands to acknowledge from the microphone. Finally, while at the pulpit holding the mike, Reynolds noticed Flint sitting quietly on the third row.

"Hello, Darin," he said with a confident, humorous smile from the pulpit for all to hear. Reynolds opened his arms to the congregation. "My friends, we have among us a good friend of mine from the Garden District of New Orleans." He again looked toward Flint. "Darin, come on up here. I don't know if you've ever stood before a church full of Christians like we have here today. Come on up here and let everyone see you," Reynolds repeated the invitation like the spider to the fly.

Flint, surprised and embarrassed, felt himself rise and move toward the aisle. He struggled to appear composed and at ease as he walked up the alter steps and stood towering over the smiling Reynolds but feeling awkward and gawky. He looked out over the twelve hundred faces smiling at him from the packed assembly and balcony of the cavernous church.

"Darin here decided a few months ago to leave the Garden District of New Orleans and discover Louisiana for the first time."

A wave of chuckling from the audience burned Flint's ears.

"Well, Darin, I want to personally welcome you to this wonderful church and introduce you to these wonderful friends of mine. It's a great part of Louisiana you are discovering today in this great church. You are welcome today and, if you ever leave the Garden District again, you will always be welcome in the future."

There was more pronounced laughter coming from the audience especially the first few rows where the special guests and politicians were seated. All was fair in politics. Including making a fool of your opponent. This occasion was not a church service where such an effort would be inappropriate. It was an annual fundraising event where high spirited political ribbing, give and take entertainment was the tradition. Flint forgot about the crowd, his mind working furiously for a response as he instinctively smiled and laughed along with the crowd.

"So Darin, let's put politics aside for the duration of this concert. You can help me read and acknowledge these checks and donations if you wish. The Church would even appreciate another contribution from you. You cannot be too generous. How much did you already give?"

Again, the loudest laughter came from the front rows of pews filled by the local officials, sheriffs, assessors, legislators, and various other politicians who had all seen Reynolds masterfully delight the crowd on similar occasions many times in the past.

"I donated three hundred dollars," Flint answered.

"Three hundred dollars!" responded Reynolds. "Did I hear you right? Did you say three hundred dollars?"

The laughter of the crowd continued.

"Come on Senator Flint, you're running for governor now. It's the big time. You don't want to embarrass everyone who's ever run for governor by offering a puny three hundred dollars. That's not even up to state senator standards. Don't you really mean three thousand dollars, not three hundred dollars? You don't expect this choir to sing another song for only three hundred dollars do you?"

The church loved it. The politicians loved it. The governor had placed Flint on his skewer and was slowly, mercilessly roasting him over the fire.

Flint was on the spot and everyone knew it. He could not afford three thousand dollars. If he did not give the money, then the Reynolds' challenge was left unmet. If he shelled out three thousand dollars, then Reynolds would get the credit for it.

To Flint, however, such a large donation was out of the question and he never even considered it. He reached out before Reynolds could react and eased the microphone from Reynolds' hand. Flint spoke to the crowd.

"Ladies and gentlemen, I want you to know I deeply appreciate the invitation to be with you here today. Frankly, you have the finest gospel choir I have ever heard and I wish every Louisianian would have the same opportunity to hear these people sing that I've had."

Flint hesitated as the crowd settled back in their seats, then pressed on.

"Please forgive me, but I guess I have been a little caught off guard by the good natured political teasing I've received from the governor here."

Flint looked over at Reynolds with a big smile. "Three thousand dollars! That is a good one René. You really know how to hurt a guy."

A gentle round of laughter rose briefly from the crowd. Flint paused and looked back at the audience. "Ladies and gentlemen, I'm not known as a standup comic. My wife's the only person who ever laughs at my jokes. But since the governor has been giving me such a hard time, in good fun, I'd like to try my hand at returning the favor."

Flint looked at the governor and extended his hand for a handshake. "Governor, I want to thank you so much for welcoming me to this church." He shook Reynolds' hand grandly. "It would probably do both of us a great deal of good to spend a lot more time here or in any good church instead of those political meetings we've been going to."

Again, some brief laughter rewarded his effort.

"It really was nice of you to welcome me," he said to Reynolds. "But actually I had received a very kind and thoughtful introduction from Reverend Esmond long before you arrived here late for church." He emphasized the last three words in an effort at humor.

"The governor knows I'm only joking with him. I know he goes to church just as I do. And I'm sure his very busy schedule kept him from being on time tonight. But now that he's here, I'm sure he'll be with us the rest of the evening and will not be leaving early."

The pastor, Reverend Esmond, had to stifle a smile as he remembered telling Flint before church that the governor would be leaving early for another meeting.

"The governor likes being here with us and I know he'll be staying for the entire concert," added Flint.

Flint hesitated then continued. "But, governor, it is a shame you were late because you missed a chance to meet and talk with everyone on a personal basis. Reverend Esmond and Sister Esmond were good enough to show me around the church and explain their many programs like the twenty-four hour prayer chains. This is a dynamic, exciting church that's delivering a religious education to over six hundred children every Sunday and is donating more to international missionary programs then any church its size in America." Flint looked upon the congregation. "It's been my pleasure to meet so many of you today."

The congregation responded with warm applause.

"I wanted to say one other thing to this congregation before I try to get this money business straight with René. I won't give a political pitch here because we're in the sanctuary of our Lord. It's a place for far more important things. But I do want to thank Reverend and Mrs. Esmond for inviting me to come. I've enjoyed it. During my years in the Legislature and, more recently, during this campaign, I've gotten to know many of the people of Beauregard Parish very well. Many of you are working actively in my campaign. I want to thank you for your warmth, for your courtesy and for your friendship."

There was more applause from the audience.

"And now for this money business with Governor Reynolds," Flint smiled broadly at the governor. "I'll make you a better deal and it won't cost you a cent. I'll put up the three thousand dollar donation to the church but only under one condition. But if you won't meet that condition I expect you to pay the three thousand dollars for me."

"O.K." Reynolds agreed, then asked, "What's your condition?"

"The Louisiana League of Women Voters is sponsoring a statewide televised debate in two weeks on October twelfth...at their expense...so you and I can face the people of this state and answer the important questions affecting Louisiana's future. You've refused to appear and debate those questions with me. If you'll change your mind and join me in that ninety minute debate, for the good of Louisiana, then I'll dig up that three thousand dollars from somewhere in my empty campaign account to donate to the fine cause we're promoting here tonight."

Flint paused in the silence of the church. Before Reynolds could speak, Flint looked out at the audience and said loudly in the microphone, "Don't you think we should debate?" A mixture of applause, whistling and laughter erupted in the hall. The noise was loud and sustained. Flint broke into a broad grin and held his right hand out to Reynolds for a handshake.

"How about it?" Flint asked.

Reynolds was caught off guard and was uncharacteristically hesitant in his reply. He took the microphone back from Flint.

"No sir, you know better than that. I'll donate the three thousand dollars," said Governor Reynolds in an effort to recover his rapport with the congregation. "And I'll shake your hand. But I will not donate to you the gift of a statewide television debate."

. . . .

The concert proved to be thoroughly enjoyable and Flint remained at the church shaking the hands of new supporters for an hour after it was over. Reynolds was back in the limousine headed for Lake Charles. He spoke with Neil Moulard by his mobile telephone and received Moulard's report on new poll results.

"Neil, I don't like it. We may be almost twenty points ahead but we're on the defensive and no one seems to have any ideas on how best to counter attack," said Reynolds into the telephone receiver.

Reynolds was silent as he again listened to Moulard through the phone, then replied.

"O.K. Neil. I agree. It's time to muddy him up. Let's get all details from Harriford on Flint's voting record and this Noble Airlines business and let's package it in a thirty minute program. And on that other item, lets see if he's got anything better for us than that blurred photograph he brought in last time. If we go with something like that, it might backfire on us. Things are not bad enough for us to go that far....yet. But I think the Noble Airlines item would be perfect to muddy up his image. We'll need Labor to do a piece in the program declaring Flint to be anti-working man. So get hold of Vernon Looper. We'll need somebody at the worker level in oil to include a segment saying Flint wants to put everyone in the oil patch out of work. Call Bill Beeson at Texon. He can get us a good site and the right person to do it. And get Jackson Wells in on it because we need a segment about Flint's budget cuts and wanting to cut off the blacks and poor from assistance. You got all that?"

Again, Reynolds was quiet as Moulard spoke. Then he again responded.

"O.K. You should contact Danny Ross tonight. Meet with all key people tomorrow. We need to look again at his voting record. They need to review Harriford's research. By the time I get to Baton Rouge tomorrow night, I want an outline of the program already prepared. I want the fifteen worst votes Flint ever cast. I want to have a strong plan of attack for these final weeks of the campaign."

Again, another pause while Moulard answered. Then another response from Reynolds.

"Hell, Neil. Maybe it should be an hour program. We might as well let it all rip. If the program hits about nine days before election day, there won't be time for his recovery or for a backlash. Let's make the show and if things keep getting tighter, then we'll run it."

Reynolds hung up the phone and rode on to Lake Charles in silence.

Darin Flint also went to Lake Charles after leaving the Pentecostal church. He went to visit Marsha Vick at the Doctor W. O. Moss Regional Hospital where he had arranged for her to be admitted that day for a full battery of tests. Her grandmother was also hospitalized for tests. The water from her house had contained a wide range of contaminants including excessive levels of chromium. There had also been levels of lead and mercury well over the safety limit for public drinking water.

He had learned that such contaminants are common ingredients in drilling "mud". A well ten thousand feet deep might require a million pounds of "mud" as a lubricant to help float cuttings to the surface. He had learned that the ingredients of "mud" include many different chemicals acting as foaming agents, defoamers, flacculants, thinners, viscosifers or emulsifers. Many other naturally occurring chemicals, such as mercury and radioactive isotopes of potassium may be picked up by the mud during the drilling process. Because of the tremendous expense in hauling away such materials for disposal, such waste material had often been abandoned over the decades in earthen pits adjacent to oil wells.

The next step was for Flint to have the pit near Marsha Vick's home tested. Tests were scheduled to be conducted the following week.

Before leaving Lake Charles that night, Flint discussed the day's developments by telephone with Jeff.ey Bordelon.

"Darin, things have really been popping today. We've heard rumors of a variety of polls people have been taking. Labor, oil, even Jackson Wells allegedly have statewide polls. According to rumor, all of the polls show the gap narrowing. You know how it is, rumor sometimes becomes fact. We've even heard rumors of one poll showing you over forty percent and Reynolds under fifty percent. We know its bad information but it's sure a good rumor."

"Where's all this coming from?" Flint asked.

"Variety of sources. Carey Jefferson heard about the so called oil poll from one of his LAIPRO board members. Jane Baldwin told me she heard about the Jackson Wells poll from another city councilman. Just talk. People are finally talking politics. A television reporter in Baton Rouge asked me about the so-called labor poll and passed that rumor on to me."

"Can we confirm any of it?"

"Carey's trying to follow up on the oil company poll, if there is one. But there's more. We're getting calls from the blacks. Here in Baton Rouge, we're getting lots of visits and not just from people looking for money. We're getting some black volunteer workers. Terrell and I met with two good black groups in Baton Rouge today and we'll meet with another group in Iberville Parish tonight."

"How'd you do?"

"Very non-committal. They wanted to meet but they were non-committal. A lot of smoke. Some radical, racial talk. They had complaints about some of your votes. Then some complaints about Reynolds taking them for granted. But few specifics. They told us how much they could do for us if we worked with them."

Bordelon went on to describe each meeting to Flint, the participants and what was said. Flint knew many of the people and was impressed such black leaders would be interested in his campaign.

"They all want to meet with you," Bordelon concluded.

"Do you think there's any chance any of them will support me?"

"The biggies are going to stick with Reynolds. They'll meet with you to worry Reynolds and jack up Reynolds' interest in them. Bids up the price. Labor will also influence them if they start to get out of line."

"Then what's the point?"

"We might get lucky and get some endorsements. We might at least create some splits in the ranks. Some of the less known groups have nothing to lose by going with us and might very well help. We've got to be careful. Many of these groups just take your money."

Flint thought it over for a moment. "I guess we've got nothing to lose. But I don't want to waste what little time we have left on hopeless meetings."

"I agree. The all out support of any of these groups is bound to be expensive. Together they put hundreds of people to work in the precincts during the final week. You remember four years ago Reynolds' campaign reports showed they wrote well over a million dollars worth of checks for election day."

"And he'll do that again this time, Jeffrey. There's nothing we can do about that," said Flint.

"I know," answered Bordelon. "But our finances might be improving as the polls improve. I got a call from Bill Beeson tonight."

"You mean the Texon lobbyist?"

"That's right," Bordelon answered. "I'll be having an early breakfast with him in the morning."

"Jeffrey. Beeson's very close with Reynolds. He's been the point man for the oil and gas industry for years in dealing with the governor. It's just a waste of time to work on him."

"I didn't call him. He called me. It may just be a courtesy call. I don't know. Maybe oil wants to hedge their bets by putting some money on both sides. Perhaps those polls mean the public liked your environmental stand last week a lot better than the newspapers did. It doesn't hurt to have breakfast with Beeson."

"No, that's true," said Flint. "Go have breakfast with him. Maybe you can learn if there has been a poll. Let's see what he wants and take it from there. I've always gotten along perfectly well with Beeson. But for him to come see me after my position paper on the environment just blows my mind."

"Me too," said Bordelon. "But it'll be interesting. I'll give you a full report tomorrow."

TWENTY-FIVE

"Character assassination is at once easier and surer than physical assault; and it involves far less risk for the assassin. It leaves him free to commit the same deed over and over again, and may, indeed, win him the honors of a hero even in the country of his victims."

Alan Barth
Twentieth Century American writer
The Loyalty of Free Men

Neil Moulard wasted no time pulling together the information and people needed to put together the television program to attack Flint. He telephoned Danny Ross to come immediately to start writing the program. It would be a late night. Moulard scheduled a 7:00 a.m. meeting with Vernon Looper at the AFL-CIO office and Bill Beeson promised to arrange whatever Moulard and Danny Ross dreamed up for an oil field scenario. Moulard left a message for Jackson Wells to return his call immediately no matter how late it was. The only other hitch was James Harriford, who had not yet delivered his final report. Danny Ross arrived as Moulard finished his telephone calls.

Moulard described the project and the material to Ross.

"We don't want the program to get too detailed. Only enough details to give sufficient credence to every element of the program. Just broad strokes. It will be thirty minutes. Sixty minutes is too long. We can use the environment issue as evidence of Flint being anti-business and anti-worker. That leads naturally to an oil field worker talking about Flint threatening everyone's job. That leads naturally to Vernon Looper talking about Flint being untrustworthy to the working man," Moulard explained. "Perhaps we can also include a brief interview with an oil field contractor or a company executive."

Danny Ross made notes as Moulard spoke.

"We could perhaps have Sylvia Rogers add something positive at that point by explaining everything the Reynolds' administration has done for the environment. She can say we've forged a new partnership between business and the state to clean up and preserve the environment. Any questions so far?"

"Just keep talking and I can ask questions after I get the whole picture," said Danny Ross.

"O.K. We also want to hit Flint's conflict of interest on that mother-in-law bill. We should also do close-ups of the stock certificates that Harriford is supposed to supply us with. Maybe do a close up of Flint's mother-in-law's name. I don't know. Something along those lines. We must explain his mother-in-law's interest in Noble Airlines and that Flint's vote gave her a special tax break."

Moulard cleared his throat and pulled his chair away from his desk. He opened a drawer and pulled out a handfull of Flint campaign materials, including his pamphlet, position papers and bumper stickers. Moulard dropped them on the desk in front of Ross.

"Here's a bunch of his campaign materials. Let's use it to say Flint's run a slick, Fifth Avenue type of campaign."

Ross laughed. "Hey, Neil. Sounds like you've been through this routine before."

"I have," Moulard ran his fingers over the top of his balding head then handed Harriford's report to Ross. "Read this right now Danny. It explains the conflict of interest vote. Look over these votes of Flint's. There's over a hundred key votes that have been identified as potentially the most damaging. I think we should use the ones dealing with budget cuts in order to solidify our black vote. The man must have decided to comm: political suicide when he proposed some of those. He tries to hit Charity Hospitals, the drug reimbursement program and parts of the education budget. Look them over and give me your ideas."

Moulard left Ross alone and went into an adjacent room to return various telephone calls. When he returned an hour later, Ross had finished reading and was making notes.

"You ready to talk?" Moulard asked.

Ross put the pad down. "We can use a lot of this in thirty second spots the last two weeks. Ofcourse we can use it in the thirty minute program as well. Flip-flop type of stuff. We can use humor and make it funny."

"Yeah. I was thinking of that too," said Moulard. "How about this idea? You could picture a yo-yo going down on a string. And the announcer says 'In 1982, Darin Flint voted for creationism.' Then you picture a yo-yo going up on the string and the announcer says 'Two years later he voted to repeal it.' Then show the yo-yo going down and state another vote, then the yo-yo goes and you state the contradiction. After you do that four or five times, you end with some kind of punch line like 'No one could trust Darin Flint to make a final decision in the State Senate. You still cannot trust him. Re-elect René Reynolds, governor.' What do think?"

Moulard leaned back in his chair, obviously pleased with his creation.

"It's cute," laughed Ross. "We'll try to smooth it out a little. Your punchline can use some work."

TWENTY-SIX

"Lack of money is the root of all evil."

George Bernard Shaw
(1856-1950)
Irish dramatist, critic

Over fifteen hundred people packed the lakefront home of Councilwoman Jane Baldwin for Darin Flint's fundraiser. The lack of space made the crowd seem more like ten thousand. They covered the front and back yards. A New Orleans Jazz band played old Dixieland favorites from a low bandstand erected adjacent to the backyard patio overlooking Lake Pontchartrain. The house and yard had been decorated the previous night by volunteers with Flint banners and posters. The food was a vast array of Louisiana foods, from crabmeat cocktail and fried alligator tail to crawfish and shrimp with a variety of appetizers. Dozens of picnic tables were occupied by guests enjoying the food. Again, overhead and expenses were held to a minimum by assigning food preparation assignments to various groups of the New Orleans' volunteers.

The invitations had gone out to every parish. Flint workers from all over the state had come to the function.

Flint mounted the bandstand midway through the evening and gave a rousing speech that brought cheer after cheer from the crowd as the television cameras and press people recorded the scene. It was easily Flint's biggest and most successful fundraiser of the campaign. It was perfect for building the morale of Flint's troops as they entered the final weeks of the campaign.

Flint and his family shook hands and greeted people as they arrived in front of the house during the early evening. Afterward, he spent another hour working the crowd before he gave his speech. Then Jeffrey Bordelon told him it was time to leave for the meeting with Mayor Edmund Lawrence. It took another thirty minutes for Flint to extract himself from the party before they were finally on their way downtown in Bordelon's car.

"Jeffrey, I almost hate to leave since we've waited so long to finally have a crowd like that," said Flint. "I wish Lawrence had been here to see it. Might encourage him to help us out."

"You can bet the mayor already knows how this party went tonight." Bordelon responded. "If not, he'll see it on the ten o'clock news. People are watching you closely these days."

Bordelon maneuvered the car through traffic past City Park and drove on Carrollton Avenue toward Canal Street.

"Jeffrey, how did the money come out tonight?" asked Flint.

"I know its' well into six figures. We've more than doubled Jane's goal."

"I can't believe it. Maybe we'll get our three weeks of media afterall."

"Not yet," said Jeffrey. "The bulk of that money will pay off everything on the newspaper section insert. We should be able to dedicate a decent portion to television. But Jon Douglas has allowed us enormous credit on his bills. We need to at least get him straight on his expenses and pay him something. His charges have been ridiculously low so far. With luck, we can start television by the middle of next week. That'll give us two and a half weeks worth anyway."

"Jeffrey, let's go ahead and buy the full three weeks." Flint looked at Bordelon for a moment, then again stared forward through the windshield. "If necessary, I'll make a second loan to cover it. We've worked too hard. We need the full three weeks of media. I don't want to look back after the election and regret not going the full route."

Bordelon understood and nodded his head. "We'll check our money and costs tomorrow and I'll see how short we are. We'll make the purchases. I'll let you know if and when you need to borrow more money, and how much."

"O.K. Let's hear about your breakfast this morning with Bill Beeson."

"Well, I sold him $25 thousand of tickets to Jane's fundraiser." Bordelon looked at Flint to watch his reaction, then smiled.

"You did what?" asked Flint incredulously.

"Well, actually he offered to take $25 thousand worth of tickets and sell them today," Bordelon added. "Hell, I had to really hustle to find that many tickets to put in his hands. I had them delivered from New Orleans. A number of oil people were at Jane's tonight and one of them delivered a thick envelope containing the $25

145

thousand worth of small checks from Beeson along with ticket stubs from every sale. Bill Beeson is one reason we did so well tonight."

Flint gave a long, low whistle. "What did he want?" he asked.

"He didn't specifically say he wanted anything." Bordelon went on to explain the details of his early morning meeting with Bill Beeson of Texon Oil Company at the restaurant of the Hilton Hotel in Baton Rouge. Beeson, a heavy set man in his mid-fifties of medium height, ruddy complexion and thinning red hair, had been waiting at a table when Bordelon arrived at 7:00 a.m. They had exchanged pleasantries, ordered breakfast and immediately got down to the business of the campaign.

"Jeffrey, I have nothing against Darin Flint," Beeson had said. "I've found him to be an open minded senator who's been fair enough to our industry."

"But you didn't like his environmental position paper. Right?" interrupted Jeffrey Bordelon, beating Beeson to the punch.

Beeson stopped and smiled. "Well, what did you expect?"

"We didn't expect you to like it."

Bordelon was briefly interrupted by a waitress delivering their coffee, then he continued, "But I tell you this. Flint's not an unreasonable man but he is dead serious about that environmental issue. As governor, he's going to want the mess cleaned up."

"So he's going to really go to war with the oil industry?"

"I didn't say he was going to war with you." said Bordelon. "That would probably be up to you. Flint would like to work with you. As you said, he's always had an open mind. He knows it's important to keep the energy industry strong, healthy and profitable."

"He has a funny way of showing it," said Beeson.

"Look, Bill. We've known each other a long time. Why don't you tell me why we're here," said Bordelon. "You're a René Reynolds man. You've probably raised millions for him in the past six months. So why do you want to talk to me?"

"I want Darin to know we regret that we've had to take issue with him in the press. We don't want to fight with a man we've always had good relations with in the past and who may be our next governor."

"Why do you think he may be our next governor?" Bordelon inserted quickly.

"Anything is possible." Beeson responded. "Frankly, I think

Reynolds will still beat him decisively. But Darin's done very well with very little and is making a race out of it. And, like I say, anything is possible."

"So, why are we here?" asked Bordelon.

"Flint's got some support among my people. Don't ask me why, but he does." Beeson took a drink of his coffee. "It's a distinct minority you understand. They've asked me to let Darin know that he has some support and to see if its possible for them to give him some help in his campaign."

"What kind of help?"

"Some of them would like to help a lot." Beeson went to his coffee again. "They would help him financially. For instance, there's that fundraiser tonight at Jane Baldwin's. No one's asked them to buy tickets."

"We would love for you to sell them some tickets." Bordelon reached in his pocket for a few ten-packs of tickets he was carrying with him.. "How many you need?"

"I can sell $25 thousand worth of tickets for you."

Bordelon stopped searching for the tickets because he knew he did not have near enough. He had not expected Beeson to be so generous to the Flint campaign. Before Bordelon could speak, Beeson said, "I'll sell the tickets just like anyone else. I'll need $25 thousand worth of tickets today."

Beeson was again interrupted by the waitress, who was delivering their breakfast. Bordelon realized that Beeson wanted to sell tickets so that the donations would be in individual, small amounts not reportable on campaign finance reports. When the waitress was gone, Beeson continued, "I don't know if they'll be able to help anymore after this fundraiser or not. They'd like to. I guess it depends on Flint. If he wants to talk, let me know. But give me those tickets and I'll sell them today. You'll get their checks tonight."

Bordelon had taken quick steps to have the tickets placed in Beeson's hands later that day. As Bordelon finished describing the Beeson meeting to Flint, the New Orleans City Hall building was coming into view. They drove the last block in silence, then were guided by security guards to a restricted parking lot where Bordelon parked the car beside the mayor's limousine.

147

TWENTY-SEVEN

"You're in the ocean, splashing about, doing your damndest not to drown, in spite of whirlpools and cross currents. The main thing is to do the regulation breast-stroke and if you're not a clod, never to let the life-buoy out of sight. No one expects any more than that out of you. Now if you relieve yourself in the water now and then, that's your affair. The sea is big, and if the top half of your body still looks as though it's doing the breast-stroke, nobody will say a word."

Anouih's
"The Waltz of the Toreadors"

Mayor Edmund Lawrence was on his feet when Flint and Bordelon entered the large, old office which Lawrence's wife had colorfully decorated two years earlier. Two of Lawrence's close friends and advisors were with him. Tom Taylor, a white attorney who many believed was the real power behind the mayor, and Lee Powell, Civil Sheriff for Orleans Parish and an influential black politician in his own right. The exchange of greetings was friendly. Flint and Lawrence had known one another for twenty-five years and, more often than not, had been on the same side of most political battles over the years.

Flint had not been deeply involved in Lawrence's two campaigns for mayor, although he had helped and donated to Lawrence both times. Lawrence had called upon Flint for help several times in the Senate to help with critical issues confronting New Orleans. He had learned Flint was willing to help with an unpopular, difficult issue if he felt it was important enough and you were right. He had also learned Flint would say no, with finality, if he disagreed. Lawrence liked him despite Flint's independence.

"You've run a terrific campaign, Darin. Congratulations."

"It's too early for congratulations, Ed. The toughest part is still ahead of us," Flint answered as he accepted a scotch and water proffered by Tommy Taylor.

"Yes, that's true." Lawrence moved to a large, cushioned chair near the back of the room, where a couch and other chairs were comfortably arranged for just such meetings. "These last three weeks will tell the tale."

He motioned for Flint and Bordelon to join him. They all sat down.

"Why did you want to meet with me tonight?" the mayor asked Flint when they were settled.

"I need your help, your organization and influence. I need your endorsement," said Darin.

Lawrence smiled and shook his head. "Darin, you know from our last visit that my hands are tied. I can't get involved. The city stands to lose too much if you lose. I can't afford to alienate the governor of Louisiana."

"But on our last visit, I didn't have forty percent of the vote. I do now."

Bordelon flinched just a bit at Flint's exaggeration of their poll results. But Flint continued without hesitation. "Today, we're in a position to win. You are the man who can make the difference for me."

"Hell, Darin, don't flatter me. I know what they're saying out there about me these days. Cutting spending and jobs while also raising taxes ain't exactly the way for a New Orleans mayor to win friends and influence people."

"Come on, Ed," Flint responded. "You're not the first person who ever had to make some tough decisions. Your problem isn't your personal popularity. I think you're as well respected as ever. Your problem is strictly politics. You probably do not have the votes on the Council to implement your plans."

Lawrence gazed at Flint from across the small coffee table.

"That may be true," Lawrence observed. "But political popularity and votes on the Council are related. I'm a lame duck. I have two and one half years left in my second term. People who I once controlled now hope to take my place. And I'm too old to think about running for some other office. So it's not easy for me to maintain leverage as time passes."

Bordelon entered the conversation. "Ed, you know and I know that your personal following and the strength of your political organization gives you more strength then any politician in Orleans Parish."

Bordelon stood up and walked to the cabinet and poured Coca Cola into his glass to cut the bite of the bourbon. He turned toward the mayor.

"The governor's race boils down to this," said Bordelon. "We can beat Reynolds, but we need twenty to thirty percent of the black vote to do it. We've got good people working with us to get that vote. But labor is gearing up for their final push and Reynolds is already spending untold amounts of money with the black organizations. Jackson Wells is doing his thing for Reynolds. We are here because we need you to push for us."

The mayor looked across the room at Tommy Taylor, who leaned forward in his chair to join the conversation. "You mind if I put in my two cents?"

Flint and Bordelon turned to Taylor. He was a small, thin man, well dressed and well groomed. He spoke directly to Flint.

"I don't want to be too blunt, Darin, but what's in this for the mayor? He owes you nothing. You've supported him in the past, but he's supported you too. Its a washout. Reynolds is the governor and likely to stay that way. Why should we get involved?"

There was a long silence. As Flint started to respond, the silence was suddenly broken by the unexpected female voice of Jane Baldwin.

"Two reasons," she said from the doorway. "We can get you your votes on the Council. And we can start pushing for a third term amendment to the City Charter. Reynolds has too many commitments to your opponents to do either one."

A wide grin spread over the mayor's face. "Here's a little lady who knows how to speak my language. Tommy, fix Jane a drink."

She smiled back at Lawrence. "Gin and tonic with a twist of lemon, please, Tommy." She walked in and sat beside Flint.

"Mayor, you can have my commitment right now on your program. You know I can bring at least one more with me. That'll give you your majority vote on the Council. And I'll agree to help you with the third term amendment. But I want your help with Flint. We need you to endorse him, then bust your tail for him."

Lawrence laughed loudly. "Tommy, what do you think of that proposal?"

Taylor handed Jane her drink, then smiled at the mayor. "She usually does what she says she's going to do, mayor."

"I'm serious." Jane looked back at Tommy, then at Mayor

Lawrence. "It may sound silly to you, but I think Flint's election is a hell of a lot more important than anything any of us have ever done in politics. And if he wins, you'll not only have done the state a favor but you will be stronger politically than ever before."

The mayor turned his head to look at Lee Powell, who had quietly been listening to the discussion from across the room.

"What do you think, Lee?"

Lee Powell was a young black man, only thirty-eight years old, who had been elected civil sheriff by an impressive vote from both black and white voters. He was likeable and competent. Local politicians viewed him as a possible successor to Lawrence. Lawrence trusted him completely.

"I'd love to see you beat the devil out of Reynolds," he said to Flint. "I think we could do you some good. But to crank things up and get our organization working full speed through election day would cost half a million dollars. People expect to get paid for their work. That's the facts of life."

They again sat in silence absorbing the full effects of Powell's words. Even Jane Baldwin had no response.

"Well, folks, I don't have half a million dollars. And I'm not likely to inherit it anytime soon," Flint finally said with all the humor he could muster.

Powell looked at Flint. "Man, I'm sorry but that's the way it is. Reynolds has met with us, as well as other black groups in the city. Hell, Jackson Wells is keeping everything in line for Reynolds with money. It's going to take at least some money, and someone who knows how to get the most out of it, in order to compete with Reynolds and Wells these last three weeks."

Flint looked at Lawrence. "Ed, you know more about what it costs to compete for the black vote than I do. I'm sure Lee knows what he's talking about. But I have no choice but to try some other way to get support because we don't have money. I need your endorsement, your energy and your resourcefulness. If it takes a lot of money to make the organization go at one hundred percent, maybe you can make it operate at thirty percent capacity with your personal persuasion but without money. That would be enough for me."

There was no reply.

Flint stopped talking and stood up to leave.

"Ed, we're both pretty old men for politics these days. It won't be long before our careers are behind us. Remember the old days when we worked, and we got our friends to work, because we believed in the cause? Well, let's give ourselves one more good memory."

The Mayor smiled, then stood and shook Flint's hand to say goodbye.

"Things change, Darin. I stopped joisting windmills many years ago. But I'll think about it and we'll see what happens."

Later, as Bordelon drove into the driveway of Flint's home to drop him off, he reminded Flint of Bill Beeson's final words. "Beeson said there would be plenty of contributions potentially available from the energy business. Do you want me to call him for you and arrange a meeting? That money could help with the mayor's people."

"I really don't want to see Beeson. What's he going to want?" Flint reached for the door handle.

"You'll have to ask him that question." Bordelon looked him in the eye. "Probably you'd have to at least compromise on your superfund idea. And they would want no more of the environmental or health attacks on the oil industry."

"I'd feel like I'd be selling my soul," replied Flint.

"No, you wouldn't. Darin, think of it this way. If you're not elected governor, what will happen on the environmental issue. On the education issue. Or labor or spending. Sometimes you have to give a little to gain a little. Maybe there is a reasonable middle ground."

There was no response.

Bordelon put the car in reverse. "Don't take it so serious. Go to bed and sleep on it. Things will look better tomorrow."

Flint had stepped out of the car as Bordelon was speaking. He stopped before slamming the door and looked back inside.

"Jeffrey. I'll meet with Beeson but I want you to know how I feel. We can do without Mr. Beeson, his friends and their money. And if Edmund Lawrence, Lee Powell and other black leaders we need will join us, then they'll have to scramble with us for contributions, volunteers and free media just like everyone else has been doing for us all along. Ed Lawrence understands that and he'll have to make his own decision. O.K.?"

"O.K." Jeffrey Bordelon smiled.

"Goodnight."

"Goodnight."

TWENTY-EIGHT

"The victor belongs to the spoils."

F. Scott Fitzgerald
(1896-1940)
American novelist
The Beautiful and Damned, 1921

Vernon Looper arrived in his AFL-CIO office in Baton Rouge at 6:30 a.m. He and Joe Randall had been on the road continuously over the past month attending local union meetings with local and state candidates. It was a necessary process to personally assure the right candidates were getting union endorsements, that local labor telephone banks were functioning smoothly throughout the state, that union mail-outs were ready for that final week, and to schedule labor union and black rallies statewide for the last ten days of the campaign.

Much of the AFL-CIO's strongest influence was in the black community. Among AFL-CIO affiliates, the Bricklayers Union, the Cement Masons and the Louisiana Federation of Teachers were heavily black. Most of the higher paid building and trade unions, the oil patch unions, the chemical and refinery unions, and seaman and harbor worker unions were heavily white. The public employee union, AFSCME, was a mixture with considerable black membership.

Vernon Looper, as the president of the AFL-CIO, knew how to coordinate the long tentacles of organized labor that reached into virtually every element of society in every parish of the state. By laying the groundwork early in the political season, establishing telephone banks, providing locals with complete voter lists, training workers to be the political operatives supervising and providing manpower for all campaign activities, Looper commanded a formidable political force.

Even in fundraising, labor was a factor. The many labor political action committees were making significant contributions to all their candidates in an effort to compete with the endless numbers of business PAC's providing financial donations to their favored candidates.

After thirty years at the labor helm, Looper knew how to bring the many diffused efforts of over three hundred union organizations together into a final stretch run for the election day wire. In gubernatorial elections, the state AFL-CIO had always managed to be certain labor was totally united behind a single candidate as election day approached. Labor was totally committed to René Reynolds. Looper was orchestrating a network of cars and drivers to transport identified Reynolds voters, labor voters and black voters to the polls on election day. In a close election, the labor organization would provide the candidate with his margin of victory.

Looper was the first in the office that morning and there was no coffee ready in the kitchenette. He opened the icebox, popped open a can of V-8 juice and poured it into a small glass. He sat down sipping his juice and began reading the morning paper. His eyes quickly dropped to the headline and article in the middle of the Advocate's front page:

"WILL FLINT DEBATE ALONE TONIGHT?"
Reynolds Refuses Invitation;
League Vows "Show will go on"
by Gordon Twilley(A.P.)

State Senator Darin Flint hopes to bring his uphill "No Deals" campaign for the governorship to statewide television tonight in a debate with incumbent Governor René Reynolds, who probably will not appear. Governor Reynolds refused the invitation of the Louisiana League of Women Voters two weeks ago and has not changed his mind. The League sponsors the debate. The League president, Louise Harrison, declared again yesterday the debate will proceed with Senator Flint alone if Governor Reynolds fails to appear.

The debate will begin at 8:00 p.m. tonight and will be televised from the stage of the LSU Student Union Theater where a packed house is expected.

The uncertainty of Reynolds' participation lends an air of mystery to a campaign that is reaching a fever pitch as election day looms only ten days away.

The campaign has been spiced up this week as new campaign ads of both candidates began on television. The Reynolds' ad campaign depicts Flint, a twenty-seven year veteran of the Legislature, as a man who has flip-flopped on key issues. Flint has struck back on issues like the environment, the need for better highways, unemployment, education reform, government waste and graft.

Governor Reynolds, the youngest governor in Louisiana history, was not expected to even have an opponent three months ago. But Senator Flint of New Orleans has surprised the political world by building an enthusiastic campaign organization across the state which now claims over forty percent of the vote according to its recent polls. Reynolds dismisses those poll figures as "overripe imagination" and declares his polls show him with a commanding lead.

The Reynolds-Flint campaign has proven unusual by Louisiana standards for several reasons. It would be an extraordinary upset for a state legislator to defeat an incumbent governor. Furthermore, spending has fallen below previous levels, mostly due to the anemic campaign budget of Senator Flint. Spending reports filed last week indicate Reynolds is outspending Flint by a ten to one ratio. Reynolds has spent $5.5 million compared to over $8 million he spent four years ago. Senator Flint's reports indicate he has raised only $543 thousand so far and spent $660 thousand. The Reynolds' campaign has over $3 million on hand, according to the campaign reports.

In an interview earlier this week, Senator Flint explained he had already paid for his television, radio and media expenses for the final weeks of the campaign so he does not consider his budget to be too deeply in the red. He has borrowed one hundred thousand dollars personally to cover deficits and he is continuing his fund-raising efforts.

If Senator Flint wins the governorship, he will be the first governor in recent memory to spend less than a million dollars in his election campaign.

However, Governor Reynolds is confident of re-election. He has received the strong endorsements of the AFL-CIO and the Legislative Black Caucus. He is expected to receive a black vote of landslide proportions. Meanwhile, the Louisiana Business League, the traditional opponent of the AFL-CIO, declared months ago that it would concentrate on legislative races and would not endorse anyone for governor. L.B.L. apparently made this early decision based upon the conventional wisdom at that time that Governor Reynolds would easily win re-election.

Tonight's debate may provide the challenger with an opportunity to further advance his chances to upset the incumbent.

Louise Harrison stated this week that the League of Women Voters were offended by Governor Reynolds' failure to answer their invitation to participate in the debate. The League was further offended to learn of his refusal from a news program instead of by personal contact. Harrison stated the ninety minute debate will proceed in its entirety tonight with Senator Flint alone, if necessary. Original plans for two debates apparently will not be pursued.

The League will proceed with five members of the press designated to present questions, and with Mr. Kevin Lowenthal of the Louisiana Institute of Politics acting as moderator.

Vernon Looper looked up from his paper as he sensed the presence of someone watching him from the doorway.

"Good morning, Vernon," said Jeffrey Bordelon. "It's been awhile."

Looper stood up with an obvious look of surprise on his face. The two men shook hands.

"Hey Jeff. It's good to see you. Have a seat. Let me fix you some coffee."

Looper took coffee from the cabinet and began brewing a fresh pot. "Well, we've gotten down to nut-cutting time in this campaign, haven't we?"

"Yes, we have," Bordelon acknowledged. "Darin Flint can be our next governor and there's no reason in the world for you to oppose him."

Looper did not respond immediately. Then his response avoided the subject.

"I thought you were finished with politics. Why did you get involved in this campaign?"

Now it was Bordelon's turn to sidestep the question. Bordelon chuckled and picked up the newspaper Looper had left on the table. "I see you've been reading about my candidate. What's Twilley attacking Flint about this morning?"

Looper took two coffee cups from the cabinet and placed them beside the percolating coffee pot, then answered, "Actually, I think that article is very favorable to Flint and gives the so-called debate some pretty strong publicity. People will watch just to see if René shows up."

"Will Reynolds show up?"

"No. Why should he?"

"Because Reynolds is in trouble and I think he knows it," Bordelon said as he withdrew a thin, bound computer printout from his briefcase and dropped it in front of Looper. "I don't know what Reynolds is telling you about his polls but I brought an extra copy of the essential part of our latest one for you."

Looper picked it up and began reading through it.

"Keep reading and I'll pour the coffee." Bordelon got up and began pouring coffee for them both. Then he stood quietly sipping from his cup until Looper had finished. Several minutes passed as they sat in silence.

Finally Looper stood, poured his by now cold coffee in the sink and poured himself a hot cup.

"I know its tightening up, Jeff. But Flint's still more than ten points down. My man is still a winner. What do you want me to do, jump ship?"

"I'm not asking you to do anything. I'm here on my own. Flint would probably shoot me for giving you those poll results. But I think I know you. You're practical enough to put up with Reynolds because he'll usually do what you want. But I don't think you like him or the sleazy way his people run the state. I'm here to remind you that you still have a choice."

Looper said nothing as he stared down into his coffee cup.

It was Bordelon who broke the silence. "Vernon, you asked me awhile ago why I got involved in this campaign. I realize now I was probably a coward to have retired from office. I was disillusioned and sick of the hypocrisy. People like you know what you want from a president or a congress. You know what you want from a governor and legislature. That's fine. But how many dishonest politicians have you helped gain power because they gave you the right commitments on the right issues?"

"Aw, come on Jeff. Don't give me that holier than thou crap."

"You know it's true," Bordelon persisted. "How else do people like Reynolds get in office. He doesn't give a damn about labor or business. He doesn't give a damn about blacks. He doesn't give a damn about Louisiana. He might casually believe in all those things. He'd like to see the state do well I'm sure. But that's his politics. He doesn't really care in the true sense of the word. What he cares about is himself. Period. And the same thing's true of those around him. Power for power's sake. Reynolds wasn't in power when I retired. I had never even heard of him. But people just like him were in power at that time. That's the way its been for as long as I can remember."

It was obvious from the expression on Looper's face that the conversation was over. Looper would not budge. Bordelon placed his cup in the sink, picked up his briefcase to leave and turned to again face Looper.

"I got so sick of it, I quit. Now, I'm sorry I quit. Now I'm fighting back. I thought maybe you were sick of it too. Maybe you would want to fight back also. At last, we have a chance to elect an exceptional man. And more importantly, an honest man. He told me you'd made a commitment to him early in the campaign to not attack him, to at least acknowledge he was an able man and not an enemy of labor. I thought you might want to go further than that."

"I never knew how naive you really are, Jeffrey."

"I understand politics, Vernon. But I regret all the concessions I made to the game. The things I tolerated because I was being realistic. I never really accomplished great and lasting things for that very reason. What was the purpose of my career? When Flint wins, I'll start enjoying my retirement at last. My conscience will be clear. Think about it, Vernon."

A moment later, Bordelon was gone. Vernon Looper picked up the newspaper and the computer print-out, then walked into his office. He dropped the paper and poll on his desk and stared at them quietly for a full minute. He thought about the segment of Reynolds' thirty minute political television program he had participated in video-taping last week. The program would be aired tonight prior to the Flint debate on statewide television.

"Aww, shit!" he muttered. Then Looper pushed Jeffrey Bordelon from his mind and went to work at his desk.

TWENTY-NINE

"Facts are to the mind what food is to the body....The wisest in council, the ablest in debate, and the most agreeable companion in the commerce of human life, is that man who has assimilated to his understanding the greatest number of facts."

Edmund Burke
(1729-1797)
English political writer, orator

Darin Flint felt absurdly calm in the back seat as his son John parked the family car in front of the L.S.U. Student Union among the throng of friends, political workers, students and interested people who crowded the union entrance. Jenny was in the front seat and his wife Susan sat beside him. Darin squeezed Susan's hand and kissed her.

"Well, here goes nothing." he said.

She smiled. "Let's go."

The mobile television cameras and lights were upon them immediately. As they worked their way through the crowd, Flint kept Susan beside him. Terrell Franks reached them at the top of the stairs and guided him across the front area of the union toward the theatre entrance. Flint found himself answering the questions of reporters as he made his way along. He was greeted by Greg Hawkins, Jane Baldwin, Eric McKay, Carey Jefferson, Joel Whitney among others as he entered the crowded theatre. Jenny and her friends had put his banners on the walls. Dozens of his placards were being held overhead by supporters in the audience.

But Reynolds buttons, signs, and banners were equally in evidence. Reynolds may not show up, Flint thought to himself, but he certainly has his people here in force.

Terrell Franks hollered in Flint's ear that they were going back stage. As Flint stepped into the full view of the audience, applause arose from the Flint partisans. He shook the hands that were being extended toward him from all sides. He worked his way toward the stage, keeping one eye on Franks. Security officers finally ushered him to a doorway and they made their way backstage. Franks showed him into a dressing room where he could have a few final moments of privacy before the debate program began.

Jon Douglas and Jeffrey Bordelon were seated inside the dressing room watching a small black and white television set. They stood up as he entered.

"Reynolds is running a hatchet job program on you right now, Darin," Bordelon pointed to the screen. "Instead of showing up to debate you, he's decided to damage you as much as possible before you ever go on the air. So far, you've been denounced as a blue blood from New Orleans, a friend of the rich and the enemy of the poor," he said sarcastically.

Jon Douglas then spoke up. "They've also branded you as a radical environmentalist who's out to destroy the oil industry and put people out of work. They also had a cute little portion of the program devoted to seven or eight votes in the Legislature where you have reversed yourself two or more times. They're calling you a flip-flopper and a yo-yo."

"Vernon Looper said you've opposed better salaries for teachers and state employees, and your labor record is unreliable. He says your campaign has fooled people with its slick Fifth Avenue position papers and mail-outs," summarized Bordelon.

"He didn't mention the millions of dollars of budget cuts I proposed to fund payraises, did he?" Flint asked knowingly.

A deep voice then interrupted them from the back of the room. "They did include black legislators in the program who said your proposed budget cuts were racist." Flint turned and was surprised to find Mayor Edmund Lawrence leaning against a table. "I wonder what they'll say about the budget cuts I'm preparing in New Orleans," he said with a smile.

Flint's concern over the Reynolds hatchet job was suddenly wiped from his mind. Lawrence had been behind the door, unseen, when Flint entered the dressing room.

"Well look who's here," said Flint as he walked across the room with a broad smile to shake Edmund Lawrence's hand.

"We thought having Ed here would be a nice boost for your confidence before the debate," said Bordelon.

"I'm with you all the way, Darin. We'll lose it or win it together," said Lawrence.

160

"Thank you Edmund. Your endorsement will turn this campaign upside down. If we win, I don't think the politics of this state will ever be the same."

Sandy Myer of WXTZ television interrupted them as she knocked on the open door. "Senator Flint, we need to get you in place. The program will begin in about six minutes."

Everyone stood to leave.

"There's one more thing you need to know about Reynolds' television program before the debate starts," instructed Bordelon. "They are attacking you as being dishonest. They've attacked you for a vote giving Noble Airlines a tax exemption. In a nutshell, they say you voted for the bill and they showed copies of your mother-in-law's stock certificates to illustrate that you had a clear conflict of interest. There may be questions on that during the debate."

Flint glanced back at the television as Senate president Sonny Stokes concluded the program, declaring that he had known Flint for years but could not let "personal friendship interfere with the best interest of the state." Stokes told the television audience it would be a great mistake to vote for Flint, whose "spotty record leaves him unprepared for higher responsibility." He praised Governor Reynolds as a great governor and ended with his endorsement of Reynolds.

"Well I suppose no red blooded Louisiana campaign would ever be complete without a good hatchet job," Flint said. "Let's talk about it after the debate."

Flint turned back to his friends with a smile, "Say a little prayer for me." Then he followed Sandy Myer to the stage behind the closed stage curtains, where he was seated on a dais at a small desk. A small microphone was clipped to his tie. The heat from the plethora of bright television lights radiated upon his face. He made a mental note of the location of the three television cameras that were being readied.

A second desk for Governor Reynolds was located immediately alongside his own, with an empty chair and another small microphone lying on the desk top awaiting his absent opponent.

To his far right, a longer desk was in place for the five reporters who would question the candidates. Flint unclipped his microphone and went to greet every newsperson on the panel, including Gordon Twilley of the Associated Press. Sandy Myer would also be one of the questioners. Flint also greeted Louise Harrison of the League of Women Voters and Kevin Lowenthal, who would serve as moderator for the debate. Then he returned to his seat.

Within minutes the stage curtains opened and the program was under way. Reynolds remained absent. Kevin Lowenthal was explaining to the statewide televison audience the rules of the debate. Flint heard himself being introduced, then he heard the enthusiastic applause and cheers of his supporters.

"Senator Flint." Flint's attention was suddenly concentrated on the lips of Gordon Twilley who was asking the first question.

"Why are you a candidate for governor of Louisiana?"

Flint's concern over the Reynolds hatchet job was suddenly wiped from his mind as he instinctively responded to the question.

"We have the essential elements to make our beautiful state a great state. Natural resources of oil and gas, rivers and streams, natural ports, geographical location, mineral resources and a large workforce are only a few. Unfortunately, our potential has been squandered too often in the past by a petty brand of politics that encourages those in office to use their elected positions for self enrichment and the enrichment of those around them. For decades, hundreds and even billions of dollars of oil and gas revenues have flowed endlessly into the state's treasury. Compare what our state government spends to the budgets of other states. We spend more for a state our size than virtually any state in America.

"Yet our educational accomplishments trail other states; our road system is a mess; our oil and gas production is dwindling leaving the tax burden to be shifted gradually onto the shoulders of the average wage earner. Yet the average earnings of our people is far below the national average.

"So how will they afford it? And who will restore our wetlands that have been damaged by fifty years of energy exploration? What about the thousands of miles of criss-crossing pipelines; the dredged canals and spiderweb of channels for oil barges and rigs. How will we revitalize our economy? How will we diversify and attract manufacturing business to replace the energy jobs being lost today?

"I'm a candidate because the time has come to face the future. We need more than humorous and colorful politicians. We cannot wait any longer to build a modern and lasting highway system. That's why I've proposed a Highway Master Plan in great detail. That's why I've proposed a superfund be established to clean up the mess that energy exploration is leaving behind. And to avoid the creation of further mess as energy exploration continues. That's why I've proposed a reform of the civil service system to bring us better services at less expense from government while also reforming the classification system that is unfair to employees.

"Frankly, my purpose is to change the entire personality of Louisiana politics. I've been accused of being unrealistic, idealistic and naive. I assure you, I've been in public office too long to be naive. Petty politics penalizes and punishes every element of the fabric of this state. Our budget ends up being far larger than it need be. Services end up being delivered in an ineffective manner. Even the governor of the state ends up being preoccupied with rewarding his friends instead of simply administering government, protecting tax dollars and delivering services on the most economical basis possible. If we improve our politics, we will see education improve, highways improve, our economy improve, government service improve, and it will be easier to balance the budget.

"Louisiana's future can be much better than her past. I'd like the opportunity to help Louisiana reach her potential. That's why I'm a candidate for governor."

Flint was interrupted several times by applause. Lowenthal intervened at the conclusion of Flint's answer to request quiet from the audience.

Twilley's followup confronted the oil and gas issue.

"Senator, you've been outspoken about environmental concerns in your campaign. A moment ago you made reference to a superfund to clean up the environmental mess. Are you anti-oil? Will your policies cause thousands of people to lose their jobs in the oil industry?"

"The answer to both questions is no. During my twenty-seven years in the Senate, I've often sided with the oil interests. Especially on taxation issues.

"For Louisiana, the energy industry has been a lost opportunity. During the past fifty years, many billions of dollars of oil royalties, bonuses and severance tax money has poured through the treasury. Most recently, we enjoyed huge windfalls from oil deregulation by the federal government. Two governors and two legislatures had opportunities to protect that windfall before and during it's accrual, but it didn't happen. The money was quickly spent, much of it on recurring expenses that have bloated the state budget. When the money was no longer there, consumer taxes were increased dramatically to cover those new programs. The current administration has increased those taxes to even higher levels. A billion dollars of new tax money has seemingly disappeared into thin air.

"We've actually managed in many ways to make the asset of oil and gas revenues a liability in Louisiana. But that's not the fault of the oil people. That's the failure of political leadership during the 1970's right up through today.

"Other oil states with greater vision have put their opportunities to far greater use. The state of Texas, for instance, now has a huge endowment fund to assure its current and future generations of a sound educational system because its been setting oil and gas money aside for many decades. Both Alabama and Mississippi have similar plans. So does Alaska.

"Meanwhile, over the decades, the search for oil has cost us environmental penalties. Twenty years ago, we didn't know what we know now about chemical wastes, PCP's, toxic metals and chemicals used in the drilling process and the wastes produced by that process. We didn't understand the effects on our soil, the destruction of fertility, it's contamination of water aquifers, streams, our wetlands and the effects on the fragile ecology of our marshes. We didn't know the danger of salt water intrusion, of erosion of our coastlines. We didn't understand what was going to be happening to our fishing industry, our fur industry and our agriculture. We didn't understand the effect on wildlife and natural habitats. We didn't have the knowledge or understanding of the impact chemical dumping by refineries, petro-chemical plants, fertilizer plants and by others would have on the Mississippi River.

"We have that knowledge today. Accordingly, the oil industry and our regulators are doing a better job than ever before to prevent even more damage from occurring.

"But what's to be done about the mess accumulated by fifty years of frenetic production when those safeguards were not in place? There are thousands of chemical dump sites, brine pits, and waste pits in this state near old drilling sites that are not going away by themselves. The oil industry is still spending a billion dollars per year on drilling "mud" used in the drilling process. If we spend a billion dollars on the mud, how much should we spend on appropriate disposal of waste and in cleaning up the mess of the past?

"Furthermore, the record still stands that the state of Louisiana has never said no to a single industry application to dredge canals in the wetlands. Oil and gas waste products are still not regulated as hazardous waste either by the state or federal government because their lobbying efforts to be exempted have always succeeded. Louisiana continues to support still more EPA applications by industries that want to dump their waste product into the Mississippi. For instance, there are currently four fertilizer plants applying for permits to annually dump millions of tons of gypsum waste, containing uranium, radium and other toxic materials into the Mississippi River. Louisiana is supporting all four of those EPA applications.

"Our public needs to be aware, and fully understand the implications. Once water aquifers are contaminated, carcinogens can never be removed. There may well be some connection with the excessive levels of colon cancer and pancreatic cancer we have in Louisiana. In fact, the densest cluster of pancreatic cancer deaths in the United States is in South Louisiana. New Orleans has a death rate from cancer twenty- one percent above the United States average. There's evidence of carcinogens in the New Orleans water supply. In communities like Kaplan or Port Barre, there's a clear indication of either brine contamination, dissolvable solids contamination; cromium, zinc or barium contamination.

"I favor creation of a superfund financed by moderate increases in virtually every fee charged energy, mining, petro-chemical production and related undertakings for such activities as dredging permits, drilling permits, state mineral lease contracts, pipeline construction and the like. Perhaps these fees could be subject to a five or ten year life. Therefore making it a temporary fund until we clean up the mess. If sufficient progress is made to resolve these problems, then the new fees could be terminated and not renewed. The cost of these fees would by and large be passed on to consumers, who for the most part reside outside the state of Louisiana.

"I am not anti-oil. I acknowledge that many of our largest oil companies have taken dramatic steps and spent large sum of monies to prevent any further creation of such damage. Many of these companies have even gone back and tried to cleanup their abandoned dump sites. I recognize and appreciate that fact. I also recognize the huge employment base these industries provide. I recognize the hundreds of millions of dollars of tax revenues paid to our state treasury. I hope the energy industry will always find prosperity in our state. But none of those facts are reasons to ignore this terrible damage from the past that threatens our future.

"I want to do two things: First, I want to provide better management of our oil revenues so that these funds are not exhausted each year, with no lasting benefit to future generations.

"Second, I want the oil industry and the state to work hand in hand to clean up the environmental mess left by our predecessors."

Sandy Meyer asked the next question. "What improvements do you propose in the field of education?"

"Again, petty politics have penalized us severely. We spend over one-third of our state budget on education, but much is lost on non-classroom expenses having little or no impact on students. The minimum foundation formula, which is used to disburse education dollars, should be altered to mandate a greater proportion of teachers to students. From kindergarten through the third grade, we should never have more than twenty-two students in the room. At higher grade levels, the numbers should be no higher than twenty-five. A teacher can do a better job. The student can learn more under those conditions. Frankly, I'd propose the goal of reducing our pupil-teacher to 18 to 1. But that would be enormously expensive unless deep cuts are made elsewhere. We are spending too much money on out of classroom personnel. I hope to redirect spending into the classroom.

"I've also proposed the implementation of sixth grade centers in urban areas throughout the state so that a new concentration on this transition grade level can be made. By having all sixth graders attend school together in sixth grade centers, implementation of new programs in music, arts, foreign languages, remedial programs for those that are lagging behind can be implemented. The sixth grade students can have specialists to teach them math, or English, or history and geography instead of having a single teacher try to teach them all of those courses. In my mind, the sixth grade gives us a last opportunity to bring our grammar school kids up to the appropriate level before they begin their junior high and high school curriculums. Therefore, I think there should be a new emphasis on the implementation of sixth grade centers.

"I favor the testing of teachers before they are certified. I therefore want to retain the NTE or some similar measure as a pre-requisite to certification. I favor a system of re-certification every five or six years. However, this re-certification should not involve the NTE or any test. It should be based more on continuing education, quality of job performance, classroom technique and classroom effectiveness. If a teacher is competent in doing the job, then that teacher should be receiving fair pay increases each year. Teacher salaries are much too low and must be increased.

"Frankly, beyond those things, my tendency is for the governor and the Legislature to get out of the educators' way. Let the experts decide the curriculum, with the Board of Elementary and Secondary Education's approval. The Legislature and governor should play a watchdog role. I do not favor the Legislature involving itself in curriculum decisions except as an absolute final alternative."

The questions and answers flowed for another ten minutes. Without an opponent present, there was little to excite the crowd.

"Senator Flint, are you surprised Governor Reynolds has not appeared to participate in the debate tonight?" asked Sandy Myer from the press table.

"Yes, I am. I felt reasonably certain he would appear."

"Why?"

"Because this is a serious effort to discuss the future of our state. And whether René likes it or not, this is going to be a very close election featuring two candidates with quite different ideas about what's wrong in state government and what must be done to correct problems. He should be here."

"Maybe he'll still show up," one panelist laughed.

"It's getting late. Maybe later than he thinks," Flint replied with a smile that brought laughter and applause from the audience.

As the next question was being asked by another panelist, a stir in the crowd began near the theatre doorway. People were being moved away by security officers. The attention of the audience was diverted from the stage. People began standing, trying to see what was happening. Members of the State Police entered. Flint caught a glimpse of Neil Moulard's balding head. Then a chorus of mixed cheers and boos began rising from the audience as Governor René Reynolds entered the theatre shaking hands and waving to the crowd. The television cameras turned from the stage and followed René Reynolds as he shook every hand, slapped backs, appeared to laugh at jokes as he worked his way to the front.

Moments later, Reynolds leaped up the stairs two at a time onto the stage. He turned with a smile to bow deeply to the crowd, bringing an increased barrage of boos, cheers, applause and laughter. Reynolds shook Lowenthal's hand, he greeted every panelist, then walked across the stage to shake Flint's hand. Flint rose to his feet to meet him. Then Reynolds stepped behind his table, sat down and picked up his microphone.

"Is this for me?" he exclaimed into the microphone bringing laughter from the audience and from everyone on the stage. Even Flint had to smile.

Reynolds had upstaged him and effectively stolen the show.

THIRTY

"The greater the truth the greater the libel."

Edward Law
(1750-1818)
1st Baron of Ellenborough
English jurist

Kevin Lowenthal interrupted the proceedings by demanding silence from the audience. Forty-five minutes of debate time remained. He welcomed Governor Reynolds to the debate, briefly explained the procedures being followed and recognized Sandy Meyer for the first question.

"Governor Reynolds, I'd like to ask you the same question we asked earlier to Senator Flint. Why do you believe the voters of Louisiana should re-elect you governor?"

"As governor, I've had to make many difficult decisions in wrestling with very difficult problems. We've done that competently in the best interest of the state. The budget has been balanced each year. We've funded a meaningful statewide drainage program. We've pushed construction of the new North-South Interstate-49 highway to completion. We've undertaken and funded important new initiatives in industrial development to create new business and a stronger Louisiana economy, including scientific research and loan programs which have aided the growth of new Louisiana industries such as crawfish and catfish industries. Despite severe financial limitations, we've fully funded an aggressive highway construction program and maintained state services. We have funded an ambitious education reform program. We're working hard to reduce unemployment. We have assisted the economic recovery of our energy industry. We have expanded and strenghtened our effective Department of Environmental Quality to enforce our environmental laws.

"Very frankly, our state government is operating smoothly and is in good hands. We feel proud and justified in standing before the people of Louisiana and asking to be re-elected."

Reynolds remarks brought applause and cheers from his supporters. Lowenthal again asked the audience for order.

The following question was then asked to Reynolds. "Do you believe Senator Flint is an honest and able man who would serve well as governor?"

Reynolds laughed. "I think Senator Flint has been a successful politician who has served a number of terms in the State Senate. I think he'd be well advised to stay in the Senate."

Again, Reynolds' remarks brought loud laughter and applause from his supporters.

Then an opportunity for rebuttal was presented to Flint. "Senator, Governor Reynolds listed a number of accomplishments of his administration a moment ago. Do you agree with his summation?"

Flint cleared his throat and looked into the camera. "Frankly, no. Governor Reynolds says he's balanced the budget each year. That's not true."

Flint glanced at Reynolds with a smile and jokingly said, "Your nose grew ten inches when you said the budget was balanced. Governor Reynolds covered most new spending by passing enormous levels of new taxes and squandering windfall revenues on recurring expenses. Even with that, the budget has been unbalanced the past two years. This year the deficit may exceed $150 million. There has been no fiscal restraint at all. The Reynolds Administration has opposed almost all budget reduction proposals that have been made. The budget has grown by more than ten percent annually during the Reynolds' years although the cost of living and inflation rate has been only four percent.

"The governor talks about education reforms. I disagree. He's created expensive new education bureaucracies and commissions with important names like the Education Administrator's School and the Merit Scholarship Commission. But we already had an executive training program for administrators and we already had numerous other scholarship programs. These are examples of questionable new bureaucracies at a time when the state can least afford luxuries. Meanwhile, petty politics have been allowed to continue dominance in the Education Department. We've had a stream of indictments stemming from favoritism in awarding contracts on everything from textbook contracts, warehouse contracts, office leases to cafeteria food contracts. Political patronage in education is a way of life. We've even had abuse of education grants where such education money is mis-used to give political friends high-priced do-nothing consultant contracts and political jobs.

"Frankly, I've seen precious little done by state government over the past four years to improve the actual education of students in the classroom. We should be using those wasted funds to reduce the teacher-student ratio, improve teaching materials, raising salaries and other steps of direct benefit to students.

"As for highway construction, Governor Reynolds should be apologizing for the role he has played in damaging our model highway priority program, which requires highway construction on basis of need and priority, not exercise of political muscle. Every year, Governor Reynolds has traded away low priority, political highway projects to legislators in exchange for their support of his new taxes and other dubious legislation.

"The biggest problem we have in building a good highway system and a good education system is petty politics. Instead of even trying to solve that enormous problem," Flint hestitated and looked Reynolds squarely in the eye, "You, Mr. Reynolds, have simply made the problem much worse."

This time the cheers were for Flint. The two candidates glared at one another. Neither smiled.

"Governor Reynolds, you're entitled to a reply," said the moderator.

"Thank you," responded Reynolds. "I certainly would like to reply. Leadership is not easy to deliver. Yes, I have had to bargain with legislators. That's the give and take of the process. You cannot succeed unless you are successful negotiating. Senator Flint offers a 'holier-than-thou' solution to our education and highway problems then accuses me of abusing authority. I don't break laws. But if a contract is to be awarded, I frankly prefer it be given to a friend as opposed to someone I don't know. That's politics.

"Now let's look at Mr. Flint," Reynolds turned and looked Flint in the face. "You are not the Mr. Clean you pretend to be. Three years ago, you quietly worked for a bill and voted for a bill in which you had a blatant financial conflict of interest. You supported tax exemptions for Noble Airlines, a business in which your family own-ed stock and would directly benefit from your vote. In the State Senate, your record is a perfect picture of political bargaining, vote swapping and compromise."

Reynolds pulled a piece of paper from his shirt pocket. "You have changed your vote on many issues over the years. Creationism and workers' compensation are two good examples. You authored an income tax cut then voted three years later to partially repeal it. You have consistently voted for teacher payraises but against the taxes to fund them. Aside from dishonest, that's downright hypocritical."

This time the audience was silent. The governor's attack on Flint had included serious charges that left even Flint's vocal supporters stunned. Most of them had not seen the Reynolds television program prior to the debate.

Flint broke the silence. "I'd like to answer those incredibly wrong and incorrect accusations."

Kevin Lowenthal responded, "Proceed."

Flint looked directly into the television camera. "I do not know where Mr. Reynolds gets his information but he should fire his researcher." He turned to face Reynolds. "If you can offer any reliable proof that I ever had a conflict of interest on the Noble Airlines issue or any other issue, and wrongfully voted to financially help myself or my family, then I will drop out of this race immediately, terminate my candidacy and instead I will vote for you. However, I also demand that you agree right now that if the records of the Legislature reveal you are wrong and, believe me, you are wrong, then you will resign your candidacy for reelection. You will drop out of the race and instead vote for me."

Flint stopped talking and stared at Reynolds for several moments, then turned back to the camera.

"During this campaign, I have tolerated false ridicule and blatant lies like those phony handbills produced and periodically distributed statewide by Mr. Reynold's campaign. I've been accused of conflict of interest on this Noble Airlines vote along with various other accusations. These hate-sheets accuse me of ignorance in farming issues and a variety of other fake charges. Thousands of citizens have been lied to in those handbills.

"This Noble Airlines issue is a perfect example. I never voted on that bill. Instead, I complied with Senate rules and submitted a statement to the Senate President's office prior to that vote declaring that I had a family member who owned stock in that corporation, that I therefore would recuse myself and not vote on that issue. And I did recuse myself, Mr. Reynolds. I did not vote. You are wrong when you say I voted for that bill. Senate records will back me up. The records of the Senate proceedings will show that I recused myself and never voted on that issue either in committee or on the floor of the Senate. It will also show that I never spoke to any committee or took part in any way in any debate on the issues."

Again Flint looked at Reynolds. "Now, René, I demand an apology instantly from you or I challange you to drop out of this race when you learn you are wrong. I am prepared to drop out if I'm wrong. But I know I'm right. What about you? What do you say? Are you willing to drop out of this race if you are wrong about the accusations you made toward me?"

The silence in the auditorium was deafening. Flint's eye was attracted by Neil Moulard standing backstage shifting his weight from foot to foot. Flint had never seen Moulard's face so blank, his skin so flushed. Lowenthal stated, "Governor Reynolds, you have the floor."

Reynolds kept his poise. "Mr. Flint, my information is that you did, indeed, vote on the Noble Airlines bill. If my information is wrong, and I will have it rechecked again, then I do indeed owe you an apology. I hereby give it." Reynolds hesitated, smiled weakly and tried to inject a little humor. "Of course, if my researcher is right, then I'll be pleased to have you drop out of the race and vote for me for governor. If my information is wrong, then I'll take your advice and fire my researcher."

The Governor's effort at humor brought no laughter from the audience this time.

Reynolds hesitated again. "Meanwhile, I believe you still owe us an explanation on all those votes you flip-flopped on."

Flint did not even wait to be recognized by the moderator but immediately responded. "Governor, I don't owe you anything. I have voted in the State Legislature over forty thousand times over the past twenty-seven years. I've never claimed to always be right. In fact I have acknowledged making mistakes in retrospect on many occasions. I have changed my mind on some issues as time, information and experience improve my understanding and viewpoints. For instance, I now believe I was wrong years ago on the Superintendent of Education issue and on the creationism issue as well. That's why my votes in the Senate changed on those issues. As I say, I voted over forty thousand times. I've done the best I can. When I've recognized an error, I've tried to correct it the next time the issue came up. Some of those votes you cited occurred ten years apart."

The debate continued for the remainder of the hour. But the high point had passed. The rest was downhill and uneventful. At the conclusion, Flint was surrounded by his family and his campaign leaders. Reynolds was joined by his wife, Neil Moulard and a bevy of state troopers. Both groups gradually dissolved into the audience as it milled about and moved toward the exits.

The front pages of Louisiana newspapers confirmed the following morning that Senate records revealed Darin Flint had properly recused himself on the Noble Airlines vote. Darin Flint had been right. René Reynolds had been dead wrong in his accusations.

THIRTY-ONE

"Gnothi seauton (Know thyself)
Meden agan (Nothing in excess)"

Engraved by the Seven Wise Men,
Temple of Apollo, Delphi

Events went spinning around Darin Flint so fast those final ten days of the campaign his only recollection was of reacting to crisis after crisis.... never an opportunity to think things through, to plan, to evaluate.

His memories overlapped and were already confused as to sequence, time and place. His campaign team had been ecstatic the morning after the television debate. Mayor Lawrence had joined his group this time when they met in Jon Douglas' home in Baton Rouge.

Their voices were still clear and embedded in his memory.

"Darin, these last ten days are the most important of the campaign," Congressman Bordelon had said. "We've got to go for it. Maximize our television."

"Darin, we haven't hit the newspapers like we need to. These ten days are our last chance to get your name and issues in every paper before election day," Terrell Frank had declared. "You've got to spend what it takes. We're too close!"

"Darin, you can be governor. It's your race to win. The blacks can make the difference," he remembered Mayor Lawrence saying. "I've endorsed you. But that won't mean a thing unless we follow it up with the black organizations that are willing to help. They've got workers, canvassers and haulers that must be paid for their time and gasoline. We'll negotiate their budgets down, but we need to tell them that enough money is coming to do a decent job."

"We're not on the radio like we need to be," he had listened to Rodney Libscomb. "In the rural areas, people are listening to that radio between five and seven-thirty in the morning. They need to hear your ads over and over every morning for these last ten days."

"Yeah. Reynolds is all over the black radio stations all day long," Terrell Franks had told him.

Then as an after thought.... "We can win this thing. You can be governor," Libscomb had added.

"You can win. But it's not cheap. You gotta pay. We've gotten this far on a shoestring budget. Now we've got to hit it hard for a week," they had all said over and over and over.

"But there are over twenty television stations, over three hundred radio stations and over two hundred and fifty newspapers in Louisiana. It'd take a million dollars to do a full media campaign these last ten days," Flint had protested.

"Sign notes... Borrow the money..... We can raise it after the campaign.... Even with this last push, your budget will be small compared to past campaigns for governor.... the black drivers and haulers control thousands of votes; if we don't take what we can get, Reynolds will sure pay for them.... We've got to get our share.... Our television is having a good impact but we only have a short time left; we must step it up.... having only two or three radio ads on a station each day does no good; its got to be on at least ten times a day per station to make an impact.... if we're going to get our votes to the polls, we've got to mail your letter out statewide, at least to the voters who voted in the last election.... You've got to roll the dice, Darin.... You've put too much time, effort and money into this campaign to lose it because the necessary money is not spent the last week.... everyone's worked so hard, they're counting on you.... Reync 'ds is trying to buy the election."

From all sides, the arguments and advice spun around Flint's head.

Gradually, it had happened. The budget grew out of control. He had first stepped up the television by increasing the number of spots each day. Thirty seconds on prime time cost him nine hundred dollars each time it was telecast. Massive mailouts were approved across the state. Just the postage was exorbitant. Then three newspaper ads were approved to alternate each day for the final week in the state's major newspapers. One ad would run in each of the major weekly newspapers. Then a special ad was cut for the black radio stations and it was running ten times daily. Early morning radio ads were added on.

Then the black organizations started presenting their "budgets" to Mayor Lawrence and Terrell Franks for election day expenses. Virtually all sixty-four parishes had at least two black organizations that wanted to help Flint. Rarely did any organization submit a budget as low as twenty-five hundred dollars. Virtually all were above seventy-five hundred dollars. Many were over twelve thousand dollars. Typically the budget would include fifty dollar payments to "haulers" who would drive voters to the polls. An average size organization might budget payments to twenty-five to thirty-five "haulers". Some proposed to employ hundreds on election day. The larger organizations in New Orleans and Baton Rouge each wanted over $100 thousand to do their work.

Mayor Lawrence and Terrell Franks worked feverishly to get the budget figures down. A typical black organization budget might be sliced from fourteen thousand dollars down to three thousand dollars overnight, bringing Mayor Lawrence back to Flint for approval. "We've cut their budget to a nub. Now we must tell them yes or no," he remembered Mayor Lawrence telling him over and over again. Flint had decided to try to pick only one organization.... the most reputable group..... in each area. On this limited basis, he started approving many of the "reduced" black budgets.

By midweek, Flint had no idea how much he was spending. He was signing blank notes and hundreds of checks were written. He would worry about it later. Everything was in place to win. TO WIN! TO WIN! TO WIN!

Finally the election arrived. He was confident. Everyone was confident. The polls looked good. He had good black organizations on his side. Expensive, but they assured him of victory.

Now the headline made no sense to him. It couldn't be. Everywhere he turned, the same headline confronted him .... sometimes sideways, sometimes straight, sometimes upside down. Big, bold, huge headlines screaming at Flint:

"Reynolds over Flint in Landslide!" Another read, "Reynolds Re-elected!"

Flint had lost. Not even close. Reynolds had stomped him six to one in the black boxes. Reynolds swept fifty of sixty-four parishes statewide and received fifty-nine percent of the votes.

Susan consoled him, reminding him of the fine race he had run, how well he had done in the debate. Just not enough time or money, that's all …. but he had done so well under the adverse circumstances.

"How much money do we owe?" Susan had asked.

"I'll find out tomorrow. It looks like it'll be about $500 thousand we owe."

"How can we pay it?"

"I don't know. I really don't know. We thought we were going to win. I don't know. I'll talk to Congressman Bordelon about it. $500 thousand. I don't know what we're going to do about it.

"I JUST DON'T KNOW!"

Flint saw a red balloon being inflated, growing larger and larger. He saw the figures "$500,000" on it's side, growing larger, larger, larger and larger until it exploded with a wrenching, horrendous "BANG!"

And Flint awoke in his bedroom and thanked God he still had those ten days ahead of him …. not behind him.

THIRTY-TWO

"I desire to so conduct the affairs of this Administration that if, at the end, when I come to lay down the reins of power, I have lost every other friend on earth, I shall at least have one friend left, and that friend shall be down inside of me."

Abraham Lincoln
(1809-1865)
16th President of the United States
(Remarks to a visiting delegation in 1863)

The final ten days of the campaign left an indelible imprint on Louisiana's political consciousness. Flint received the editorial endorsement of five major, daily newspapers and a long list of weekly and bi-weekly newspapers. Vernon Looper and the AFL-CIO carried out their commitment to René Reynolds. Labor's telephone banks, the rallies and the mail outs all were carried out according to schedule. But the enthusiasm was not there. The rallies were not well attended. The election day "get-out-the-vote" effort was only half- hearted. Rank and file sentiment had turned against the governor; Vernon Looper's struggle to rebuild labor's impact had only mixed results.

Mayor Edmund Lawrence publicly endorsed Darin Flint the morning after the debate. He began fundraising efforts immediately and successfully put together a good volunteer effort for Flint within the black community for the remainder of the campaign.

Prior to the debate, Governor Reynolds had received almost all the endorsements of the state's major political organizations in both the black and white communities. They demanded and received hundreds of thousands of dollars from Reynolds to cover their campaign expenses, but their leaders (even Jackson Wells) were almost apologetic as they carried out their efforts for Reynolds among voters.

Reynolds' "hatchet job" television program and the erroneous accusations during the debate backfired. The ceiling of public opinion had fallen on Reynolds' head.

Flint met with Bill Beeson and other representatives of the oil and gas industry, the petro chemical industry and other groups vitally concerned with Flint's environmental stands. They came to him with a moderate proposal to implement a superfund program. The Legislature had earlier enacted a constitutional provision to protect funds that might eventually come to the state treasury from settlement of the federal-state dispute over oil and gas tax revenues produced from offshore mineral production in areas overlapping the federal-state boundary. The constitutional provision had provided that the great bulk of the funds (perhaps as much as $500 million) would go to education. However, the Legislature did not protect the first $100 million of such funds; these funds could be used in any manner. It was a political grab-bag the governor and his favored legislators would largely control. The oil industry now proposed to Flint that at least one-half of these unprotected funds ($50 million) be dedicated to the new superfund. Furthermore, they indicated a willingness to accept for five years a one-half cent increase of Louisiana's natural gas severance tax to be dedicated to the superfund. This five year tax would bring an additional $15 million each year ($75 million over five years) to repair environmental damages. The major oil companies assured him that their private efforts to clean up their own abandoned well sites would become even more pronounced.

Although Flint agreed only to take the proposal under serious consideration, privately he was pleased. A feeling of understanding and cooperation had been established with the oil industry; a decent plan to begin a strong attack on Louisiana's environmental problems, the result of prior decades of careless energy exploration, would be pushed through the Legislature.

The tragedy facing Marsha Vick and her family could not be avoided. Her father's illness was serious and probably terminal. The good news was that Marsha Vick and the rest of her family were given a clean bill of health. The Vick family's privacy was preserved and their plight never became a campaign issue. Flint was successful in having state health officials evaluate the pollution problem in her family's community. In an effort to begin mending fences, Bill Beeson initiated volunteer efforts among oil companies to haul away the waste in the old waste pit adjacent to the Vick home and to do their best to treat ground-water contamination and provide a healthy water system for the community.

Flint's campaign fund was suddenly flooded by contributions. Potential contributors lined up to meet with Flint, or his key campaign leaders. Flint had known many of these new contributors for years. Realtors, bankers, businessmen, nursing home owners, attorneys, lobbyists, labor leaders, LBL leaders, police jurors, mayors, legislators, members of the congressional delegation, black leaders, physicians, and pharmacists were among those joining the campaign effort. Many of the new contributors had close dealings with the governor's office throughout Reynolds' term in office. Understandably, they wanted to establish good terms with the man likely to be the next governor.

Flint's campaign schedule would have been destroyed if he had tried to meet with so many people during those final two weeks. It was important not to offend his new friends. So Flint assigned the task of organizing these appointments to Jeffrey Bordelon, who in turn put John Flint, Rodney Libscomb, Jane Baldwin, Terrell Franks, Joel Whitney and Eric McKay to work attending such meetings. Jeffrey Bordelon decided what meetings Flint would personally attend those final two weeks.

Flint's orders were explicit. They would graciously accept contributions from these new contributors, but the size of contributions were limited to two thousand dollar maximums.

Darin Flint stayed on the road and continued his campaign schedule through election day. The crowds grew larger and larger. The polls grew in his favor until he finally forged into the lead. As his name recognition grew, so did his support. Flint's headquarters operations in each community were filled with volunteers. They blanketed every community with door to door efforts distributing Flint campaign materials. The yardsign campaign they had planned for the final ten days exceeded their best expectations and urgent orders for more signs were submitted to printers.

When the polls closed on election day, John Flint's campaign accounts indicated $860 thousand had been spent in the campaign. All debts had been paid. Flint had a campaign surplus totaling more than $200 thousand. The surplus of the deposed Governor René Reynolds' $11 million campaign budget totaled over $500 thousand. Reynolds had salvaged a surplus from his otherwise wrecked campaign.

The people of Louisiana had witnessed the spectacle of an enormously powerful, popular governor (who had seemed so recently to be politically invincible) being transformed into a virtually helpless, destroyed politician almost overnight.

But it had not occurred overnight. The seeds of the Flint victory had been sown from the first day of his candidacy. And the political earth had been fertile from the public's frustration with decades of larcenous politicians running their state. This was true despite the wealth of campaign funds retained in Reynolds' campaign accounts and the long list of political endorsements he had secured prior to the debate. In effect, Reynolds had wasted his own talents and, in the end, destroyed himself. It was an election decided by the people, not the traditional political leaders.

The vote totals were startling. Flint received over fifty-six percent of the total vote, his victory therefore approaching landslide proportions. He split Acadiana and the River Parishes with Reynolds, but won decisively from Orleans through the Florida Parishes and across central and north Louisiana.

Perhaps most gratifying was the so-called black vote. According to the post-election analysis of Jon Douglas, slightly over forty percent of all black voters supported Darin Flint. There had always been a very small splinter of independent black voters who were not automatically in the corner of the organizations and their haulers, the labor unions and the money politics that in combination had dominated black precincts in the past. This splinter of independence had grown into a huge oak tree reaching forty percent of black voters who could not be budged by the deluge of paper endorsement ballots spread throughout the black community the day before the election.

Louisiana's past tolerance of self-serving and even corrupt politicians ended on that election night. Not only was Flint's victory complete, but a thorough house cleaning of both Houses of the Louisiana Legislature occurred. Reynolds was joined in defeat by many of his closest supporters in the Capitol. It was the largest turnover of the Legislature's membership since the benchmark year of 1972. Of the 105 members of the House, only forty-one would return. There would be seventeen new state senators among the Senate's thirty-seven members.

Colbert Freeman survived and would return to the State Senate as no one had qualified to oppose him back in July. But Senate President Sonny Stokes was not so lucky. Stokes was defeated.

Darin Flint's protege Tony Ciaccio was elected to take Flint's place in the State Senate.

The unlikely, the unexpected, the impossible had occurred in Louisiana. Louisiana's future lay before her like the clean pages of an unwritten book. The author's pen had been placed in the fingers of Darin Flint and his new Legislature.

EPILOGUE

"Sing Goddess, of the wrath of Achilles."

Virgil

"He (Theodore Roosevelt) got down on his knees before us. We bought him and he did not stay bought."

Henry Clay Frick
(1849-1919)
American Industrialist
(A reference to the 1904 campaign.
An uncensored version reads:
"We bought the S.O.B. but he didn't stay bought.")

James Harriford turned the steering wheel of his 380 SL Mercedes Benz and drove into the parking lot behind the New Iberia law office. He parked in his reserved parking space and switched off the ignition. Harriford glanced in the rearview mirror and noticed his white hair had been windblown. He combed his hair, grabbed his newspaper, then walked to the back door of the office where he inserted his key and entered the building. Harriford walked down the hallway to the door marked "INVESTIGATOR" and entered his office.

It was almost 7:30 a.m. He was supposed to drive his boss, who was the senior partner of the law firm, to Darin Flint's inauguration in Baton Rouge. They were to leave by 8:00 a.m. Harriford had never met Darin Flint. His boss had told him he never would. Observing the inauguration would be as close as he ever got to Darin Flint. Harriford expected his boss to arrive shortly.

He sat behind his desk and thumbed through the newspaper. Harriford read an editorial on the ed-op page which capsulized the recent Flint —Reynolds gubernatorial campaign. The author attributed the final collapse of the Reynolds candidacy, and the landslide victory of Darin Flint to the faux pas of the Reynolds research staff on the Noble Airlines vote.

Reynolds' thirty minute television "hatchet job" had backfired.

It had been exposed as an effort to exaggerate harmless elements of the Flint record to smear Flint's name. Even if Flint had voted for the Noble Airlines bill, the editorial observed, "So what?" Flint's mother-in-law had held only a minor amount of stock in the troubled airlines. No appreciable financial gain was in store for either Flint or his mother-in-law. Yet Flint had recused himself. The incident served to prove Flint's honesty, not his dishonesty.

The Reynolds people had searched Flint's background exhaustively, determined to find something .... anything .... to build a "hatchet job" television program upon. This effort of exaggeration and distortion had worked many times before in Louisiana history during the heated, frenzied, final days of many campaigns. This time it had failed. Some incompetent researcher had made a mistake. Either that, or the accusations had been an intentional smear. Afterall, Flint had not voted on the bill and his statement recusing himself was in the Senate Journals. Reynolds had put his foot in his mouth, said the editorial, and justice had prevailed.

Harriford leaned back in his chair and smiled broadly. His eyes approvingly surveyed the paneled walls, the nice painting, the carpeted floors. "First class," he muttered to himself.

Harriford put the newspaper aside and reached for a pen and began writing a letter on stationary entitled "From the Desk of James Harriford." He addressed the letter to René Reynolds.

"Dear Ex-Governor Reynolds,

You probably don't remember a pretty girl you took advantage of awhile back. She worked in the Secretary of State's office. She quit shortly after she met you. You almost ruined both her marriage and her life.

She is my daughter. She's had enough guts to get her life back on the right track. Until your campaign gave me the chance to do some special research for you, my daughter was the only decent thing I ever had anything to do with in my life. I thoroughly enjoyed helping you show the world what a creep you really are.

James Harriford"

Harriford put the pen down, reread the letter, then placed it in an envelope. He addressed and stamped the envelope and slipped in into his coat pocket. He would mail it that morning.

His thoughts were interrupted when he heard his employer walking down the hallway. He looked up as former Congressman (now attorney) Jeffrey Bordelon appeared in the doorway.

"Good morning, Jimmy," Jeffrey Bordelon said. "Are you ready to go to Baton Rouge?"

THE END

*"How Long, Louisiana .... How long must
we wait?"*

Edward C. Scogin
Louisiana State Representative
District 76
Speech during proceedings of the
Louisiana House of Representatives
immediately following passage of the
unbalanced state budget, July, 1985.

ABOUT THE AUTHOR

John Wyeth "Jock" Scott is a native of Alexandria, Louisiana, where he is a practicing attorney. He is a ten year veteran in the Louisiana House of Representatives, and was a second place finisher in a 1985 special election for Congress in the legendary 8th District. As a Democrat, the author has served on the party's state central committee and as its National Committeeman. He resigned the latter post last summer to become a Republican.

Mr. Scott holds a degree in government from Tulane University (1969) and his law degree from Louisiana State University Law School (1972). He is married to the former Cynthia Henderson. They have three children.

Mr. Scott is a veteran editorialist and radio commentator. This is his first book.

GLOSSARY

Acadiana — region of south Louisiana known for its unique French Acadian culture and language and officially comprised of the following parishes (counties): Acadia, Avoyelles, Ascension, Assumption, Calcasieu, Cameron, Evangeline, Iberia, Iberville, Jefferson Davis, Lafayette, Lafourche, Pointe Coupee, St. Charles, St. James, St. John, St. Landry, St. Martin, St. Mary, Terrebonne, Vermilion, and West Baton Rouge. (See also CAJUN.)

Act — a measure having the effect of law which has passed (been adopted by) both houses of the legislature and been approved (signed) by the governor or becomes effective without his approval.

Advertising or public relations agency — a business engaged in the promotion and marketing of a particular product, business, individual, or issue to the public through publication or broadcast.

Agency shop — labor-management contractual relationships in which the union serves as the agent for and receives dues and assessments from all employees in the bargaining unit regardless of an individual's union membership. Passage of Louisiana's Right to Work law in 1976 made agency shop illegal in the state.

Amendment — means of modifying a legislative instrument (bill or resolution) by adding or deleting language or changing wording or intent.

AFL-CIO — abbreviation for the American Federation of Labor-Congress of Industrial Organizations, the largest and most influential labor organization in the country, a federation of over 130 unions. The AFL-CIO has over 13 million members who comprise about 70 percent of organized labor today. The remainder of organized labor is in independent unions such as the Teamsters, Longshoremen, and a number of smaller unions.

Aquifer — A water-bearing layer of the earth's crust. The water may be drinkable, or too filled with salt and other minerals.

Associated Press (AP) — one of the major wire news service agencies, the AP receives and transmits on a continual basis national and international news from its correspondents around the world to a variety of subscribers in the field of communications (newspapers, television, and radio). (See also UNITED PRESS INTERNATIONAL)

Bank charter — grant of authority by an appropriate federal or state governmental entity to a bank to do business. A charter defines the institution's general corporate powers, responsibilities, and organization. A bank doing business in more than one state must be chartered by the federal government, as well as by each state of operation and is referred to as being "nationally chartered"; a bank doing business in a single state is chartered therein only and is referred to as "state chartered."

BESE — acronym for the state Board of Elementary and Secondary Education, the constitutionally created body responsible for supervision and control of the state's public elementary and secondary schools, vocational-technical training programs, and special schools for the handicapped. Private elementary, secondary, and proprietary schools in the state also receive state certification of their various curriculums through BESE.

Big oil — refers collectively to the largest of the nationally owned oil companies in the United States which comprise one of the most powerful business and political forces in the country. The group is particularly active in government at both the federal and certain state levels, including Louisiana.

Bill — a document by which one or more members of the legislature seek to effect some change in statutory law, to enact new law, or to repeal existing law (which, if successful, becomes an Act) or seek to propose changes or additions to the constitution (which, if successful, becomes a Joint Resolution).

Budget — the coordination of estimated expenditures and expected revenues in the form of an annual fiscal plan providing for the manner of operation of state government. The state constitution requires that the governor submit and the legislature approve a proposed operating budget for the upcoming fiscal year in the form of a General Appropriations Bill. The constitution also requires submission by the governor to the legislature of a proposed five-year capital outlay program and that implementation of the program's first year of legislatively approved projects be included in the comprehensive state capital budget, called the Capital Outlay Bill.

Cajun — slang for a Louisianian descended from Acadians, French settlers exiled by the British from their Nova Scotia homeland in 1755 and finally resettled in Spanish Louisiana after

30 years of homelessness. Also means the dialect of French spoken by this group. Known particularly for their cuisine, music, and *joie de vivre* (joy of life), Acadians have contributed significantly to Louisiana's rich cultural heritage. (See also ACADIANA.)

Carcinogen — A substance or agent that can produce a cancerous growth. Examples: acrylonitrile, asbestos, chromium and benzidine.

Central purchasing law — requirement that state procurement of all supplies, services, and major repairs of items for use by its agencies be centralized in a single procurement authority within the executive branch and be conducted in accordance with law and specific administrative regulations.

Civil service — a term encompassing most persons employed by federal, state, or local government, more generally understood to apply to those gaining governmental employment through a merit system. In Louisiana the state and certain city civil service systems are established in and protected by the state constitution, which includes provisions restricting the political activities of civil servants while protecting them from arbitrary dismissals and requiring that job appointments and promotions be based on efficiency, fitness, and length of service.

Civil service job classification — grouping government employment positions on the basis of duties, responsibilities, and qualifications such that a position is classified in accordance with the nature of the job rather than the individual holding the position. (See also CIVIL SERVICE.)

Code of Governmental Ethics — code of conduct governing the activities of all state and local elected officials, appointed officials, and employees, except judges. It contains ethical standards for these public servants ranging from restrictions on receipt of payments from nonpublic sources to prohibitions against participation in certain transactions or contractual arrangements involving the individual's agency, gifts from lobbyists, abuse of office, illegal payments, and nepotism.

Compulsory arbitration — requirement that an unresolved labor-management dispute be submitted to an impartial board whose decision is binding upon the parties to the dispute. Many collective bargaining agreements provide for compulsory arbitration, and a large number of labor disputes are submitted to private professional arbitrators, thereby avoiding a strike. Although required by law in some states (Louisiana is not one) for settling certain types of disputes, both labor and management typically prefer to keep government out of labor disputes and to pursue their ends through collective bargaining.

Consultant contract — contractual agreement involving expenditure of public funds by any state agency for work, other than professional (such as legal, medical, or accounting) or personal services (creative or artistic work), rendered by an individual possessing certain specialized knowledge or skills. State law requires that state procurement for professional, personal, and consulting services be awarded, managed, and controlled by a central contract review agency in accordance with specific administrative regulations so as to foster competition and provide fair treatment to all potential contractors. (see also PROFESSIONAL SERVICES CONTRACTS)

Dual officeholding and dual employment law — state law defining and regulating dual employment and defining, regulating, and prohibiting dual officeholding in state and local government, the underlying principle of which is to prevent or curtail the accumulation of power occuring when one individual holds a number of public offices.

Exclusive franchise — a privilege conferred by government upon a single private company to operate a public utility and to use public property as a monopoly in order to satisfy the public welfare or convenience. In Louisiana most such grants are by local governments, particularly municipalities, for services such as water, cable television, or garbage collection services.

Fault — a fracture in the earth's crust in which one or both sides of the fracture move. Environmentalists worry that such fractures may afford a pathway for hazardous waste to move into a drinking water aquifer.

Feasibility study — socioeconomic research conducted to determine the need and/or potential effectiveness, generally both programmatic and economic, of a proposed project, program, or idea.

Floorfight — an argument on either floor of the legislature between at least two factions concerning an issue that is ultimately resolved by a vote of the legislative body.

Fundraiser — an activity, usually of a social nature, conducted as a means of soliciting funding for a political candidate, group, or issue.

Garden District — an 80-block, primarily residential area in the city of New Orleans bounded by Jackson, Carondelet, and Magazine Streets and Louisiana Avenue boasting a concentration of fine antebellum architecture set in beautifully landscaped grounds. Characteristic architectural styles include raised cottages, mansions with two-story galleries, and "shotguns." During the 1970's the term came to be used generically to describe older residential neighborhoods in central city areas comprised of homes over 50 years old and well established landscapes, and today several Louisiana cities have designated garden districts.

Gasoline tax — tax on the first handler in Louisiana, that is, the importer or the manufacturer, of all gasoline or motor fuel sold, used, or consumed in the state for domestic consumption. The present state gasoline tax rate is $.16 per gallon.

Grandfather clause — language inserted in a bill to make its provisions inapplicable to activities or individuals involved prior to the enactment of the new legislation, thus exempting those certain specified activities or individuals from the new law.

Haulers — paid political workers who transport voters to polling places on election day.

Hazardous waste landfill — hazardous waste that may come from refineries, petrochemical plants or old waste pits is "stabilized," usually with kiln dust, and buried in deep pits.

Highway passing lanes — in areas where highway visibility is obscured, such as in hilly terrain, an additional lane in a two-lane highway extending for a short distance and designated only for one lane of traffic to pass slower moving vehicles.

Highway priorities act — state law enacted in 1976 creating a program of state highway construction based on established scientific need which is nationally recognized as a model for highway planning.

Hospital permit — a finding (or failure of finding of conformity) by the state that a proposed health care facility meets certain criteria and standards related to the need for the facility in the service area. Such a finding makes the facility eligible for capital expenditure reimbursement under the federal Social Security Act. Also referred to as a "certificate of need."

Independent oil producers (LAIPRO) — Louisiana Association of Independent Producers, a state association of self-employed individuals in the oil industry whose work entails "packaging," and in some cases overseeing, the entire process of drilling and production of a well. (See also BIG OIL)

Indictment — a formal written statement of accusation drawn up by a prosecuting attorney and found to be valid by a grand jury charging an individual with commission of a crime.

Injection well — a well used to dispose of oil field waste, salt water that may contain chemicals used in drilling, or commercial hazardous waste. The waste is pumped deep into the earth, usually into salt water layers below the drinking water aquifer. Environmentalists worry, however, that waste may find its way from the lower level into potable aquifers.

Jim Crow laws — laws requiring segregation of the races enacted by several states after the War Between the States, upheld by the U.S. Supreme Court in 1896 under the "separate but equal" doctrine, and finally struck down in 1957 by the Court holding that segregation based on color denied equal protection under law. During the early 1960's the Louisiana Legislature attempted to circumbent that ruling by enacting variations on these segregation statutes, but by the mid-70's the state's Jim Crow laws were finally repealed.

Legislative fiscal office — the agency headed by the Legislative Fiscal Officer which serves as primary advisor to both houses of the state legislature on fiscal matters. The agency's primary duties generally are the development and presentation of fiscal information to assist in legislative deliberations and specifically the review of budget requests, analysis of the governor's proposed executive budget, and fiscal recommendations with a view toward state governmental efficiency, economy, and improvement in service provision.

Licensure law — a certificate granted under law by administrative officials permitting private individuals to engage in certain business or professional activities. Primarily licensing power is exercised by state and local governments to regulate professions such as physicians, cosmetologists, and architects to ensure certain standards and, in certain cases, to restrict competition in the field.

Literacy test for voters — a suffrage qualification used to determine fitness for voting by means of a reading or "understanding" test. Because they were frequently used to discriminate against prospective voters, Congress suspended their use in the Voting Rights Acts of 1970 and 1975.

Lobbyist — one who attempts to influence legislators to support his stance on an issue, usually a person acting as an agent for a particular interest group who seeks to bring about the passage or defeat of legislation, as well as to influence decisions of executive officials and administrators. Louisiana law requires paid lobbyists to register with the legislature.

Merit pay for teachers — a type of differential teacher pay program in which salary levels are based upon a teacher's demonstrably better performance in the classroom. Merit pay programs tend to utilize such mechanisms as pupil achievement scores or teacher assessment models to measure teacher performance. For a number of reasons, few states have established a true merit pay program; recent legislative attempts in Louisiana to enact a "career ladder program" — a similar type of differential pay scheme — were unsuccessful, largely as a result of opposition by teacher groups.

Minimum Foundation Program (MFP) formula — basis for funding Louisiana public elementary and secondary education in accordance with an annually revised standard to determine how much state money will be allocated to each school system in order to provide a minimum educational program to all children. Program components include teacher salaries, transportation costs, teacher and employee benefits, utilities, and insurance. (See also TEACHER-PUPIL RATIO)

Modified open range pay scale (civil service) — a type of salary scale for a particular job classification which provides designated "step" increases in salary from the minimum entry salary level to the midpoint of the scale but no designated increases from the midpoint to the maximum level. This type of scale is said to afford both job advancement security for the entry level employee and flexibility for management to reward outstanding work.

Multi-parish banking law — authorization for a bank holding company in Louisiana to acquire and own more than one bank, subject to certain specific limitations on its acquisition activities. Contrary to its name, the law applies only to multi-bank holding companies and does not allow a single bank to establish branches outside its parish of domicile or to merge with another out-of-parish bank.

National Teachers' Exam (NTE) — national standardized test designed to measure academic knowledge and educational skills of teachers. In Louisiana and many other states, the NTE is the testing instrument used to certify prospective teachers. The state superintendent of education, with approval of the State Board of Elementary and Secondary Education, has established minimum scores necessary for certification.

New tax — a charge imposed by government on particular persons or property upon which or in a manner in which a charge has not previously been levied. In Louisiana, for example, the city of New Orleans recently attempted to enact an "earnings tax" on wages earned within its jurisdiction as a means to tax the incomes of its relatively large white-collar suburbanite workforce.

Open meetings law — requirement that every meeting of any state or local governmental entity in Louisiana in which a majority of its members are present be open to the public and that prior notice of the meeting be given and its proceedings recorded.

Personal privilege — according to Mason's *Manual of Legislative Procedure*, refers to all questions affecting the rights, reputation, and conduct of legislators in their capacity as such. However, in practice in Louisiana it is used as a device for allowing a legislator to take up an item off the regular agenda for a brief period of time.

Poll tax — a tax levied against a voter in order to vote in an election. Typically utilized in the South after the War Between the States to exclude minorities from participation in elections, the tax was declared unconstitutional by the U.S. Supreme Court in 1966.

Precinct — basic element of the election process, the smallest unit of political geography from which elections are held. Generally contains between 200 and 1000 voters and a polling place.

Prevailing wage — state law requiring private contractors on state construction projects to pay employee wages on the same scale as that paid for similar work in the area. Enacted in 1968, the law was repealed by the legislature but vetoed by the governor in 1985.

Previous question on the amendment — motion to end debate and vote on the particular amendment being discussed (pending) before the legislative body. A motion aimed at a particular action, it prevails over a general motion such as that of the "previous question on the entire subject matter." Since it ends debate only on the amendment pending and not on the entire subject matter under discussion, this motion is frequently used as a stopgap for attempts to bring the entire issue to a vote by opposition members wishing to continue debate. (See also AMENDMENT and PREVIOUS QUESTION ON THE ENTIRE SUBJECT MATTER)

Previous question on the entire subject matter — motion to end debate on the issue before the legislative body (an amendment or the bill itself) and to bring the body immediately to action to resolve the entire issue in question, that is, the pending amendment, if any, and then the bill. (See Also AMENDMENT and PREVIOUS QUESTION ON THE AMENDMENT)

Professional Improvement Program (PIP) — program to provide enhanced salaries and retirement benefits for Louisiana educators who participate in programs of professional self- improvement. Involves development by each participant of his five-year plan of work in accordance with program requirements, submission of the plan and approval by a local committee, and completion of the program as outlined in the plan prior to receipt of salary enhancement. A highly touted program initially, PIP became controversial, with most criticism focused on the nonacademic nature of many of the courses offered in its curriculum, and in 1984 the legislature provided for its phaseout by 1989.

Professional services contract — a contractual arrangement involving expenditure of public funds by any state agency for work rendered by an independent contractor possessing certain specialized knowledge or professional expertise, as distinguished from mere skill, in such fields as law, medicine, or accounting. State law requires that state procurement for professional, personal, and consulting services be awarded, managed, and controlled by a central agency of contractual review in accordance with specific administrative regulations so as to foster effective competition and provide fair treatment to all potential contractors. (See also CONSULTANT CONTRACTS)

Public bid law — requirement that all public construction work and all material or supply purchases in excess of certain specified amounts by public entities, that is, agencies of the state or of local governments, be advertised and let to the lowest bidder in accordance with specific procedures.

Public employee union — labor union whose membership is composed of nonmanagerial state or local governmental employees.

The American Federation of State, County, and Municipal Employees (AFSCME), located in every state, is the largest such union, with a membership of 1.1 million.

Public records law — requirement that all documentary materials relating to the business of any state, parish, or municipal governmental entity in Louisiana be made publicly available for inspection or reproduction.

Public Service Commission — state regulatory agency charged with regulating the rates and services of common carriers and public utilities operating within the state.

Qualifying dates for election — deadline for a person to become a candidate in a state, parish, or municipal primary election by filing proper notice of his candidacy. State law establishes various specific qualifying periods, or timeframes, for various types of elections.

Reapportionment — reallocation of legislative seats in the U.S. House of Representatives following the decennial population census. In Louisiana refers to the redrawing of electoral districts following the census, including both houses of the legislature and certain local governmental bodies, in which case it is called "redistricting."

Recusal — the act by a public official or employee in the course of exercising the duties and responsibilities of his office of refraining from voting on any matter in which he has or could potentially have a conflict of interest.

Right to Work — state law that prohibits making union membership a qualification for employment. First enacted in 1954 and repealed in 1956, Louisiana's right to work law was reenacted in 1976 and has remained in effect since that time. Labor interests continue to work for its repeal, and business interests recently began efforts to more firmly establish the law by placing it in the state constitution.

Rules review law — officially known as the Administrative Procedure Act, the major state law governing the procedures of state regulatory agencies and providing for standards of judicial review of administrative determinations. Provides specifically for public input into proposed agency rule changes, for appeal from agency decisions to the courts, and for other safeguards for private rights of individuals affected by administrative agencies.

Sales tax — a tax on the sale, lease or rental of property and on the sales of services that is payable by users and consumers, lessees, or persons receiving services taxable under the law. Levied by the state and local governments at the maximum rate of 4 percent and 3 percent respectively in Louisiana.

Scientific creationism (creation-science) — theory that man originated as a species according to Biblical teachings, as opposed to the theory of evolution of the species. State law enacted in 1981, but never implemented due to continuing litigation as to its constitutionality, provides for "balanced treatment" of both theories in the state public school system.

Senate journal — a record of daily proceedings of the Senate published for each legislative day during each session. The House of Representatives journal is the comparable daily record of that body. A complete journal for each house is printed after the close of the session.

Senate president — in Louisiana the presiding officer of the Senate who officiates over the proceedings of that body. Prior to 1976 the lieutenant governor served as Senate president, but the state constitution now provides that the president be elected by the Senate membership. In the House of Representatives the Speaker of the House is the presiding officer.

Special fuels tax — a tax on special fuels (diesel, LP gas, butane) sold, used or consumed in the state for the operation of motor vehicles licensed or required to be licensed for highway use. The tax rate is $.16 per gallon.

State bonds — certificates of indebtedness issued by state government to finance capital improvement needs that cannot be financed out of current revenues. No bonds may be issued by the state, its agencies, or local governments without approval by the State Bond Commission. The two major types are general obligation bonds secured by the full faith and credit of the state and revenue bonds issued to finance construction of a revenue-producing facility and secured by and payable from the revenues produced. In addition, industrial development bonds (IDB's), often called "tax free bonds," are those issued by local governments to encourage economic development or employment through financing facilities for private businesses and whose rental payments pay the bond's debt service requirements; the tax exempt status of these bonds to finance private projects has been the subject of controversy at both the state and federal levels.

Supply contracts — state agreements for the purchase of supplies, defined as property such as equipment, insurance, and property leases, that are subject to state procurement requirements through the central purchasing agency. (See also CENTRAL PURCHASING LAW)

Tax exemption — a privilege granted by government legally freeing certain types of property, sales, or income from general tax-paying obligations. They are used to encourage certain activities such as economic development, energy conservation, or trade and commerce, as well as to recognize that within certain taxpaying categories exceptions must be acknowledged in the interest of fairness. For example, the elderly or low-income groups are frequently granted sales tax exemptions for that reason.

Teacher-pupil ratio — the manner in which teacher positions are allocated to each Louisiana public school system. The present ration is 25-to-1 for grades 4-12 and 24-to-1 for grades kindergarten-3; for example, for every 25 fourth grade students a school has, the state will pay one teacher's salary. (See also MINIMUM FOUNDATION PROGRAM FORMULA).

Teachers' minimum salary schedule — schedule under state law by which Louisiana teachers are paid based on an individual's educational achievement and years of teaching experience.

Telephone bank — a mass of telephones connected to a central system and utilized during a election campaign by a political candidate or party in order to generate support for its candidate(s) and votes on election day.

Third Congressional District — one of the eight political-geographical divisions of the state from which a member of the U.S. House of Representatives is elected, stretching across the coastal area of south Louisiana from below New Orleans west to the Vermilion River.

Toxic substance — any chemical which when present in excess causes harmful biological effects in living organisims.

Unemployment insurance — a program of insurance under the Social Security Act of 1935 administered by the states under national supervision that provides for payment of funds for a limited period of time to workers who are laid off or discharged for reasons beyond their control. Employers pay into a fund from which each state determines the amount to be paid each of its unemployed persons, for how long, and under what conditions. Louisiana's unemployment insurance benefits are some of the highest in the nation.

U.S. House Rules Committee — standing committee of the U.S. House of Representatives that can provide special rules under which specific bills will be debated, amended, and considered by the House. The committee functions as a valve to control the flow of bills from House standing committees to the floor for consideration, a power which can be abused by its selective use.

United Press International (UPI) — one of the major wire news service agencies, the UPI receives and transmits on a continual basis national and international news from its correspondents around the world to a variety of subscribers in the field of communications (newspapers, television, and radio). (See also ASSOCIATED PRESS)

Veto — a legislative power vested in the governor by the state constitution to disapprove a legislative Act. Such action has the effect of killing the bill unless the legislature subsequently acts to override the governor's action (requires two-thirds vote to override).

Worker's compensation — an insurance program, in effect in all states, that provides compensation for workers injured on their jobs and for dependents of workers who are killed in the course of employment. The program is financed by the employer, who must take out insurance for this purpose.

"Young Turks" — group of members of the Louisiana House of Representatives first organized during the 1968-1972 term, many of them freshmen, who sought legislative and substantive reforms and are particularly noted for efforts at reform of legislative procedure, fiscal responsibility, and the establishment of the legislature as a co-equal branch with the governor. One of their earliest successes was the establishment of defined subject area jurisdictions of each legislative standing committee. In 1972 the group, augmented by additional newly elected freshmen, succeeded in rule changes removing lobbyists from the floor of each legislative chamber.